A KNIFE THROUGH THE HEART

BRIAN O'SULLIVAN

Since I'm running out of proper dedications to make, this novel is dedicated to coffee. I'm not sure I would have crossed the finish line without you.

This is a work of fiction. Names, characters, places, and incidents either are the product of the author's imagination or are used in a fictitious manner. Any resemblance to actual persons, living or dead, events, or locales is merely coincidental.

A Knife Through The Heart

Copyright @2022 **Brian O'Sullivan**

All rights reserved.

ISBN: 979-8-9853830-1-0

Published by **Big B Publishing**

San Francisco, CA

❀ Created with Vellum

A KNIFE THROUGH THE HEART

PART ONE: THE INVESTIGATION

CHAPTER 1

I t took three phone calls and two meetings before I agreed to take the Archer Keats case.

A man accused of the brutal murder of his wife.

I'd like to take credit and say I originally balked because I smelled a rat, that I knew the case stunk to high heaven.

In the end, I accepted their offer.

So I don't deserve any credit.

But I do deserve some of the blame for all that followed.

∼

"Hello?"

"Quint, this is Gene Bowman again."

I knew this third call was coming at some point. And on a random Wednesday morning, as I sat in my office, it came.

"I know who you are by now," I said.

"I'd like to make one last pitch to see if you'll take the case."

"Give it the old college try because this is your last opportunity."

"Meet with Archer's attorney."

"That's it?"

"That's it. I haven't been able to convince you. Maybe his attorney can. If that doesn't work, you won't hear from me again."

"Can I get that in writing?"

I heard a slight chuckle on the other end.

"You have my word."

"Fine, I'll do it," I said. "But this is all likely for naught. I don't see myself working under a lawyer and spending time in court. I'm more of a lone wolf."

"You won't have to go to court. Unless you find something important and his attorney decides to put you on the stand."

The truth was that I didn't like the idea of having a boss for the next few months. It's one of the reasons I'd been so reluctant to accept his offer. One of the perks of being a P.I. was working alone. Sure, I had to deal with shady people a good deal of the time, but if mistakes were made I only had one person to answer to. Myself.

And yet, as the days had turned into weeks, and I learned more about the prospective case, the more fascinated I'd become.

"Alright, I'll meet with Keats' attorney," I said. "What's his name?"

"It's not a he. Her name is Ellie Teague."

I hated to admit it, but this piqued my interest. He hadn't mentioned the attorney was a woman. It shouldn't have made a difference, but somehow, it did.

"She's one hell of an attorney," he added.

Then he came in for the kill.

"And she's beautiful."

"You don't have to lay it on so thick. I've already agreed to meet with her."

Gene Bowman laughed.

"Point taken."

"When and where?" I asked.

"I'll let you two figure that out. You ready for her number?"

"Hold on a second," I said, grabbing a pen from my desk.

"Go."

"925-555-2052. I'd suggest reaching out today. The trial is approaching faster than you think."

"Didn't he just get arrested a few weeks back?" I asked.

"He's asking for a speedy trial."

"I'm no attorney, but..." I said.

Bowman knew where I was going.

"I thought it sounded crazy too."

Gene Bowman was an old friend of Archer Keats. I'd gathered that much from our earlier conversations. Why he had been the one calling me was harder to ascertain. My gut told me that when Archer Keats was arrested, he'd given Bowman carte blanche to hire whomever he wanted.

I guess I should have been honored.

Instead, I had been annoyed.

When Bowman called me the first time, I'd instantly been turned off by the name Archer Keats.

Was I judging someone I'd never met? Sure, but who names their child Archer?

People who like archery or people who are way too rich. And I doubted the Keats were known for their bow and arrow skills.

As my mind wandered, I realized Bowman had spoken last.

"Why is he going for the quick trial?" I asked.

"That's something you'll have to discuss with Ellie."

Bowman was already pawning me off to her. He'd done his job and now it was out of his hands whether or not I took the case.

"I'll give her a call later today," I said.

"Thanks. You won't hear from me again unless you take the case."

"Thank God for small favors."

I heard another short, courtesy laugh.

"Hope you take the case. I promise you won't regret it."

It was the first of several lies I'd be fed about this case.

Archer Keats had killed his wife Gracie.

That was the consensus among the local press.

As well as the people who'd voiced their opinions to me. Of which, there'd been many. The case had been a talking point around the Bay Area since the news broke. You couldn't avoid it. It had been water cooler talk since the savage details became public.

I hadn't formed an opinion yet.

Everyone else was talking about it. I was fine sitting this one out.

The intrigue in the case seemed to grow larger by the day.

A husband killing his wife was a crime as old as time, but this one had a few aspects that kept the public enraptured.

One, the Keats were a rich, well-known family.

Two, and maybe more importantly, was the way in which Gracie Keats had been killed.

Someone took a ten-inch carving knife and stabbed her with it.

Repeatedly and unmercifully.

Twenty-seven times in total.

And that wasn't even the most egregious fact.

Her killer stabbed her so many times through her breastplate that eventually the skin, tendons, ribs, and whatever else was there had been pushed aside. The final stab was unimaginable.

A knife through the heart.

That's right.

The final stab - the twenty-seventh overall - went directly through Gracie Keats's heart.

~

The local news had covered the case like it was the crime of the century.

If the murder had occurred in New York, or even twenty-five miles away in San Francisco, I think it would have become a national phenomenon, if not global.

Since Walnut Creek is a fairly innocuous city, most of the coverage was limited to the Bay Area. At least for the time being.

Once the trial started, who knew if 20/20 or one of those news programs would descend on our city.

If that happened, all hell would surely break loose.

And I'd regret having taken the case.

Which now seemed like a distinct possibility.

~

My meeting with Ellie Teague was looming so I pondered all the information I'd read about the case.

Archer and Gracie Keats had been married for twenty-four years at the time of her death. He's fifty-three years old and she was forty-six at the time of her death.

They were very active in Walnut Creek's social life. Archer was a businessman, involved mainly in the hospitality business. He was the majority owner of eighteen restaurants and three bars. Every time one of his restaurants had a grand opening, it was a big event with a ribbon-cutting photo-op and plenty of local news coverage.

And like clockwork, Gracie was there to host the shindig.

She was a very statuesque woman, tall and thin, with undeniable energy about her. Gene Bowman had described Ellie Teague as beautiful. I'm not sure that's how I'd characterize Gracie, but in every picture she was in, you couldn't help but be drawn to her. Maybe that's more alluring than beauty.

Archer Keats was a handsome man who didn't look to have an ounce of fat on him. Together, the Keats were a couple you wouldn't easily forget.

And that's merely what I got from looking at pictures. In person, I'm sure they were even more dynamic.

Archer was born in San Ramon, ten miles south of Walnut Creek, and after graduating college at UCLA, came back up north and went to Haas

Business School at Cal-Berkeley. Two years after graduating from business school, at the ripe old age of twenty-seven, with the help of his parents, he opened his first restaurant. There never seemed to be a doubt what Archer Keats was going to do with his life. He was born to be a restaurateur.

Gracie was born and raised in Los Angeles and came north to attend college at St. Mary's College in nearby Moraga. St. Mary's was a very safe, some might say staid, college. If parents were afraid to send their kid into the gauntlet of a metropolitan city and the risks that came with that, St. Mary's was a nice alternative. It's basically hidden away in the East Bay suburbs and as safe as a college can be. A parent wouldn't have to worry at night.

From what I gathered, Archer and Gracie met sometime while she was attending St. Mary's. She was only twenty-two when they got married, so it's not like they'd dated for very long.

They had a very happy marriage. At least, from the outside looking in. The people interviewed about their marriage said all the right things.

'They were great together.'

'Archer never could have done this.'

'He worshiped the ground that Gracie walked on.'

I didn't put much stock in those answers. Nor did the public, judging by their opinion. Ninety percent of the people I talked to thought Archer Keats was guilty.

Plus, what was someone going to say?

'There was a dangerous undertone to their marriage. Her murder didn't shock me.'

Now, that would have gotten my attention.

~

Gracie Keats was killed on December 22nd.

Gene Bowman called me on Christmas Eve, the day after I finished taking down the serial killer in the Ronnie Fisk case. I was certain that was no coincidence.

He called me a few weeks later, early in 2022, and I brushed him off again.

Finally, on January 23rd, he called a third time, this time talking me into meeting Ellie Teague.

Well, that's not exactly true.

I didn't take much convincing.

And I knew what had changed.

I'd been exhausted in the days after the demise of Ronnie Fisk's killer. I couldn't imagine accepting another case so soon thereafter.

But now a month had passed and I knew this was going to be different.

There would be no chasing a serial killer.

This was simpler. Straight and to the point.

A yes or no answer.

Did Archer Keats savagely murder his wife? Did he stab her twenty-seven times?

Was he responsible for the unthinkable?

A knife through the heart…

CHAPTER 2

Gene Bowman had described Ellie Teague as a beautiful woman. He'd understated it.

Stunning or striking would have been more appropriate adjectives.

I met her out front of her law offices on Newell Street in downtown Walnut Creek. She greeted me at the door, wearing a form-fitting navy blue dress suit.

She looked to be in her thirties, but I couldn't tell if she had just entered them or was bearing down on forty.

The sign behind her said, "Tiller and Teague, Attorneys-At-Law."

Unlike my P.I. firm, which was hidden in the corner of a strip mall, Ellie Teague's law firm was smack dab in the middle of the main street.

She extended her hand.

"I'm Ellie," she said.

"Quint. Nice to meet you."

She had short brown hair with a few blonde highlights. Her body was impressive, but I was drawn to her face; high cheekbones, full lips, and as pretty a woman as I'd seen in a long time.

Her skin was flawless.

She was of average height, but that was the only thing average about her.

She reminded me of Angelina Jolie, which included a bit of the bad-girl look.

"No last names. It's like we're old friends," she said.

I smiled.

"That doesn't mean I'm necessarily taking the case."

"Good," she said. "I don't want someone who is just taking it for the paycheck. If you take this case, I want you all-in."

I nodded, trying not to stare at the woman in front of me.

She opened the door and led me through the law firm. There was a young male secretary at the front desk and along the left side, two large offices. One said, "Wyatt Tiller, Attorney-At-Law" and the other, "Ellie Teague, Attorney-At-Law." She bypassed the two offices and led me to a giant conference room near the back. It had the requisite allotment of old, stale-looking legal books.

Couldn't lawyers just research all their bylaws and motions and measures and statutes online these days?

Maybe it was all for show. To bring an aura to the room. As if to say, *"Look at all these legal books, I must be a great attorney."*

Ellie motioned for me to sit down. She did the same, sitting in the seat next to me on the massive, mahogany table.

"I'm glad you're giving me this chance," she said.

"Was this your idea or Gene Bowman's?" I asked.

I wanted to know how and why they'd picked me.

"Originally, it was his. The day after Archer's wife was murdered, the news broke about you helping take down that serial killer. Gene thought you'd be a good person to have on our side."

Just as I'd suspected.

"But you took some convincing?" I asked.

"I hadn't heard of you."

I laughed.

"Good. I prefer that."

"Gene kept extolling your virtues, but said he hadn't been able to convince you to take the case."

"That's true."

"Finally, he said he was going to call you one last time."

"And he decided to name-drop you?"

This time, Ellie smiled, replete with the whitest teeth imaginable. I wouldn't have expected anything less.

"That was my idea," she said.

"Because you're used to getting men to say yes to you?" I asked.

"You're pretty upfront, Quint."

"I just want to know where I stand."

"I'll put it this way. I thought I had a better chance of convincing you than Gene Bowman."

"I'm going to tell him you said that."

And there was that smile again.

"How exactly does he fit in with the Keats family?" I asked.

"You know how some mafia families have a consigliere?"

"I've seen *The Godfather*," I said.

"Well, Gene Bowman is the consigliere for a completely legal, law-abiding family."

"It's a cute analogy, but what exactly does it mean?"

"He advises Archer. He's the guy who will find out if a potential business partner is doing too much cocaine. If a location Archer wants to build a restaurant has some noisy - or nosy - neighbors, Gene will know."

"Sure he's not a PI like myself?"

"You share some similarities. His firm also utilizes some financial planners."

"Does Archer Keats need one?"

"Everyone in the restaurant business needs one."

"Did Archer have ups and downs financially?"

"Everyone in the restaurant business does now and then."

"Point taken."

Ellie shifted in her chair and crossed her left leg over her right. I had to remind myself to keep my mind on the case.

The prospective case, Quint.

I had to remind myself I hadn't taken it yet.

"You'll learn about all this stuff as we progress, but why don't I describe in detail what happened to his wife. That seems more pertinent."

I noticed that neither Gene Bowman nor Ellie had ever mentioned Archer's wife by her first name. That seemed odd.

"Her name was Gracie, correct?" I asked.

"Yes," she said succinctly.

"You've got the floor," I said. "Convince me that your client didn't stab his wife twenty-seven times. Convince me that he's not a cold-blooded killer. And then, convince me why I should accept your offer."

"Let me start by asking you a question. How much do you know about the case?"

"Just what I've read in the papers and seen on T.V."

"No offense, but that ain't much. They've made his wife out to be this saint in waiting."

"She wasn't?"

"No, although I can't blame the media. After a woman is stabbed through the heart, you can't just come out and say she was a two-timing whore who was about to file for divorce."

At that moment, I realized the woman in front of me was much more than a pretty face. Ellie Teague was cutthroat. If you were on trial for your life, you'd want her in your corner.

"Wouldn't the two-timing give him a motive?" I asked.

"Yes, I guess it would. Don't worry, the jury won't be looking at Archer's motive."

"Seems like something that would be pertinent."

"Peripherally, they'll be aware of it, but I'll be too busy making them examine the motives of the other suspects I'm going to throw at them."

I vocalized what I'd internalized earlier.

"Archer Keats is lucky to have you on his side."

"Yes, he is."

There was no denial or playing it down by Ellie. Her confidence was on par with her beauty.

"So, is that where you want to start? Your other suspects?"

"No, I'm going to start at the beginning. And once I finish, I'll tell you what I expect from you."

"If I take the case," I said.

"When you take the case."

I smiled, in spite of myself.

Ellie took a deep breath and started talking.

"I'll try to only focus on the bullet points."

I nodded and she continued.

"Archer met Gracie when he was twenty-seven and she was twenty. They fell head-over-heels for each other almost immediately and they knew they'd get married eventually. She was still in college, however, so they waited two years until she graduated and married a month later. They had two kids within their first twenty-four months of marriage. Archer Jr., who is now twenty-three, and his younger sister Grace, who is twenty-one. The first twenty or so years of their marriage sounded idyllic. Archer claims the last few years were when things started going downhill. Gracie had begun to enjoy her Chardonnay just a bit too much and was drinking at least a bottle at home every night. More when they went out on the town. She was the consummate flirt, but Archer overlooked that. Truth was, it helped his business. Gracie could schmooze with the best of them and when you're opening restaurants and bars, that is beneficial."

She looked up at me.

"So far, so good?" she asked.

"I don't know about good, but I'm listening," I said.

We had our own little back-and-forth going. I imagined it was something that Ellie had with most people. Even conversations were a competition with her.

"Any questions?" she asked.

"Their children are named Archer Jr. and Grace?"

"Yeah, although their son is known as A.J."

"And I'm going to assume Grace is named after Gracie?"

"Yup."

"Both kids are named after their parents? Pretty douchey, I'd say."

"You won't get an argument out of me," Ellie said. "A bit conceited for sure. That doesn't make Archer a killer, however."

"No, it doesn't," I conceded.

I could tell Ellie didn't want to talk about the children. She changed the subject.

"As I mentioned earlier, Archer had some financial ups and downs. The last few years had been a little tough. Several restaurants went under because of Covid."

"Was there a prenup?"

"No. And probably not in the way you meant either."

"I'm not sure what you mean."

"She was the richer one."

I hadn't seen that mentioned anywhere.

"Really?"

"Archer was very successful, but he'd also lost probably a third of his net worth in the last few years. And his wife had received twenty million dollars on the day she turned twenty-one."

"Jeez. What business was her family involved in?"

"Movies. They produced some of the biggest blockbusters of the '80s and 90's."

"I'm afraid to ask, but is Archer the sole beneficiary?"

"Yes. And that's surely going to be the prosecution's motive once the trial starts. That he killed his wife for the money."

"You really don't like mentioning her name do you?" I asked.

"Gracie. Gracie. Gracie. How's that?"

"You're too much," I said.

She smiled.

"You're going to hate hearing this, but I view her as the enemy."

"Because she was stabbed twenty-seven times?"

"Because her death might put my client in jail for life. An innocent man."

"That doesn't make Gracie Keats the enemy," I said.

"Once you hear more about her, you might change your mind."

"I doubt it, but continue."

She gave me a quick staredown. Ellie Teague didn't like being told what to do.

"Things were on the rocks, but they remained married, both sleeping in different living quarters. There's a courtyard terrace that separates the main house from a guest house. His wife remained in the master bedroom of the main house and Archer started sleeping in the guest home."

"And you said this started about two years ago?"

"Their marriage started going downhill two years ago. I'm not sure exactly when Archer moved to the guest house. I'll find out."

"I'm going to guess that on the night in question, Archer was in the guest house?"

"That's right. And he never stepped foot in the main house. And unless he has some otherworldly skills I don't know of, that would preclude him from being Gracie's killer."

She accentuated Gracie's name, obviously for my benefit.

"Why did the cops arrest Archer?"

I found myself referring to him by his first name. It just seemed easier. I still despised the name Archer.

"Haven't you watched *Dateline* or *48 Hours*? They always suspect the spouse."

"That's for sure," I admitted. "I'll rephrase. What evidence did they have, besides him living on the premises and being her husband."

"Rephrase sounds like something an attorney would say."

I smiled.

"So did they have any direct evidence?"

"I think whoever killed Gracie knew the Keats well."

It was a bit of a non-sequitur from Ellie.

"What do you mean?"

"After the killer stabbed her to death, he left the main house and walked the fifty yards or so to the guest home, spilling Gracie's blood all over the terrace as he did. When he arrived outside of Archer's, he raised his hands - which were surely covered in gloves - and spilled blood all over the door to the guest home. And yet, police never found a drop of Gracie's blood in the guest house. I think someone was trying to frame Archer by leaving a trail of blood. Maybe he was even hoping he could get inside and leave a few more drops of blood. The door was locked though, so he had to settle for it looking like Archer was trailing blood as he walked back to his place."

There was a lot to digest.

"For now, I'll accept your premise that Archer wasn't involved."

"It's not just a premise, but sure."

"Did he sleep through the whole thing?"

"Yes. There's no way he could have heard his wife being murdered. When you see the crime scene, you'll realize how far it is from the guest house. Anyway, Archer woke up the next morning and saw all the blood when he stepped outside. He immediately entered the main house and found his wife dead in bed, the knife still sticking through her heart."

"My God," I said. "Obviously, I'd heard that she'd taken a knife through the heart. I didn't know the killer left the knife in her."

"He sure did."

Something clicked.

"You've said he several times. Are you sure the killer is a male?"

"No, I guess not. It's just kind of become my default. It feels weird to say 'he or she' every time you mention the killer."

"I understand," I said.

"And if we're being honest, it's much more likely to be a male. She was stabbed twenty-seven times."

"That's fair."

We looked at each other, but no one said anything for several seconds.

"Are you intrigued?" Ellie finally asked.

"Intrigued is probably not the word I'd use. I just finished working on a case of a serial killer with victims dating back decades. That was intriguing. This seems more like a '*Did he or didn't he*' type of case."

"I've only pulled back one layer of the onion. I promise you there is more."

"Now see, that sounds intriguing," I said.

"Well then join me on this case. And let's peel that onion together."

Was she hitting on me or just trying to get me to join her?

Maybe there wasn't much of a difference. She wanted to get her man, one way or another.

"I'd like to do one more thing before I agree to take the case," I said.

"Anything."

"I'd like to meet Archer Keats."

"Done. How about tomorrow?"

"Sure."

"I'll call him and we'll set up a time. You know he's been bailed right?"

"Yeah, I read that."

"I'm glad you'll get to see the scene of the crime. And even better, you'll get to meet the man being framed for murder."

Ellie Teague was damn convincing, but I'm not sure I fully trusted her.

I vowed to keep my eye on her.

And not just for her looks.

"Set it up," I said. "I'll be there."

CHAPTER 3

A million dollar bail would be out of the question for most people. Archer Keats wasn't most people. He'd posted $100,000 - 10% of the overall bail - and been released from jail a day after he was arrested.

Maybe his financial situation was unstable, but it certainly wasn't dire.

He'd agreed not to leave the county as part of the agreement. They put on an ankle bracelet to ensure that didn't happen.

And from what Ellie had told me, Archer had rarely left the house. I couldn't blame him. Would you want to hit up Trader Joe's and have everybody pointing fingers and calling you a murderer?

Not that Archer Keats was a Trader Joe's regular.

From the outside, the Keats' home didn't look all that spectacular. For a guy who owned twenty-plus restaurants and whose wife was worth millions, I was expecting something more extravagant.

I parked my car on the ample driveway and made my way towards the front door. They must have seen me coming because the front door opened before I got there. Archer Keats and Ellie Teague stood waiting.

The defendant and the defender.

The older man and the younger woman.

I imagined that's one of the reasons Archer Keats wanted Ellie to defend him. If you're accused of stabbing a woman to death, it couldn't hurt to have a woman defending you.

'Look! Here's a woman who knows I didn't do it.'

I approached Archer Keats for the first time. He looked older than I'd expected. I shouldn't have been surprised. He'd been through a lot. I'm sure anyone would age a little bit after his wife was stabbed to death.

Either from the heartbreak of it all or, if you'd committed the crime yourself, the guilt.

He was wearing jeans and a white t-shirt. He looked very ordinary.

Was that part of the plan to convince me?

Did they think if he came out in a $3,000 dollar suit that I'd be turned off?

Truth was, I probably would be.

"Hello, Quint. I'm Archer Keats."

I shook his hand. He was around six feet tall and I was a good two inches taller.

"Thanks for meeting with me."

"Ellie tells me you two had a nice meeting, but you wanted to meet me before deciding whether to take the case."

"That's true," I said.

"Well, then I better lay on the charm," he said.

He smiled, having as white a pair of teeth as Ellie.

"Just don't make me suspect it's all a show," I said.

This time I only got the courtesy, no-teeth smile.

"Oh, boys," Ellie said. "You're going to get along just fine. Shall we go inside?"

We entered the house and Archer shut the door behind us.

I immediately realized my mistake.

I'd judged a book by its cover.

Or, in this case, a house by its exterior.

The inside of the home was magnificent. Extravagant. Opulent.

There were pillars that rose from the floor to the vaulted ceiling. A stairwell that seemed to curve three or four times on its way to the second story. And a chandelier that might have occupied more square footage than my apartment.

"Wow," I said.

"That's what I said the first time I saw this place," Ellie said.

I was trying to get a read on Archer, not congratulate him on a gorgeous home. It was magnificent, however.

"You have a fantastic home," I said.

"Thank you, Quint," he said.

I had a feeling he'd be calling me by my first name today. Make it seem like we were old friends.

"And I'd like to congratulate you on catching Leonard Rolle over Christmas. And the Bay Area Butcher a few years back. You're very good at your job."

"Is that why you wanted me?"

"Yes. When I was arrested and Gene Bowman came to visit me, I asked him to try and secure your and Ellie's services. You two are my dream team."

It was an odd reference to make. O.J. Simpson had assembled what was called the dream team and most people believe he violently stabbed his wife - and Ronald Goldman - to death.

I looked at Ellie and she realized his faux pas.

"Let's not use that phrase anymore," she said.

It took Archer a second until he realized his mistake.

"I apologize. That's not what I was referring to."

"Maybe not intentionally," Ellie said. "But you say something like that while you're on the stand and believe me, the jury will remember."

"Should I show Quint upstairs?" Archer said, eager to change the subject.

I knew that Gracie Keats had been killed in her bed upstairs. They were leading me to the scene of the crime.

"Yes, I'd like to see it," I said.

We started walking up the majestic spiral staircase. I looked at the pictures lining the walls as we made our way up. There were several of Archer, Gracie, and their two children. It was a very photogenic family.

We arrived at the top of the stairs.

"Are you ready for this, Quint?" Ellie asked.

I would have imagined it was twenty times more difficult for Archer. I don't care how many times he'd been up there since Gracie was killed.

"I'm ready," I said.

We entered the gigantic master bedroom. It was all hardwood flooring.

We took several steps in and stood at the base of a king-sized bed with a massive golden headboard. The bed was fully made up with four gold and four white pillows pressed up against the headboard. An off-white duvet with ruffles extended over the length of the bed.

You'd never guess that a horrendous crime had been committed feet from us.

I couldn't imagine the agony that Gracie suffered in this bed.

It was almost inconceivable.

They talk about some murders being more personal than others. I'd say twenty-seven stab wounds would qualify.

And nothing is more personal than a husband killing a wife.

I looked over at Archer Keats.

Was I five feet away from the man who'd savagely butchered his wife?

My first impression of him had been a good one, but what the hell did that mean?

He was using everything in his repertoire to impress me.

I had to take my initial judgment with a grain of salt.

He seemed to notice that I was deep in thought.

"I know what you're probably thinking right now, Quint, but I didn't kill my wife."

"That's not what I was thinking," I lied.

"Yeah, you were," he said, calling me on my bluff.

There was no reason to keep the charade going.

"Alright, I was."

He didn't say anything or give me a "*gotcha*" face.

No one said anything for probably a minute as I looked out upon the bed.

Suddenly, an idea came to mind.

"Can I ask a few questions?" I asked.

"Of course."

"Did Gracie sleep on her back, front, or was she a side sleeper?"

They both looked at me inquisitively.

"I'm fascinated to know why you'd ask that," Ellie said

"I'll tell you after Archer answers," I said.

I didn't want him thinking too hard about it. He'd been married to her for twenty-plus years. He had to know the answer.

"She slept on her back almost exclusively. Maybe she'd occasionally roll over on her side, but she almost never slept on her stomach."

Ellie looked at me, longing for an answer.

"Gracie was only stabbed through the chest, correct?" I asked.

"Yes," they simultaneously answered.

"And she had no defensive wounds, correct?"

I'd read that as well.

"No, she didn't," Ellie said.

"What are you getting at?" Archer asked.

"If your wife slept on her stomach, the killer would have had to roll her over to stab her in the chest. That would have woken her up and she'd have had time to protect herself. Which means she'd have defensive wounds, but she didn't have any."

They were trying to fathom what I was saying. I continued.

"My guess was that the killer approached and saw your wife sleeping on her back and made sure the first stab was deep and it rendered her defenseless. I'm not saying she was killed instantaneously, but maybe the first stab prevented her from having the ability to raise her arms in defense. Like I said, if she'd been lying on her stomach, she'd have had defensive wounds."

They looked at me with admiration.

"Maybe I should hire you as co-counsel," Ellie said. "That's impressive, Quint."

"I agree," Archer said. "But does it actually mean anything?"

"I'd say it's good for your defense. It shows that anyone could have killed Gracie. The lack of defensive wounds means nothing."

I felt dirty saying these things, but I was trying to think as someone defending Archer Keats would think.

"Were you a lawyer in a previous life?" Ellie asked. "This is impressive stuff."

"It's just how my mind works," I said.

"You're fired, Ellie. I'm hiring Quint to try the case," Archer said, a big smile on his face.

It was a terrible look and Archer knew it immediately.

"I'm so sorry," he said. "I realize this isn't the time or the place for bad jokes."

"Don't worry about it, Archer," Ellie said.

I kept my mouth shut. I wouldn't have so easily excused him.

Having a big smile only feet from where your wife was murdered? Inexcusable.

However, and maybe I was just spinning this, it's not something a guilty man would likely do. He'd do everything in his power to look sad and distraught. Archer had done the opposite and made a tasteless joke. Weirdly, and probably contradictory to logic, this made me think it was less likely he was guilty.

We walked away from the foot of the bed, heading towards the closet/bathrooms. Archer showed me the dual sinks and a giant shower with two showerheads. They also had a massive walk-in closet. Gracie's dresses remained on her side.

His side had nothing.

The reason was obvious. He'd been banished to the guest house. And he surely wasn't coming back to sleep in this room. Not after what happened.

"Quint, would you like to see where I've been living for the last year or so?"

"Yes."

We exited the master bedroom and walked to the top of the stairs.

"I'm sorry for making that horrendous joke," he said. "I didn't kill my wife. I promise you that. But I imagine you must think I'm an insensitive asshole for what I said. I apologize."

I wasn't going to admit it had actually worked to his advantage.

"It won't be the final determinant on whether I take this case," I said.

That seemed to satisfy him.

We walked down the stairs and exited the main house into a little court-yard. There were two patio sets with long, glass rectangular tables and several chairs around each. Four or five lattices were littered throughout the courtyard, with some sort of ivy plants hanging from each. It was a very peaceful area. In better times, I'm sure they had many brunches out here.

At the end of the courtyard was what must have been the guest house. He led us in that direction.

Archer looked over at me.

"I was in the guest house the night Gracie was killed. After about seven p.m. or so, I never left. I swear on the lives of my children."

Part of me wanted to say, 'I believe you', but I wasn't ready to cross that bridge.

"And what time did you get up the next morning?" I asked.

"A little before eight. I walked out and saw the blood all over my door and the courtyard. I immediately entered the main house. There was blood on the stairwell so I ran up it to check on Gracie. And that's when I saw her."

He started to choke up. It seemed authentic.

"You don't have to describe it," I said.

"Thanks," he said, through a few tears. "It's something I'll be burdened with for the rest of my life."

Ellie decided to break up the sound of Archer's sobs.

"Archer called the cops immediately and answered all of their questions for hours on end," she said.

It was unnecessary. She was trying too hard.

"As opposed to doing what?" I asked.

The hard-headed woman in front of me looked a little sheepish for the first time.

"I'm just trying to let you know that he cooperated fully."

I had Ellie on her back heel. It wouldn't last so I was enjoying it for the time being.

Archer opened the door to the guest house.

It looked more like a man cave. There was a pool table in the middle of the room and a bar with five stools on the far end. An old school, sit-down Ms. Pac Man rounded out the room.

A door was open and you could see into a sizable bedroom. There looked to be a smaller room as well.

"What do you think?" Archer asked.

"It's not like you were relegated to Siberia," I said.

Archer smiled.

"There was definitely some charm to this place. But I'd built a life with my wife. I didn't want to be banished to the guest house. I wanted to sleep in the main house with her."

"You must have been pretty bitter?"

I was definitely pressing both of their buttons. I wanted to see how they'd react before I agreed to take the case.

"It wasn't like that. I was only pissed because I'd been exiled down here and I couldn't be with my wife."

"Is that so? Ellie made it out like you were irritated with her."

"Those aren't mutually exclusive, Quint. I could be pissed off at my wife and still want to sleep in the same bed as her. In fact, I'd venture to say that every marriage has been in that stage at one point or another."

It was a fair point.

"I'll concede that," I said.

"Ellie is correct, though. I was mad. She was an impossible flirt and there were times I thought she was cheating on me. I just couldn't prove it."

"I heard she might have been drinking too much as well?"

"Yes. It got to the point where if we went out in Walnut Creek, she'd be housed before we finished dinner."

I hadn't heard one word about their kids. From Gene Bowman, Ellie, or Archer himself.

"Did your kids turn on her?"

"No. She was smart enough to tone down her drinking when they came to visit."

"Where do they live?"

I hated involving the children, but if I was going to immerse myself in this case, I'd have to understand the family dynamic. And entertain the possibility that maybe another family member besides Archer wanted Gracie Keats dead.

I wouldn't be doing my job if I didn't at least consider it.

"A.J., that's what we call Archer Jr., lives in Lake Tahoe. His sister, Grace, lives in Napa."

I still thought it was asinine to name both kids after their parents, but I held my tongue. One name, I could understand. Two was just asking for attention.

I'd found Archer to be somewhat believable. I wasn't ready to proclaim his innocence, but I wasn't going to condemn him merely for his kids' names.

"And were either of them in town on the night your wife was killed?" I asked.

"No," he said.

Ellie, who had been oddly silent since I'd reprimanded her, finally spoke.

"A.J. and Grace both had great relationships with their parents. They are above reproach."

Her answer sounded formulaic.

"Be that as it may, if I decide to take this case, I will be looking into every member of the family. Friends like Gene Bowman as well. Your goal is to get Archer off, correct?"

"Of course, but not by throwing his kids under the bus."

"That's not what I meant," I said. "I'd want to talk to them because maybe they know of someone who had it in for their mother."

"You don't think they would have spoken up to the cops?"

"Listen, Ellie. I understand I'd be working for you, but I'd also be out there on my own, trying to find out what happened. If you're not going to allow that, maybe you should find someone else."

Archer spoke next.

"Quint, Ellie is just trying to look out for my kids. Of course, you can talk to them if you'd like. They know I didn't do this."

"I'm sorry for jumping on you," Ellie said.

"Apology accepted," I replied.

I was oddly enjoying this.

"When will you make your decision, Quint?" Archer asked.

"I'll decide by tomorrow. Give me today to think about it."

"That's fine."

There was something I'd meant to ask.

"Why are you going ahead with a speedy trial?" I asked.

"Because I want to clear my name."

"If that's true, wouldn't you want to give Ellie more time to be able to prove you're innocent?"

"You don't prove you're innocent, Quint. They try to prove you're guilty."

He was right, and suddenly, it was me who looked silly.

"Archer for the win," Ellie said. "Quint takes the L."

After my jabs at her, I knew she was relishing this.

"Ellie is reinstated as lead counsel," Archer said, doubling down on his earlier mistimed joke.

This time it was actually funny.

I laughed quietly. Ellie laughed much louder.

"You're a competitive SOB, aren't you Ellie?" I said.

"You know this already. And I think you are too. Imagine us working together, eviscerating the prosecution's case brick by brick."

She stared at me seductively. Or, so I thought.

"I do like a good battle of wits," I said.

"And we'd be saving an innocent man's life."

"That would be me," Archer said, raising his hand.

It was also oddly funny. This whole conversation had taken a weird turn.

I didn't know if Archer Keats killed his wife.

And I hate admitting this, but I almost didn't care. The intrigue of it all. The spectacle, the matching of wits versus the prosecution, even working with Ellie. It was starting to get the best of me.

I was captivated.

No, it was more than that. I was all-in. Just like Ellie had wanted.

"Fuck it," I said. "I'm in."

They both came in and gave me a hug.

What the hell had I got myself into?

CHAPTER 4

Ellie called me that afternoon.

"Should we iron out the financial details?" she asked.

"Why don't I swing by your office? You give me a couple of things and I'll sign on the dotted line."

"Sure. And what things?"

"I'd like the initial police report as well as a list of people you intend on calling to the stand."

"The police report is easy. As far as the witnesses, I'm still deciding whom I'm going to call."

"That's fine. You can give me a list of possibilities," I said.

"You do realize that you'll be working for me and not the other way around?"

"I do. If I'm taking the case though, I want to make sure I'm informed. I don't want to be ambushed and have to interview a potential witness I've never heard of."

"I'm starting to understand why you're such a good P.I."

"Probably the same reasons you're a good lawyer."

"How do you know that?"

"You're smart. You're thorough. And you're cutthroat. Just to be sure, I did a little research. It appears you've never lost a criminal case."

"That is true. And Archer Keats is not going to be the first."

"I also read that this will only be your seventh murder case."

"Murderers aren't falling off of trees in the East Bay."

"Murder suspects," I corrected.

"Yes, that's what I meant. Smartass."

As usual, we had a compelling back and forth. Part combative, part battle-of-wits. With a little flirting underneath the surface.

"How late are you at the office 'til?"

"I'll be here until six."

"Alright, I'll stop by a little after five. It will give you time to arrange the things I need."

"I'll draw up the contract as well."

"Good. See you later today."

"Bye, Quint."

I showed up a few minutes after five.

Ellie Teague was the only person remaining at her law firm. We were in the conference room again. I continued to be unimpressed by the copious amount of legal books.

We went over the boring particulars of our financial agreement. They were fair. I was to be employed until the trial came to a conclusion or if a settlement was made before the trial started. I would be paid by the hour; at slightly higher than average rates for a private investigator.

While I was theoretically employed by Archer Keats, I would answer to Ellie and she would tell me the things she wanted to be investigated. Potential jobs would include trying to find conflicting statements by prosecution witnesses and checking for alibis of people that Ellie considered potential suspects in Gracie's murder.

Whether she really considered other people suspects, or if that was just to throw people off the scent of Archer, was debatable. I guess it didn't really matter. I was going to do my job. That's what I was being paid for, after all.

"Are you ready to sign on the dotted line?" Ellie asked.

"Sure. Although it never really is a dotted line, is it?"

She looked down at the piece of paper.

"No dots," she said. "It's a long, straight line."

I don't know whether she meant to say it seductively, but that's the way I took it. Ellie Teague was a riddle wrapped in an enigma. Or, however, that phrase went.

I signed my name.

Part of me thought I'd just signed a deal with the devil.

I was going to try and exonerate a man who may have stabbed his wife through the heart.

"Can I add an addendum?" I asked.

"You just signed the papers, Quint."

"Alright, then I'll just come out and say it."

"Say what exactly?"

"If I find evidence that convinces me that Archer did kill Gracie, I'll be quitting the case."

"Lawyers can't just quit if they think their client is guilty."

"Well, good thing I'm not an attorney."

She shook her head. And followed it up with a smile.

"This is going to be fun, isn't it?" she said.

"It's going to be something, alright. I'll let you know in a month if fun is the adjective I'd use."

"Why don't you come by the office tomorrow? We'll do a little planning going forward."

"I'll be here."

She grabbed the files I'd asked for and set them in my right hand.

"Here are the police reports. I'll get you the witness list tomorrow."

She then held on to my wrist for a few more seconds than necessary.

This is going to be fun, isn't it?

What type of fun was she referring to?

I drove back to my apartment at 1716 Lofts in the middle of downtown Walnut Creek.

I lived on the fifth floor and had a nice view of the city below. It was no comparison to Archer Keats home, but it was perfect for me.

I poured myself a glass of red wine and threw on some jazz, my thinking man's music. On this day, I chose *Mingus Ah Um* by Charles Mingus.

I laid down a coaster on my end table and set the glass of wine down. Next, I took the police report and the list of potential witnesses and laid them on the coffee table in front of me. Finally, I took a seat on the couch and took a big sip from the wine glass.

And I started reading.

I'd covered most of it in my discussions with either Ellie or Archer. Gracie Keats was murdered sometime between midnight and two a.m. on December 22nd. She was found with a knife protruding from her heart the next morning by her husband. He claims to have seen all the blood and followed it into the main house, where he found his wife deceased in her bed. There was no sign of illegal entry into the house and the doors had remained locked.

It brought some questions to mind.

Question #1: If Archer Keats did kill his wife, why would he leave a trail of blood leading to the guest house?

The prosecution's answer would be obvious: He was making it look like someone was trying to frame him.

Question #2: Who else had keys to the main house?

I'd be sure to follow up on that question when I met with Ellie.

I went back to reading.

The police arrived after Archer's 911 call. Obviously, Gracie was pronounced dead at the scene.

When you have a knife sticking out of your heart, there's not a rush to try and perform life-saving measures.

Being that Archer Keats was the only other person on-site, the police started questioning him at once. This began at the house and continued when they took him down to the station for further questioning.

The police continued doing their due diligence for several days.

Gene Bowman first called me on December 24th. Archer hadn't been arrested yet, but they must have known that was a distinct possibility.

And on December 29th, the inevitable happened, and Archer was arrested for his wife's murder. The next morning, at his court appearance, he was charged and posted bail.

Although the crime was barbaric in nature, the judge allowed bail. My guess was that since Archer Keats was such a well-known member of the community, he was not considered a flight risk.

I got my second call from Gene Bowman a week after Archer was arrested. Ellie was already the attorney of record. Did they contact her the morning that Gracie was found or did they wait until Archer was arrested?

It doesn't appear that much happened between December 29th and January 12th, when I got the third phone call from Bowman.

Maybe a few court dates.

I wanted to find out when Archer had asked for a speedy trial.

Also, when was Ellie going to be given Discovery by the prosecution?

That's when you could start analyzing just how good their case was.

Sadly, I knew a little bit about the criminal justice system, having been wrongfully arrested by Ray Kintner, who became a great friend of mine and subsequently died at the hands of the Bay Area Butcher. I still wasn't over it.

I started to read the police report a second time.

In a show of solidarity, I refilled my wine glass a second time as well.

CHAPTER 5

"My guess is that the trial will start in about a month," Ellie said.

I was back at her law firm the following day.

She was wearing another pantsuit with a white blouse underneath and navy blue pants and jacket.

I was wearing some khakis and a white dress shirt. It's about as dressed up as I'd get unless at a wedding or a funeral. Or a murder trial.

This time we were in her actual office. Maybe she realized the big, bad conference room hadn't dazzled me. Or, maybe she'd got her man for the job, and no longer cared about impressing me.

"A month doesn't seem that bad," I said.

"Maybe not for you. You're just the P.I. investigating behind the scenes. I'm the lead attorney for a case that might get national attention. And it will certainly be a massive event locally. Do you think I want to look incompetent?"

"That's not what I meant."

"I know. I'm just saying that the pressures that face the two of us are entirely different. Your picture won't be plastered all over the T.V."

"It has been before," I said.

"True," she conceded. "But it's always been for something great you've done. Not for being a lousy attorney who fucked up a high-profile case."

She had a point. It was also the first time she'd shown me her vulnerable side.

"You're going to do just fine," I said. "Now, what can I do to make your job easier?"

"I've made a list of several people I'd like you to interview. Remember, our job is to defend Archer to the best of our ability. So if his daughter tells you that she thinks he did it -which I hope she won't say, by the way - that doesn't help me. I want information that will help exonerate him. Or, at the least, help call into question whether he did it. I'd also like to know if these prospective witnesses might come back and bite us in the ass. I don't want someone saying under cross-examination that Gracie told Archer a day before she was murdered that she was filing for divorce. Surprises are the enemy of a defense attorney. So I want to know everything about these people. Are they loyal to Archer? Will they turn on us at the last second? And most of all, are they an advantageous or disadvantageous witness for the defense. Sure, they might get called anyway, but I'd rather one of the prosecution witnesses point the finger at Archer. If one of our own witnesses thinks Archer did it, we're basically fucked."

"You're going to have no problem making an opening statement," I said.

Ellie laughed.

"I can be a little long-winded."

"You're in the right profession," I said.

"Did you understand what I was trying to get at?"

"Of course. You want to know everything there is to know about these prospective witnesses. Warts and all."

"That's right. And listen, I'll be talking with them before they go on the stand, but I'd much rather know beforehand if they're going to drop an atomic bomb on our defense. Plus, I've got a lot of other experts to deal with. The crime scene people, DNA, and that type of boring shit."

"You can leave me out of that."

"Don't worry, I've already got a DNA expert hired for that undertaking."

The piece of paper sat on the table in front of us, but I hadn't read it yet.

"So, stop leaving me in suspense. Who are some of the people on this list?"

"One, their son, A.J. Two, their daughter, Grace. As I said, be gentle with them. Three, Gene Bowman. Four, Donna Neal, who was Gracie's best friend. Five, Vic Parsons, who was their next-door neighbor. And last, Brad Lacoste."

"Who's that?"

"He's the tennis pro that Gracie took lessons from. And the man Archer thought Gracie might be having an affair with."

"This is quite the eclectic list."

"It sure is. I have no doubt there will be more. This is enough to start, however."

"How exactly is this going to work? Do you want me to update you every day?"

"Yeah. At least send me a daily text. I'll be busy, so we won't be meeting every day, but I'd like to know how things are progressing."

"That's easy enough."

"And then every second or third day, we'll sit down and you can talk about what you've learned about each prospective witness."

"This sounds pretty open-ended," I said.

"It is. You're obviously good at your job. While this isn't exactly the same as what you've been doing, it's not that far off. You're still trying to solve a mystery. Just make sure this mystery doesn't end with Archer being the murderer."

She exposed her teeth, but it seemed less a smile and more a warning.

"It's like a game of Clue, but we're removing Colonel Mustard as a suspect."

"I was always more of a Professor Plum kind of gal."

This time she gave me her full, unadulterated, charming smile.

"Well, we know it's with a knife and in the bedroom. Now, all we have to do is find out who."

"You're already two-thirds of the way there. The rest should be a piece of cake," Ellie said.

"Child's play. I should be able to wrap this thing up by dinner.."

Ellie laughed.

"That's the attitude. Listen, I got one of the DNA bores coming in ten minutes. Let's talk tomorrow."

"Sounds good," I said.

Before I stood up, Ellie had walked over and put her arms on my shoulder.

"We're going to make a good team," she whispered in my ear.

There was no longer a question.

She was undoubtedly hitting on me.

Now for the million-dollar question.

Was I going to act on it?

CHAPTER 6

Archer Archibald Keats II was one of the most obnoxious names I'd ever heard.

I'd figured Archer had already been shortened from Archibald. But no, there was a second "Archie" making an appearance in the family name.

I wanted to puke.

Instead, I had to play nice.

I met AAKII - my working name for him - at my office two days after procuring the list of potential witnesses from Ellie Teague.

Archer was wearing flip-flops, white cargo shorts, and a yellow t-shirt. It was January and quite chilly out. It didn't seem to bother him.

I opened the door as I saw him approach.

"You know it's January, don't you?" I asked.

"I'm hot-blooded. What can I say?"

I'd only known him for two sentences, but there was none of the snobbishness that I was expecting.

"I respect that," I said. "And yes, I'm Quint."

"Nice to meet you, Quint. I'm A.J."

"Not Archer?" I asked, poking the bear for no reason.

"Nope. And certainly not Archer Archibald or Archer Jr. or any of the other ridiculous things I've been called over the years."

I smiled. I'd incorrectly judged a book by its cover again. Or, in this case, a man by his name.

"A.J. it is. Why don't we go inside?"

"Sure."

I led him back to my office and we both sat down. I'd hired an answering service who picked up the calls to my office, but I still didn't have an in-office secretary. It didn't seem necessary just yet. Soon, hopefully.

"First off, I'd like to say how sorry I am about your mother."

"Thanks. It's now been almost a month so the surprise is starting to wear off. That doesn't mean I don't think about her many times every day."

"Of course. I'll be asking some tough questions, so I just want you to know that it's not coming from a place of malice."

"I understand. You're working for my father. I know we're on the same team."

"I was going to wait and ask this, but I might as well ask now. Do you think your father had anything to do with your mother's death?"

"Of course not. My father loved my mother. With all of his heart. Did they fight sometimes? Obviously. What married couple of twenty years doesn't? Were they living in separate quarters? Yes. I'll even admit that things hadn't been very rosy over the last year or so. All that being said, my father loved her. He never would have killed her. My father is guilty of many things - including burdening me with this terrible name - but he didn't kill my mother."

It was an odd thing to say, bringing his name into a discussion of his murdered mother. If I was playing armchair psychiatrist, I'd say that A.J. Keats tried to use humor to cope.

"Thanks. I'm sure that couldn't have been easy."

"If this had been within a week or so of the murder, I don't think I could have done this interview. As time has moved on, I've been trying to focus on all the great memories of my mother, while attempting to avoid thinking about the way she was killed. Which, obviously, is easier said than done."

"We'll have to get back to it at some point, but I'd like to get some basic stuff out of the way first."

"Sure."

"How old are you?"

"Twenty-three."

"And where do you live?"

"In Lake Tahoe."

I knew the answer to the above questions, but since becoming a P.I., I'd noticed that asking easy, throwaway questions tended to get someone more willing to talk.

"And you're two years older than your sister?"

"Some parts of the year. Other times I'm only one year older. We're eighteen months apart."

"Are you two close?"

"Close-ish. Grace can be a handful."

"I'm meeting with her tomorrow."

"Good luck," A.J. said and smiled.

"Do you want to tell me more?"

"And ruin the surprise? Hardly."

This time he laughed. My upcoming meeting with Grace Keats all of a sudden held more intrigue.

"Were you closest to anyone in your family?"

"Probably my mother. My father was very hard-charging and my mother was more laid back, so it shouldn't come as a surprise."

Ellie hadn't exactly described Gracie Keats as laid back. Then again, she said she viewed Gracie as the enemy, so maybe her representation of her was going to be jaded.

"What did you and your father butt heads about?"

"Mostly small stuff."

"Any big stuff?"

"Yeah."

"Would you mind sharing it with me?" I asked.

This had been the first time that A.J. hadn't been completely forthright.

"He wanted me to join the family business. I have other plans."

"What is it that you want to do?"

"Something in the arts. I want to create. I want to leave something tangible for when I'm gone."

"You're only twenty-three, A.J. You're going to be around for a long time."

"I know. I just don't like the idea of buying and selling my whole life."

"Some people might say that a restaurant is tangible. And creative."

"Yeah, maybe. For the architects designing the restaurant or the chefs coming up with the menu. My Dad is on the business side, not the creative side."

"Point taken. So what exactly are your plans?"

"I majored in film studies last summer. My plan is to head down to Los Angeles soon."

"Why haven't you moved yet?"

"My girlfriend lives with me in Tahoe. She's not so keen about moving to LaLa Land."

This conversation was certainly free-wheeling and not what I'd expected at all.

"I'm sure you'll make the right decision."

"I told my girlfriend I was moving down there in February. I wanted her to join, but if she won't, I have to follow my dream. But now, with my mother's death, I won't be going anywhere in February. I can't exactly ditch out on Dad and Grace right now. Especially with a trial looming."

A.J. was older and wiser than his years. Usually, that's used as a compliment, but with him, it was more of a burden. He was saddled by the worries that being older brings. He wasn't as carefree as you should be at twenty-three. Obviously, his mother's death had a lot to do with that, but I had a feeling he'd always been this way.

"Hollywood isn't going anywhere," I said. "It will be there this summer. Or later this year."

"Thanks."

"I'm going to ask another question that may hurt."

"I knew this conversation wasn't going to be all roses. Go ahead."

"I heard a few rumors that your mother may have drank too much. Are they true?"

"Yeah, I guess that's fair. To be honest, she's far from the only one in the hospitality business. Try being sober at all these restaurant openings, with everyone wanting to have a drink with you."

"Were there that many restaurant openings?"

"It wasn't just the grand openings. It was the one-year anniversary. The five-year anniversaries. If a restaurant was named 'Top 50 in the Bay Area' or something like that, my father threw a party. If a local politician wanted a fundraiser, he'd do it at one of my father's restaurants. And my mother was always the host. That's not to say she didn't like it, I just thought there were too many."

"Are we talking one a month?"

"I'd say closer to one a week. I swear there was always some excuse to host something."

"And why didn't you like it?"

"Because of what you said. My mother could get a little drunk at these things. And they'd always fight more when they were drunk."

"Did your father drink at these?"

"Sure, but not as much as Mom."

A.J. looked out past me towards the window. I saw his eyes start to moisten.

It was the first time he'd said Mom instead of mother and I think he realized it himself.

"I'm sorry," I said. "Let's talk about something else."

"Thanks. My mother was a great woman. I'd rather not remember her for her imperfections."

"What were some of her great qualities?"

He wiped a tear away.

"She'd do anything for us. Grace and I played every sport as kids. Guess who always brought the oranges or Capri-suns to soccer? Guess who cheered loudest when one of us made a basket? Guess who paid for all the uniforms in little league? I'm not sure she ever missed a game of ours."

"That's great to hear."

"And she was completely supportive. While my Dad was trying to lure me into his business, my mother was telling me to go to LA. She just made me promise that I had to introduce her to George Clooney when I made it big."

I laughed.

"Probably wanted you to take her to the Oscars."

"Yup. She mentioned that too."

I shook my head.

"I'm sorry, A.J. Well, if you ever get to the Oscars, I'm sure she'll be looking down somewhere and smiling."

"Thanks."

"Can we get a few more unpleasant questions out of the way?"

"Yeah."

"Who do you think might have killed your mother?"

"I have no idea."

"Did she have any enemies?"

"No, she really didn't. My Dad did."

His words hung in the air. I hadn't really considered the idea that Gracie Keats had been killed to punish Archer Keats, but it made some sense. The killer had tried to frame him, after all.

"Do you think your mother's death might have been because of who your father was?"

"It makes as much sense as anything else. I don't think my father did it and no one hated my mother enough to murder her, so what other possibility is there?"

"Who were some of your father's enemies?"

"Pretty much anyone in the restaurant business in Walnut Creek. He was cutthroat. I know there were examples where he hadn't even planned on opening a restaurant, but when he found out another company was involved, he'd get interested, merely because he hated them."

"Are there a few companies you can think of?"

"One stands out. Johnson and Johnson. Yes, just like the famous company. It's a father and son venture. My father can't stand them. And vice versa."

I was ten minutes through my first interview and I'd already found another potential suspect. Or two, if you counted both father and son. Ellie was going to be happy.

Not that I should be concerning myself with how she felt.

And yet, here I was thinking about her.

"This is all great information. Thanks, A.J."

"You're welcome. I've lost my mother. I hope you and Ellie can prevent me from losing my father as well."

"Do you know Ellie?"

"My father had used the other attorney in her firm a few times, so we kind of knew Ellie as well."

Teague and Tiller. But I couldn't remember the other guy's name.

"Tiller, right?"

"Yeah. Wyatt Tiller."

"Is he a criminal defense attorney as well?"

"No. Civil."

"And your father needed him for more business-related matters?"

"Yeah. Investors suing. Employees complaining. When you own that many restaurants, things happen."

"I understand. Had he ever used Ellie before?"

"I don't think so, but as I said, we all kind of knew her."

"And Gene Bowman is the man behind the scenes, correct?"

"I guess you could say that. He's not exactly a guy who likes to hide, however."

"It sounds like he was one-part fixer, one-part money manager."

"Fixer makes it sound like he was dropping bodies in the Pacific. Gene is much less sinister, I can promise you that."

I was learning a lot from A.J.

He was going to be a big help when I knew more of the cast of characters surrounding Gracie Keats's murder. For now, he'd answered the limited questions I had.

"Can we meet again in a week or so?" I asked.

"Sure. I'll be coming down every few days until the trial starts. And once it does, I'll probably live down here."

He stood up, we shook hands, and I walked him to the exit.

Tre Larson had been a friend of mine for years.

He'd long been a recognizable face in the nightlife of Walnut Creek. If you ever spent time out on the town, you'd surely been introduced to Tre.

I'd originally met him when I was still with my ex-girlfriend Cara. He was working at a place called Rooftop. It served food and drinks with a great view of neighboring Mount Diablo.

We'd kept in touch over the years as he moved from restaurant to bar, bar to restaurant. He was an in-demand manager for a few reasons. One, he was very good at his job. And two, he had so many friends that bars and restaurants knew if you hired him, dozens of his friends would be checking out your new establishment.

He seemed like the right guy to ask a few questions about Johnson and Johnson.

∼

I met Tre at a place called Modern China. It was one of the few places in Walnut Creek that Tre had never worked. I imagine that's why he'd chosen it.

"Mr. Quint," he said.

He'd always used my first name as if it was my last.

"Mr. Tre," I responded in kind.

We gave each other a hug and sat down. Over the phone, I'd mentioned that it would be better if we weren't seated near anybody else, and sure enough, we had a table in the corner. I imagine Tre could get any table he wanted in Walnut Creek.

"Thanks for agreeing to meet me," I said.

"Of course. It's been a minute."

"Yeah, it has. I've been so wrapped up in my new job, I haven't had much of a social life."

"Life in moderation, Quint. That usually refers to drinking and eating, but it also means working. All work and no play makes Quint a dull boy."

Tre was kidding around, but it did hit home. Since Cara and I had broken up, I really hadn't exactly been Mr. Personality.

"That hurts," I said. "Probably because it's true."

"Let's get you back on a regular schedule. How about every other Friday we get a drink or two. Going out two days a month ain't going to kill ya."

"Probably be good for my mental health, now that you mention it."

"Indeed. People who bring down serial killers deserve a drink or two."

"You heard about that?"

"I'll assume you're kidding. You were the talk of the town. Do you know how many people came up to me and asked if that's the same Quint that I was friends with?"

"And what did you say?"

"I'd say, 'How many damn Quint's do you think there are?' Not exactly a name growing on trees."

I laughed. Tre had always been able to make me do that.

It might have seemed an odd friendship. I was six years older. He was a black guy who'd grown up on the tough streets of Oakland. I was a white guy who, although not born with a silver spoon, never had to struggle for things growing up.

None of that mattered. We'd got along great from the first day we met at Rooftop. We liked talking about the same things. Sports. Movies. Music. Women. We even had debates about the two things you're not supposed to talk about at bars: Politics and Religion.

And our differing backgrounds and races never meant a damn thing.

I was kind of disappointed in myself for not reaching out more. Tre could be a ray of sunlight, and in my new line of work, those were rare.

"I'm sorry for not having reached out lately," I said.

It sounded like an admission of some sort.

"Stop with that. You're busy working. I understand. Plus, you've now agreed to a twice a month commitment, so we're good."

I laughed again.

"I didn't know I'd committed."

"You'll thank me in the long run. Plus, you're going to owe me for dragging me out on this Friday night. It's my one night off this week."

"You didn't tell me that."

"It's been too long. I wasn't going to miss it."

"Thanks, buddy."

A waiter came by and we put in our orders. Broccoli Beef for Tre and chicken fried rice for me.

"So, you brought me here. What's up?"

"I probably should have told you over the phone, but I figured I'd drop it on you here."

"What's that?"

"I've been hired by the defense attorney of Archer Keats."

Tre let out a quick laugh.

"I should have known. I've worked at probably four or five of his restaurants."

"Did you know him well?"

"I wouldn't say well, but we definitely say hi when we see each other."

"Did you like him?"

"I had no problem with him. He was never rude. He was the owner though, so we never exactly became chummy."

"I'm just glad he didn't come off as a jerk."

"There's a lot of those in the restaurant business. Archer Keats wasn't one of them. Now, that doesn't mean he was Mother Teresa."

His 'Mother Teresa' comment aside, it was reassuring that Tre thought Archer was an alright guy.

"Have you heard of Johnson and Johnson?" I asked.

"Sure. I buy their baby powder all the time."

I looked at Tre, realized he was joking, and started laughing.

"Oh, you must mean the Walnut Creek Johnson and Johnson," he said. "Yeah, I know them too."

I looked around and made sure no one was walking towards us. Walnut Creek was a fairly small town and I didn't want people hearing us talking about some famous restaurateurs.

"Any thoughts on them?"

"Remember when I said there were a lot of jerks in the restaurant business?"

"Yeah."

"Those two fit the bill. Complete and total A-holes."

Bingo!

"I should have said this earlier, but I have no plans of telling Archer's attorney about this. The last thing you need is to be brought into court to talk about people you've worked for. I'm sure that wouldn't be good for your employment prospects. I promise this is just between us. You have my word, Tre."

"I believe you, Quint. And thanks for saying it. If word got out that I liked to gossip about my previous bosses, I'd be looking for a new line of work."

"Just think of this as two friends talking."

He smiled.

"That's exactly what this is."

"Then tell me more about Johnson and Johnson."

"I worked at two of their restaurants. Never again. Always barking orders and rude to the staff. You know how much that irks me."

"I do. They sound terrible, but is there more to it? As you said, jerks in the hospitality business aren't exactly rare."

"They were wannabe dictators. Every little thing had to be perfect. Which might be understandable, but it's the way they'd look at their employees."

"And how was that?"

"Like they were gum stuck on the bottom of their shoes."

"That bad?"

"Worse. Not sure I've ever heard a kind word said about them."

"Then why do people remain?"

"I imagine it's the first job for most of the waiting staff. None of the people I know who have been in this game for a long time would ever work for their punk asses."

"Anything besides verbal intimidation?"

"Heard a few stories of some sexual harassment. Never anything violent, however."

"So, if this was ever Archer vs. Johnson and Johnson, you'd be on Team Archer?"

Tre leaned in closer and whispered.

"Of course. But it begs the question. Are you suggesting that J and J killed Archer's wife?"

"No, I'm not saying that," I said. "Trying to find other potential suspects is kind of in my job description right now."

Tre leaned back and a slight smile came across his face.

"You might have to start coming out three or four times a month. This is some nasty business you've got yourself into."

I couldn't exactly deny it.

"Better than chasing a serial killer," I said.

"I guess. In the same way that skin cancer is better than pancreatic cancer."

"They are both cancers?"

"Something like that," Tre said.

I decided to change the subject.

"How's Gina?" I asked.

Gina had been Tre's longtime girlfriend. She also worked in the hospitality business. Tre and Gina were really the first couple of Walnut Creek nightlife.

"She's good. Thanks for asking. Does that mean we've moved on from Johnson and Johnson?"

"Yeah. For now. I may have some more questions down the line."

"You know where to find me. As for Gina, she is great. Working at 1515 tonight. Want to stop by there after and grab a drink?"

"Why wait?" I said.

I motioned to a waiter who quickly came over.

"You still drinking Rum and Cokes?" I asked Tre.

"You know it."

I turned back to the waiter.

"Can I get two Rum and Cokes please?"

"Coming up."

The waiter walked away.

"You've never had a specific drink, have you?" he asked.

"No, I'm like a permanent free agent. Jack and Coke one year. Vodka/soda the next."

"Not me. Rum and Coke locked me down years ago."

"Gina and Rum and Coke. The two things that locked Tre down."

He laughed.

"And I couldn't be happier."

"As to your earlier question, yes, let's go see Gina after this."

"You ready to tie one on tonight?"

"I'm not sure I'd go that far. But I'm up for a few."

"That's how it starts."

"Ain't that the truth," I said.

The waiter brought our drinks back over and said the food would be out in a minute.

"Cheers, Quint."

"Cheers, Tre. Thanks for coming out."

"For an old friend? Of course."

We clinked glasses and took a sip of our drinks.

CHAPTER 7

I woke up the next morning with a mild hangover.
Nothing an Advil couldn't cure, which is a testament to me getting home before it got crazy. After dinner, Tre and I met Gina and before I knew it, a group of old acquaintances showed up. I was sure that Tre had told them I was out on the town.

After Gina's spot, we hit a few more bars, but luckily I made my exit before the clock struck midnight.

I spent most of the night answering questions about my relatively new job as a private investigator. Luckily, they all pertained to the Ronnie Fisk or the Bay Area Butcher cases. No one knew I was now helping with the defense of Archer Keats except for Tre, and he wasn't going to say anything.

At one point, he leaned in and whispered to me.

"If you have more questions about Johnson and Johnson, let's do it over the phone. These walls have ears."

I got his point.

I felt bad for putting him on the spot at Modern China. I really did want to see him, but probably should have told him beforehand what we'd be discussing.

After rehashing the night, I stumbled out of bed and took down an Advil with some water.

It was time to find out a little more about Johnson and Johnson, so I moved to my couch and opened my trusty laptop.

A few Google searches later, I'd learned the following.

Parker Johnson, 57, and Caleb Johnson, 30, were a father and son business, known as Johnson and Johnson. For two decades, it had been known as The Parker Johnson Group until Caleb joined the family business five years ago. That's when they took on their current name.

I wonder if Archer had any misgivings that Parker and Caleb went into business together, but his son didn't want to join him?

Parker was an East Bay native and Caleb had been born and raised here as well. There were several pictures of them on the internet and it was the most obvious father/son duo I'd ever seen. Parker had lily-white hair, but besides that, looked like a young man. His face was seemingly devoid of wrinkles. Caleb's face was the spitting image of his father's, with the exception that his brown hair had not turned to white just yet.

Their eyes, nose, and cheeks looked like they'd been photoshopped onto the other.

As I looked at them, I began to feel guilty for the conclusions I'd jumped to.

While A.J. Keats hadn't been a fan and nor had Tre, it was a huge stretch to suggest that they'd kill a rival's wife by stabbing her twenty-seven times.

And calling it a huge stretch probably wasn't even enough. A Grand Canyon type stretch, maybe.

I was just doing my job, looking for other suspects, but I felt dirty.

I had exactly zero evidence that Parker and Caleb Johnson could - or would - ever do anything so brutal.

And here I was, mulling that very possibility.

~

I met with Grace Keats the following day at 4 p.m.

As with her brother, we met at my office, which was getting a lot of use as of late. She was wearing jeans and a beige, lightweight hoodie. She was an attractive young woman, which came as no surprise. She came from some pretty good DNA. In the looks department, at least.

"Thanks for meeting with me, Grace."

"You got it."

We walked to my office and sat down.

"So, how can I help you?" she asked.

"As you already know, I'm working to get your father acquitted of your mother's murder."

"Are you sure he didn't do it?"

Her question shocked me.

Archer and Ellie alluded to the fact that Grace might be a little rough around the edges, but certainly, nothing prepared me for this.

"That's not what I was expecting," I said.

"Join the crew. I wasn't expecting my mother to be stabbed twenty-seven times."

"Do you really think your father committed murder?"

"I didn't say that. I just asked if you're sure he didn't."

"No, I'm not sure," I answered honestly. "That's why I'm meeting people like your brother and yourself. I was hoping to get confirmation that your father never could have done something this horrible."

"It's hard to give confirmation when I wasn't there."

"Maybe confirmation wasn't the right word."

"Then what is?"

Instead of asking the questions, I was playing defense.

"I don't know. Maybe I was just expecting a little sympathy towards your father."

"He has my sympathy. That's not what you're looking for though."

I was starting to dislike the young woman across from me.

"Then why don't you tell me, Grace. What am I looking for?"

"People who will make good witnesses."

She wasn't wrong.

"That's partly true, but I'm also looking for people who think Archer is innocent. I'm not some biased hack who wants your father to be acquitted even if he committed the crime."

"Are you sure?"

It was a fair question. Was I already so involved in the case that I'd do anything to prevent Archer Keats from getting convicted? No, I wasn't at that point. If I knew - or even thought - he was guilty, I'd recuse myself from the case. I'd already told Ellie as much.

"I'm sure," I finally answered. "I've already told Ms. Teague that if I think your father is guilty, I'm off the case."

"That's admirable. I doubt there's going to be a smoking gun confirming his guilt, though. Or in this case, a smoking knife."

She was oddly nonchalant when she mentioned the word knife. If it was someone I'd loved, the last thing I'd do is make a joke about the murder weapon. It would conjure up too many disturbing images.

"I'm pretty good at my job, Grace. I may not need a 'smoking knife' to conclude that your father is guilty."

"What job? Working on an upcoming court case? I didn't know you'd done that before."

I looked out on Grace, half expecting some sort of smile. It wasn't to be.

"I was referring to my job as a private investigator in general. I'm pretty good at that."

"The guy who got his revenge at sea. The Bay Area Butcher. Saving the Vegas girl. Catching and killing Leonard Rolle."

I was taken aback.

"You sure know a lot about me. Although, I'm not the one who killed Leonard Rolle."

"Your investigation led to his death."

It was hard to argue with that.

"So you've been researching me?"

"I want to know who's helping out my father."

"Even a father you think might have killed your mother?"

"I still never said that."

"You've alluded to it."

For the first time, Grace Keats smiled. It was a devious smile.

"Are you enjoying this as much as me?"

"Not really," I said. "I was expecting a daughter who was going to be loyal to her father."

"Someone needs to be loyal to my mother as well."

We had already gotten off on the wrong foot - to say the least - so from now on, I was going to view her as a hostile witness.

"So you were close to her?"

"I wouldn't say that."

"What would you say?"

"I'd say we had more fights than most mothers and daughters. And because of her murder, I'll never be able to have the ability to get close to her. Isn't that what happens to most mother/daughter relationships as the daughter gets older?"

"Yes, that probably is true."

This was the point where we should have found a common ground. Where she realized I wasn't the bad guy and I understood how tough this was on her.

"I'm sorry, Grace. For the loss of your mother."

"Thanks," she said matter-of-factly.

That's all I was going to get out of her.

"I'd like to move past your father. Who else did you think could have possibly killed your mother?"

"A spurned lover. Anyone who would benefit financially."

"A spurned lover? Was your mother having an affair?"

Archer had alluded to it. Maybe Grace actually knew one was going on.

"Shouldn't that be something that you are looking into? I mean, that's one of the reasons that people kill."

"So is money," I said.

"Which is why I included people who would benefit financially."

"And who would that be?"

"Jeez, Quint. You really are behind the eight ball."

It was the first time she'd said my name. And boy, what a time. She was talking to me like I was a child in a game for adults. Maybe she wasn't wrong. I was quickly realizing how little I knew about this case. And this family.

"You and your brother are the first people I've interviewed about the case," I said, intentionally leaving out Tre Larson. "I'm trying to learn about it from you two."

"Then you should appreciate all the knowledge I'm dropping on you."

I once again half-expected a smile, a show of sarcasm. As I looked out on Grace, it was obvious none was coming.

"You're a tough little girl, aren't you?"

I didn't like my choice of words, but I blurted them out without having time to think.

This time, Grace did smile.

"Finally, you got something right."

"But why? What exactly did I do to you?"

"You'll find out at some point. I promise."

"What does that mean?"

She stood up from her chair.

"I think we're done here."

"I have no idea what's going on here," I said.

"No, you don't. Come back and talk to me when you do."

And with that, Grace Keats walked out of my office.

CHAPTER 8

I was dumbfounded by my meeting with Grace Keats. I'd never had an interview go so poorly. I'd been on the defensive from the opening moment and it only went downhill from there.

Hopefully, the day wouldn't get any worse.

I walked the three blocks back to my apartment, deciding I wanted to sit on my couch for an hour and decompress.

I stepped off the elevator on the 5th floor and made my way towards my apartment. As I approached, I saw a piece of paper was taped to my front door.

I shut the door behind me, deciding to read it inside. I'm sure it was some maintenance issue they were alerting the tenants to.

Sitting on my couch, I unfurled the paper and started reading.

"You're so far out of your league. You don't know what the fuck is going on. Why don't you investigate Dickie Faber? Maybe learn a little."

I was wrong.

The day could get worse.

~

I felt like I was in a washing machine, indiscriminately being thrown to all sides, having zero choice of where I was headed next.

In a world of Kings and Queens, I was a pawn.

I called Ellie who agreed to meet with me, so I headed down to her law office.

So much for decompressing on my couch.

~

"Who is Dickie Faber?"

Once again, Ellie was waiting outside the door to her law firm. I asked her the question immediately, wanting to read her reaction.

"I've never heard that name in my life," she said.

I handed her the letter and she looked it over with a quizzical look on her face.

"And why didn't you tell me that Grace Keats is a little witch?"

"I somewhat warned you, but part of me wanted you to find out on your own."

"I'd prefer to have more info next time. I was ambushed."

"Like you inviting yourself over and immediately asking about some guy named Dickie?"

I gave her a slight smile.

"That's fair," I said.

"Let's talk inside."

We walked into her office, bypassing the secretary, who was talking to a tall, skinny, blonde man.

"Was that Wyatt Tiller?" I asked.

"Yeah. Do you know him?"

"No, but I heard that Archer used him on different occasions."

"He sure did. Give me a second."

Ellie left her office and a minute later, returned with Wyatt Tiller. His blonde hair looked like a mop on the top of his head. Boris Johnson came to mind.

"Wyatt, this is Quint Adler. He's helping with the defense of Archer."

He extended his hand and I shook it.

"Nice to meet you," I said.

"Likewise," he said. "I know you a bit by reputation. You're good at what you do. Which will lead to you helping exonerate Archer, because I know he didn't kill Gracie. I was friends with both and while they had their problems, they still loved each other."

"I'll do my part," I said.

I wasn't going to promise anything.

"I'm sure you will. If you ever have any questions about Archer, just come knocking. If I had any criminal law expertise, I'd be helping you guys. I'm merely a civil litigator, however."

"He's being modest," Ellie said. "Wyatt is one of the best civil attorneys in the Bay Area."

"I think I'm going to keep you around a little longer," Wyatt said.

Ellie laughed. I wasn't as enthralled with his sense of humor. It reminded me of Archer joking about hiring me as lead counsel.

"Just come knocking if you have any questions," Wyatt reiterated.

"I might take you up on that offer."

"Please do."

And with that, Wyatt Tiller walked out of Ellie's office.

Ellie and I both sat down.

I saw her typing away at her computer.

"I'm sorry, I do know who Dickie Faber is. At least, I know of him. The name hadn't rung a bell."

"Who is he?"

"He was Gracie Keats' psychiatrist."

"Hmmm," I said rhetorically.

When she didn't answer, I asked a follow-up question.

"Have you talked to him?"

"No, of course not. I'd have remembered the name if I had."

"Then how'd you know he's Gracie's psychiatrist?"

"I just Googled his name and he's a psychiatrist from Walnut Creek. Once I saw that his name rang a bell."

"You forgot about Dickie?" I joked.

Ellie laughed.

"Must have been a little Dickie."

I laughed as well.

"For shrinks, does the attorney/client privilege continue after death?" I asked.

"It's complicated, just like it is for lawyers. The attorney/client privilege survives their deaths in both, meaning the lawyer or psychiatrist can't say anything. However, once the person dies, the holder of the privilege is actually the personal representative of the deceased."

"Does that mean the person who holds the estate?"

"In most cases, yes. And Archer currently is Gracie's quote-unquote personal representative. Since he's been charged with her murder, there's a zero percent chance that the State would allow him to make decisions for Gracie. So there is no way that Dickie Faber will be compelled to talk."

"That's too bad, but it does make sense."

"For sure. If not, Archer would be in the position of allowing/disallowing certain info to become public knowledge, which might give him an unfair advantage in court."

Ellie was gorgeous, but damn if she wasn't also as intelligent as hell.

Was I smitten?

No.

Was I attracted to her?

Yes.

I told myself to say something before Ellie saw right through me.

"Do you think he'd still agree to meet with me?"

"Maybe, but if he's worth his salt, he won't say anything that matters."

"Any idea who would have posted this note to my door?"

"None. Are there cameras where you live?"

"No."

"Maybe Archer's daughter found out where you lived."

She smiled, but it wasn't all that crazy. Grace would have known that I was waiting for her at my office if she'd wanted to leave it beforehand. And she did seem to know a lot about me. How hard is it to find out someone's address these days? Not very.

I thought of something else I'd forgotten to mention.

"Do you know who Johnson and Johnson are? And don't use some cheesy joke about baby powder. I already heard it."

"Damn, that's where I was going. Yes, I know who they are. And I also know that A.J. is not a big fan of theirs. Let me ask you a question, Quint."

"Shoot."

"Do you actually think one of Archer's rivals would go and stab his wife twenty-seven times?"

"It's highly unlikely. And yet, I seem to remember this attorney who told me that she wanted to flood the jury with other potential suspects."

"She sounds like a good attorney."

I smiled.

"She is."

"Keep digging on the Johnson's. I'm willing to throw it out there, but only if we have something that would stick. Being bitter business rivals isn't enough."

"Understood."

The phone rang in her office. Ellie kept the speaker on.

"Ms. Teague, your 3:30 appointment is here."

"I'll come and get her."

Ellie hung up the phone.

She walked behind me and put her arm on my shoulders.

"Sorry, Quint, you've got to go. I did enjoy all the talk about Dickie and Johnsons, though."

As I stood up and turned around, she smiled seductively.

Nothing was going to happen at that moment, not with her 3:30 waiting.

But I had a feeling it wouldn't be long…

CHAPTER 9

I decided against trying to set up a meeting with Dickie Faber.

One, it would give him time to prepare for my questions. Two, he would likely stonewall me and tell me about doctor/client privilege, etc.

If this letter I'd received - which I still had many doubts about - really was pertinent to my investigation, then I couldn't give Faber the advantage of knowing I was coming.

So I set about "ambushing" Dickie Faber.

~

Originally, I was going to wait outside of his office before eight or nine a.m. and hope to catch him walking in.

I was sure he'd say something like, *'I have a client coming in right now.'*

So I waited until four p.m. to scope out his work, hoping to catch him as he was leaving.

He was located in a fairly large office building. There were a few dentists, orthodontics, and orthopedics listed on the sign outside.

Luckily, there was only one entrance and exit to the building and I'd googled Dickie Faber so I knew what he looked like.

At 5:15, after seventy-five minutes of sitting in the parking lot, I saw him leave his office. My car was only twenty feet from the entrance/exit, so I quickly pounced.

Faber was in his early-fifties, short, and had a long, slender goatee that looked ridiculous. As I got closer, it looked more like a Fu Manchu than a goatee. It's like he was trying too hard to look like an old-school psychiatrist. He looked more like Vladimir Lenin.

"Mr. Faber," I said.

He turned around suddenly, a suspicious look on his face. I'd certainly caught him by surprise.

"Can I help you?" he asked.

I was a good six inches taller than him.

"I hope so," I said. "Do you know a woman named Gracie Keats?"

He took a few seconds to look me over. I thought he was going to deny knowing her, but I was wrong.

"If you're here in front of me, I'm assuming you already know that we knew each other."

"You're right about that."

"And I'd also assume that you've heard of doctor/client privilege?"

"You're right about that also," I said.

"Then what are you doing here?"

He was a little conceited for me. Yes, I'd ambushed him, but he was very dismissive and I didn't like it.

"I'm here to ask you a few questions that don't break the doctor/client privilege."

"Good luck with that. Most everything is going to impugn on that in one way or the other."

"Did Gracie fear for her life?"

"You know I can't answer that."

Someone walked out of the building and I let him pass us before asking my next question.

"If she felt her life was in jeopardy, aren't you obliged to tell the police?"

"I'm not obliged to do anything. It's up to my discretion."

"So you're admitting she was scared?"

"I have done no such thing."

"You seem a little nervous, Dickie," I said, intentionally using his first name.

"I'm not a big fan of someone lying in wait for me."

I began to think I'd made a mistake. I was usually able to get people to like me and open up. I never gave Dickie Faber that chance, choosing to go the antagonistic approach instead.

"What if I told you that someone asked me to investigate you?"

"That's preposterous," he said.

"Why?"

"Because I'm not allowed to talk."

"Maybe so, but I'm not very good at just letting things go."

"I was Gracie's psychiatrist and that's it. I certainly had nothing to do with her murder."

"Do you think her husband murdered her?"

Now that I had him on the defensive, I hoped he'd unwittingly give me a few answers.

"I have no comment on that."

"Maybe I'll get a warrant forcing you to talk."

"Good luck with that."

"You haven't even asked who I am. I find that odd."

"Your name is Quint Adler and you're working for Ellie Teague. Why should I ask questions I already know the answer to?"

I was taken aback.

"Been keeping up on Archer's defense it appears. Why so interested?"

"A client of mine was murdered. And more than that, a friend. You'd keep tabs also."

It was hard to argue with that.

"Were you having an affair with her?"

He just shook his head. It wasn't exactly a denial.

"Is there anything you'd like to tell me about Gracie?" I asked.

"Maybe if you hadn't ambushed me."

It might have been too late, but I had to try and play nice.

"I'm sorry, I thought it was the only way you'd talk to me."

"Too late. You better go get that warrant, Quint, because I'm done talking to you."

I didn't like him calling me by my first name. Two could play at that game.

"I'm not done with you yet, Dickie. Be seeing you around, I'm sure."

"I can't wait," he said.

With that, he ran fifty feet to a red Tesla, quickly got in his car, and sped off.

I was stuck standing in the middle of the parking lot, kicking myself over a missed opportunity.

The chance of getting any information from Dickie Faber was likely gone forever.

I drove back to my office, trying to take in everything that I'd learned.

I remembered thinking this was going to be a pretty easy case. '*Did he or didn't he?*'

It was becoming a lot more convoluted than that.

I did a quick rundown of people associated with the case.

Gene Bowman. Nice and polite, but still a bit of a shadowy figure. I needed to set up an appointment with him soon.

Ellie Teague. Very intelligent. Very beautiful. Very flirty. And I still couldn't tell whether she was using me or not. Despite our many interactions, I didn't have a great read on her.

Archer Keats. The defendant. I was not yet in a position to judge his guilt or innocence, but If I had to choose, I'd lean towards the latter. It was odd, but he wasn't even one of the more interesting people in the case thus far. And he was going to be the man on trial.

A.J. Keats. He'd been likable and helpful.

Grace Keats. The exact opposite of her brother.

Dickie Faber. An arrogant, unlikeable, little man. And yet, he was just doing what any psychiatrist would do. So while I didn't like the guy, I had no reason to suspect him of anything. Yet.

I put Tre Larson in a different category. He's the only one I didn't consider a suspect. Yes, that even included Ellie. I know she was just Archer's attorney, but she wasn't being completely forthcoming and that got my attention.

The trial was still several weeks away, so I had time to gather more information on everyone. Plus, meet a few more people.

I made a few phone calls and was able to secure two more interviews in the days to come.

Gene Bowman and Donna Neal, who was Gracie's best friend. I assumed that was going to be a rough one.

Hopefully, it would go better than my ambush of Dickie Faber.

I called Ellie and told her of my plans for the next few days. I asked about meeting with Archer again, but she said let's wait until after I talked to Bowman and Neal.

CHAPTER 10

I met Gene Bowman at his office.
    I'd extended the offer to meet at mine, but he chose his own.
    Maybe he felt he had some home-field advantage. It was odd, but that's how I was viewing a lot of these interviews. As if everyone had something to hide and these were all one-on-one battles with yours truly.

Bowman Consulting was in bright, red letters across the top of a wide, one-story office building. I opened the front door and was greeted by two separate secretaries and a busy office, with several people milling around. It was bigger than I'd expected with what looked like five or six offices.

"I'm here to see Gene Bowman," I said.

"Your name?"

"Quint Adler," I said.

"Have a seat. He'll be out shortly."

He was obviously a busy man, but I was a little disappointed I wasn't sent back to meet him immediately. I was the guy doing him a favor by taking this case, after all.

Five minutes later, Gene Bowman made his way to the front of the office.

"Quint, how are you?"

It was at that point I realized we'd never actually met in person. I felt like I knew him after several talks on the phone, but he wasn't exactly what I expected.

Bowman was probably 6'6", maybe taller, and only around my age.

I'd been expecting someone older and certainly wasn't expecting someone so tall.

I stood up from my chair.

"Nice to finally meet in person, Gene," I said.

"You as well. Follow me."

We bypassed offices on the left and right until we arrived at the biggest office of all. "Gene Bowman, Founder" was in large, gold, engraved letters on the door.

He opened it and we walked in. I took a seat across from him, a large, expensive desk in between us. There were papers scattered everywhere, which somewhat surprised me.

"Excuse the mess," he said. "My secretary just dropped a shit ton of paperwork on me."

"You don't have to apologize. This office seems pretty hectic."

Gene Bowman smiled at me.

"Never a dull day. Which is the way I like it."

My office was almost always quiet. I'm not sure which I'd have preferred.

"Thanks for meeting with me," I said.

"It's the least I could do. I appreciate you taking the case."

"Ellie is a pretty woman."

Gene laughed.

"We thought that might do the trick."

"We? She made it out like it was her idea."

"That's probably true."

"Just to be clear, that's not why I took the case."

"Well, that begs the question. Why did you?"

"I'm fascinated by the competition of it all. The defense vs. the prosecution."

"I get that. Maybe we'll get lucky and there will never be a trial."

"I'm not holding my breath," I said.

"No, I guess not. So, what did you think of Archer?"

I decided to keep things close to the vest with Gene. He seemed like a man who tried to accumulate all the information he could. I wanted to keep some for myself.

"I took the case, so I guess I think there's at least a chance he's innocent."

"Not guilty."

"That's the second time I've been corrected on that," I said.

"Good thing you're a P.I. and not the attorney of record."

Gene Bowman smiled, but I was a little perturbed.

Was I on my way to another combative interview?

"I'll give you a one-time pass on that," I said.

He gave another sly smile.

"I'm just busting your balls," Gene said. "Shall we get down to business?"

"Yes."

"What did you want to know?"

"First, I want to know exactly what you do for Archer?"

"A few things. First and foremost, we do the research before he decides when and where to launch his next endeavor. Restaurants are a tricky business, so we do all the legwork for him."

"What does that entail?"

"Finding out the history of the location. Have any places done well there or do they always go under? If he's opening a Mexican restaurant, find out how many similar restaurants are in the area. Check to see if there will be enough parking. Is it too close to another one of his businesses and might potentially cut into their profits? A lot of boring things like that."

"Sounds like it could be interesting," I said.

"It's all number-based. We're not like you, getting to be out in the field and interviewing people."

It was hard to tell if he was trying to wind me up again. I didn't think so, but Gene Bowman was tough to read. He was the male version of Ellie.

"I was told you also help handle some of his finances."

"We've got a few financial planners in this office."

"Does he use them for the monetary ins-and-outs of opening a business? Buying stocks? His retirement plan? What?"

"He uses us for all of the above."

"Are you involved in any of the financial dealings with Archer?"

"It's my firm, so I'm involved in everything, but no, those things are not my bread and butter."

"I ask because I know Archer has had some financial issues that started during Covid. And there's no question in my mind that the prosecution will use Gracie's estate as Archer's motive for her murder."

"You're right about that, Quint. But I don't expect you to bore yourself with the financial aspects of this case. Ellie has an expert for that."

He was once again bordering on belittling me.

I decided to hold my tongue one last time.

If it happened again, I'd call him out.

"Then maybe you can answer me this. Who else would gain by the death of Gracie?"

"Just Archer. He was the sole beneficiary."

"Not the kids?" I asked.

"No, but obviously they would get it when their father eventually passes away. Hopefully, forty years down the road."

"What happens if Archer is convicted of Gracie's murder? Who does the estate go to? Surely, it's not his to keep."

"Maybe I haven't given you enough credit, Quint. Now you're asking the right questions."

I ignored his backhanded compliment.

"So, where does the money go?"

"There would likely be a hearing with the executor of the will, but I imagine it would go to A.J. and Grace."

I could tell he didn't like admitting that.

I almost said something and then realized it would be better to stay silent. It appeared like Gene wanted to say something.

He took the bait.

"Look, Quint. We're here to get Archer off. That's our first order of business, but we are not going to do that at the expense of throwing his children to the wolves. There will be no mention of them at trial."

"I can't mention them at trial. Remember, I'm just the P.I. and not the attorney of record."

Gene laughed loudly.

It felt good, I had to admit it.

"I deserve that," he said. "That's a damn good comeback, Quint."

"I noticed your zingers. Was just biding my time."

"Revenge is a dish served cold?"

"Something like that," I said.

"Is there anything else?"

I decided to end on a positive note.

"Not for now, but I'd like to set up another meeting as the trial approaches."

"I can't wait," Gene said, and I actually think he meant it.

CHAPTER 11

In my never-ending stretch of interviews, Donna Neal was next.

I met her on a Tuesday at her house. I'd offered to meet at my office which she'd turned down and also at Ellie's law firm, which she'd vehemently turned down.

I wasn't sure if she didn't want to deal with lawyers in general or just lawyers defending Archer Keats.

As long as she'd agreed to meet with me, I didn't really care.

Donna Neal opened the door after I'd knocked twice and I was greeted by a woman wearing dirty, faded jeans, a gold buckled belt, and a black and red flannel shirt. She looked more like she belonged in Texas than in Walnut Creek. It surprised me, being that she was best friends with Gracie Keats.

I'd expected someone more regal looking. It was less a judgment on Donna and more on the perceived vanity of Archer and Gracie.

"You must be Quint," she said eagerly.

"I am. Thanks for meeting with me, Donna."

I used a trick that I thought Archer used on me. Calling someone by their first name in hopes that would open them up to you.

"Why don't you come inside?"

We entered her one-story, likely two-bedroom home. It was nice and clean, but smaller than I expected. I'd assumed Donna Neal had been married and likely raised some kids. Here I was, jumping to conclusions again.

I looked around and didn't see any pictures of any husband or any kids.

"You can sit here," she said, pointing to the dining room, a foot to the left of the front door. She took the seat next to me.

"Should we just get down to it?" I asked.

"That means something different where I come from."

She smiled and I laughed.

"I'm sorry, that's not what I meant."

"I know. Just thought I'd give you a little shit."

That seemed to be the trend with these interviews.

She motioned her hand as if I should begin.

"I've heard that you were best friends with Gracie Keats. Is that fair to say?"

"Yeah, that's fair. There were four of us who hung out together all the time, but Gracie and I were probably the closest."

"What are the names of the other two?"

"Two sisters. Pamela and Bunny Arden."

"What brought all of you together?"

"Entirely different reasons. Pamela and Bunny both had kids who grew up with A.J. and Grace."

"You didn't?"

"No, I'm the black sheep of her friends, or hadn't you heard?"

"In all fairness, I've been interviewing so many damn people, that I kind of came into this one with a blank slate."

"Well, I better let you in on a big secret," Donna said and smiled. "I'm in my early fifties and never been married or had any kids."

"Nothing wrong with that," I said.

"I know. The elite of Walnut Creek might beg to differ. They look at me like I'm from Mars. *A woman your age who isn't married? And hanging out with all married women with kids?* Trust me, I've heard all those comments thousands of times."

"Must not have been easy."

"If I gave a fuck about their opinions, I guess it could have gotten to me."

I laughed. "There's the attitude."

"To be honest, I think it made our friendship all that much stronger. She had enough friends she could talk about her kids with. Or their kids. Or what was going on at school that day. When we went out, she knew I didn't care about the kids. So we could just have fun and talk about anything and everything else."

"What did that usually entail?" I asked.

"Guys. Soap operas. Fashion. Rodeos. The last was my personal favorite as you may have guessed," she said, motioning to her outfit.

"Gracie didn't strike me as the rodeo type."

"She wasn't. At least, not at first. Until I described some of those rodeo men, and then she took a big interest. I even got her line dancing at some local dive bar. She loved it. And you know why?"

"It was probably the opposite of what she and Archer would do on a night out."

"That's exactly right, Quint."

"Gracie ever fall for one of those guys line dancing?"

"Oh, come on now. You've been so good thus far. Don't have me dish the dirt on Gracie just yet."

I found it an odd thing to say, considering her best friend had just been murdered a month ago. I was getting a sneaking suspicion that Donna Neal liked to gossip. I decided I'd come back to it.

"My fault," I said. "So tell me more about this local dive bar."

"You reckon you'll find yourself line dancing there one day?"

"Are all the girls as pretty as you?"

Donna laughed. She was an attractive woman in her fifties, but she knew I was likely pulling her leg.

"Not many of them," she said and then laughed at her own joke.

"You would be fun to party with. I'm sure of that."

"I think that's what Gracie saw in me. As I said, no kids talk. Just good clean fun. And some dirty fun too."

"That's the best kind," I said.

We were doing our own version of a line dance, only it involved delving out information. Much as I'd already done with Ellie, Grace, and Gene.

"So what do you think of Archer?" Donna asked.

I wasn't expecting the question.

"It's hard to say. I haven't come up with an opinion on whether he did it."

I didn't have to say what 'did it' meant.

"To tell you the truth, neither have I. I know Gracie didn't love him near the end, but Archer didn't seem like such a bad guy. Then again, he was the only one there when she got murdered. I guess that's what we'll find out at the trial."

"Yeah. I'd like to prevent it from getting that far, though. If I could find something that helped exonerate Archer, we could save the taxpayers a lot of money."

I didn't like it when it came out of my mouth. Donna's expression only confirmed that.

"I don't give a shit about no taxpayers. The only thing I care about is finding out who killed my friend and seeing them rot in jail."

"A perfectly understandable position. I'm just doing my job, Donna. If Archer didn't kill her, I want to find that out."

"Sorry, can't help you there. I'm enjoying talking to ya, but there's not going to be some magic get out of jail free card coming from me."

It was time to double back to our earlier conversation. Archer's guilt or innocence wasn't going anywhere.

"I know you don't want to badmouth Gracie, but how about telling me a few things that made her fun to party with."

Donna laughed.

"Oh, but you see, those two are one and the same."

"Give me a little something," I pleaded. "Who knows, maybe it will lead to something bigger. Possibly even lead me to her killer."

"I doubt that. A damn good try, though."

I was trying to get some information on a possible Gracie affair, but Donna didn't want to divulge it. I went in another direction once again.

"How did you first find out Gracie had been killed?"

"I heard about it the next morning."

"Do you remember who told you?"

"I'm pretty sure I first heard it from Bunny Arden. I got about eight calls that day."

"When you first heard, who did you think had killed Gracie?"

"I probably thought Archer. He was the only one who was at the house, after all."

"The only one that the police know about," I corrected her. "Is there anyone else you suspected?"

"There were rumors that Gracie may have been cheating around. I remember thinking that maybe one of the men had killed her to prevent her from making it public."

"Or one of the wives out for revenge," I said.

"Doubtful."

"Why is that?"

"How many women do you know who want to stab another woman twenty-something times?"

"How many women do you know who don't take kindly to another woman cheating on her husband?"

"Point taken," Donna said.

"Listen, you're probably right. I think it's likely a man as well. I'm just trying not to overlook anyone."

"You've got a shitty job. You're either defending a guilty man or chasing after a sinister murderer."

"You can say that again."

Donna stood up.

"You want a beer, Quint?"

It was 11:30 a.m. and I most assuredly did not want a beer, but I felt Donna wanted to open up more. And maybe having a beer with her might do the trick.

"I'd love one," I said.

"Two Miller Lite's coming up."

She walked past me and down the hall toward what must have been the kitchen. The configuration of this little house was quite odd.

Donna returned a minute later with two Miller Lite cans. I can't imagine that Gracie Keats drank many beers in the can with Archer. Maybe that was the fun of hanging with Donna.

We both took a sip of our beers. Donna made a point of accentuating the sound of the beer hitting her lips.

"So, where were we?" she asked.

"You were telling me that I had a shitty job."

She laughed.

"That's right. And after my first sip of beer, let me confirm that I still believe that."

"If Archer killed Gracie and is found guilty, I have no problem with that, obviously. What I fear the most is that I miss something, and he gets convicted because of me. I couldn't live with myself if that occurred. That's why I'm asking all these questions. Why I'm trying to find out if you might have any suspects."

Donna took a long sip of her beer. For a second, I thought she was going to pound the rest of it.

She looked at me and I knew something consequential was coming.

"When we went out, she flirted with the guys that we line danced with. I remember her even kissing a few, but she didn't sleep with any of them. I'd have known."

"I believe you."

"I'm pretty sure she was having an affair with her psychiatrist, though."

That hit me like a ton of bricks.

"Dickie Faber?"

"That's him. Quite a name, right?"

It wasn't the time to rehash Ellie's 'Little Dickie' jokes.

"Sure is. What makes you think she was having an affair with him?"

"Call it women's intuition."

"Anything else? I can't exactly take that to the jury, even though I know it's a real thing."

"There were a few times I'd ask her to come out and she'd tell me she was going to meet with Dickie."

"Is that so odd?"

"When there wasn't a scheduled appointment, yeah it was."

"Did she ever say anything more about him?"

"What she said was enough. I was her friend and if she didn't want to open up about it, I wasn't going to pry."

I wasn't sure if I believed her. Donna Neal seemed like the prying type. I felt like she'd enjoy the drama of infidelity and would certainly ask a follow-up question or two if Gracie was sleeping with her shrink.

I'd save that for a later meeting. There was no need to offend her and call her bluff at that moment.

"Did you get the feeling that she loved Dickie?"

"No. My gut feeling is that it was early on in their affair if that's what it was. She only mentioned him a few times and they were both within a month of her death."

"Curious timing," I said.

Donna didn't touch my comment.

"Had she ever mentioned how Dickie was as a psychiatrist? Devoid of all the other stuff."

"He'd been helpful getting her through a difficult time in her marriage."

"Yeah. A little too helpful," I said.

Donna laughed.

"That's not what I meant. He helped her talk through some of her misgivings about Archer."

"Which where?"

"When they'd first married, he was a hard-working, hard-driven man. Those first ten years together, he'd opened like fifteen restaurants or something like that. And then he really slowed down."

"Why?"

I had a feeling I knew where she was going.

"Gracie thought he was relying a little more on her family money and less on his own wherewithal."

"He still opened quite a few restaurants in the last five years."

"Until Covid hit. He hasn't opened one in the last two years or so."

"It's understandable. We are in a global pandemic after all."

"Agreed, but Gracie felt like he was starting to use her. Archer had lost quite a bit of money and he was coming to her for loans. And you'll probably say it's not a loan if it's between man and wife, but her family money was separate from him, so it was like a loan."

"How much did he borrow?"

"Over a million dollars."

"That's a lot of money. I'll concede that. She inherited twenty million, though. It's not like she was living in the poor house."

"I never said that. You asked me what were some of her misgivings about Archer. And that was one of them. That he was getting lazy and reliant on her money."

We'd covered so much in our conversation, I didn't know what to ask next.

She seemed to sense it.

"How about one more beer before you get out of here?" she asked.

"Let's do it," I said.

I grabbed my beer and realized there was still a good three-quarters left.

I tilted it towards my throat and did the best imitation of my college years. Four seconds later, I'd pounded the rest of it.

"Impressive," she said.

"You should have seen me at twenty-one."

"I'll bet. Give me a second," she said and disappeared down the hallway once again.

When she returned, I still didn't know what I was going to ask. I just knew we were on our second beer and if she was ever going to talk, now was the time.

"Did she tell the Arden sisters about Dickie?" I asked.

"I'd bet my life against it," she said.

"Why?"

"Because those were her domesticated friends. Archer knew their husbands and their kids. Gracie wouldn't have risked it getting back to them."

"It sounds like you're the fun friend who she could tell anything."

She held up her second beer, signifying she was exactly that.

"I'm starting to see why you guys were so close," I said.

"Gracie liked Walnut Creek but felt it was a little stuffy. She liked being able to gossip with me. To drink cheap beer and not expensive White Zin's. Yeah, she was a rich girl from a rich family, but she was a lot more blue-collar than you'd think."

"I wasn't expecting to hear that when I came here today."

"Today? It feels like you've been here for a week."

I don't know if it was the beer in me talking, but now I thought Donna Neal was hitting on me.

This case was making me crazy.

"I'll be out of your hair in a minute," I said. "I'll ask you point-blank. Do you have any other suspects besides Archer and Dickie Faber?"

"I never said I suspected Dickie of murder."

That was true. I was projecting.

"Anyone else that had a gripe with Gracie?"

"With her personally? Probably not. With Archer? Most certainly."

"Do you know who Johnson and Johnson are?"

"Sure, they caused Gracie a headache or two. Always in competition with her husband. And it seems like J & J might have gotten the upper hand over Archer in the last few years."

She took a big sip of her beer and I followed suit.

We both knew our meeting was winding down.

"I've got one last question," I said.

"Let's hear it."

"What did Archer think of you?"

"I don't think he was my biggest fan. He knew what kind of friend I was to Gracie."

"Did he know that you two would hit dive bars together?"

"Probably not. This all started after he moved into the guest house. Gracie was free to do what she wanted at that point."

"Would you ever go to her house?"

"I've been there a few times. But I think Gracie preferred meeting me out. If she needed to do the whole kids/husband shit, she had ten other friends she could do that with. Remember, I was the undomesticated friend, so what's the point of bringing me home?"

Donna laughed when she said it. I wondered if there was any resentment on her part towards Gracie. You're best friends, but she'd rarely have you over.

My gut told me it didn't bother her very much. Plus, I was up to my neck in suspects already. I wasn't going to be adding Donna Neal to the list.

I stood up, getting ready to go.

"You asked for that second beer," Donna said. "The least you can do is pound it for me again."

She smiled a bit seductively and I knew a third beer would be a bad idea.

I pounded the beer, this time even quicker than the first, and Donna Neal had a smile on her face as I turned to go.

I'm not sure if the two beers were to blame for what followed next, but it certainly didn't help.

When I arrived at my office ten minutes later, Ellie Teague was waiting outside.

She was wearing a light brown skirt and a tan blouse. She looked beautiful. As always.

"Hey, Quint."

"What are you doing here, Ellie?"

It sounded more accusatory than I'd intended.

"I knew you were interviewing Donna Neal at eleven. Figured I'd intercept you here."

"It was an interesting interview, to say the least."

"I'd love to hear about it."

"Come on in," I said, opening the door to my office.

She nudged her way by me to enter first. I had no idea why.

"You smell like beer," she said.

"I went above the call of duty," I said.

"What does that mean? Getting drunk with a prospective witness?"

"I didn't get drunk. She suggested having a beer and I thought I might get more out of her if I joined her."

"That's good thinking, Quint. Get the witnesses drunk so they bare their souls to you."

I couldn't tell if she was being sarcastic or complimentary. As usual, it was hard to tell with Ellie.

We were standing in the waiting area of my office. She'd started questioning me as soon as we walked in, which had prevented me from making my way to my office.

Ellie sat down on the lone couch in the room.

I sat my butt on the desk where my non-existent secretary would be sitting once I made it big.

"Remember Dickie Faber?" I asked.

"Of course," Ellie said. "How could I forget our little Dickie joke."

"Donna thinks they were having an affair."

"That's intriguing," Ellie said, but I could tell it wasn't what was on her mind.

What was on her mind was me.

She rose from the couch and started walking seductively towards me. This is where the two beers might have clouded my judgment just a little bit.

"What are you doing?" I said, but it was hardly an order to stop.

Ellie walked closer. She was within five feet of me.

She unbuttoned a button on her blouse as she slowly, methodically moved in my direction.

"This is a bad idea," I said, more to myself than to Ellie.

She unbuttoned one more, showing off her ample cleavage.

"This is a bad idea," I repeated, with even less aplomb this time. My defense was weakening.

"We're just two attractive adults, about to have some fun," Ellie said.

She inched closer. I did too, in my own way.

"Why?" I said, this time my voice barely a whisper.

I was no longer objecting, just putting it on record that I'd said something.

She unbuttoned the last two buttons on her blouse and took it off. She was now standing there in a skirt and a bra.

This time, I removed my butt from the table and stood up, facing her.

Ellie put her hands on my chest and started taking off my shirt.

I said nothing, knowing it was past the point of no return.

She took my shirt off.

I glanced towards the blinds to make sure no one could see in.

And then I took off her bra and saw two beautiful breasts staring back at me.

She kissed me on the neck a few times and went for my pants. Apparently, extended foreplay wasn't a big thing for Ellie.

Once she'd removed my pants, she took off her skirt.

We were facing each other, me in my boxers and her in her panties.

I leaned in to kiss her.

After only a few kisses, she leaned over and grabbed the outside of my boxers.

She whispered in my ear.

"This is the only Dickie I care about."

⁓

Ten minutes later, it was over.

There was virtually no foreplay and when it was over, it felt cheap.

That's not to say I didn't enjoy every second of it.

Ellie was gorgeous and our bodies worked in unison, a minor miracle considering it was our first time having sex.

I finally knew what women meant by a "Wham Bam Thank You, Ma'am."

We'd started with her bent over the desk and finished with her on top of me on the couch. Two positions, about five minutes each.

And now, a million uncomfortable moments surely to follow.

Sex was odd sometimes.

A few minutes of ecstasy, but for what price?

As Ellie put on her blouse, she uttered the first word between us since we'd finished.

"So what exactly did Donna say about Dr. Faber?"

It was so matter-of-fact, I almost laughed.

We'd finished having sex less than three minutes previous and it went unacknowledged.

Ellie was already back to business.

"She said Gracie was going to meet him during unscheduled times."

"Sounds tawdry," Ellie said.

I didn't mention that this meeting could be described in the same way.

"Why don't we meet with Archer tomorrow?" Ellie said. "Ten a.m. at his house, alright?"

"Sure. Listen, Ellie, are we even going to talk about this?"

"No, we're not."

She leaned up and kissed me on the mouth.

"You were great. Now, let's forget it happened."

Two minutes later, she was walking out of my office.

CHAPTER 12

I woke up the next morning with a pounding headache and it had nothing to do with the two beers I'd consumed.

My head hurt thinking through all the possibilities following my carnal interlude with Ellie.

Had it all been a set-up?

Did Ellie want to sleep with me in hopes of having me under her thumb?

Had she encouraged Donna Neal to serve me a couple of beers first?

What the fuck was going on?

Whatever it was, I didn't feel like I was in control.

Maybe Ellie just really wanted to jump my bones.

Maybe.

But my mind was taking me to a much darker place. I continued to feel like a pawn.

And I didn't like it.

I needed to take things into my own hands. Did that involve following Ellie? Following Dickie? Following Donna? I'd have to wait and see, but everything was now in play.

～

First, I had to meet with Ellie and Archer.

I had to make sure that Archer had no idea what had occurred between Ellie and me. Nothing good would come from that.

I arrived outside of his house a few minutes after ten a.m. He opened the front door wearing khaki pants and a red shirt with an oversized polo logo.

"Hello, Archer."

"Nice to see you, Quint."

"Is Ellie here?"

"She has an important meeting at her office today and won't be joining us."

It took me by surprise and added another wrinkle to the craziness of the last twenty-four hours.

"Okay, no problem," I said.

"No, it's not. You and Ellie should be sharing everything with each other, anyway."

Does that include bodily fluids?

"Let's get started then," I said.

Archer escorted me to the courtyard where he'd set an outdoor stand-up heater for us to sit next to.

It was a bit breezy out and my choice would have been to sit inside, but maybe Archer still didn't feel comfortable in the main house. I know I wouldn't. And his little townhouse didn't have much room to sit and talk.

"Do you want water or a coffee?" he asked.

"I'd love a coffee if you've got one made."

He walked toward the townhouse and emerged a minute later with two cups of coffee along with cream and sugar.

"Need any of this?"

"No, I take it black. Thanks."

He added both cream and sugar to his and took the seat across from me.

"So, how's the investigation going?"

It had only been about a week since I'd first met Archer, but so much had happened.

His son. His daughter. Hearing about Johnson and Johnson. Gene Bowman. Donna Neal. Having sex with Ellie Teague.

"I've got a million questions," I said.

"That's why I agreed to meet with you. Let's get this started."

I decided to just throw random questions at him and see how he reacted. If I went person by person, it would be easier for him to be prepared for a stock answer. I didn't want that.

"Do you hate Johnson and Johnson?"

"Yes."

"Would you care to elaborate?"

"They are scavengers. Whenever they see a restaurant or bar deal in trouble, they swoop in and pick up the scraps. They never have any great ideas on their own. It's always someone else's who is in trouble and they just come in with their big money and take credit as if it was their own."

"And that's happened with you?"

"Yeah, quite a few times. For some bigger endeavors, I'd have to call in some financiers. It didn't always work out. And when it didn't, Johnson and Johnson came in to sabotage my deal and create one of their own."

"Is there a specific one you dislike more?"

"The father, Parker Johnson. The son, Caleb, is just a chip off the old block. He didn't stand much of a chance. Parker Johnson is his own self-built asshole."

Parker and Archer. Archer and Parker. Usually, I'd want nothing to do with such rich-sounding, WASPy names, but here I was.

"Would they ever go to extreme measures?"

"Sure. A lot of people around town were scared of them, mainly because they'd start spreading bullshit rumors. I know one case where a restaurateur was close to getting a prime location and Parker Johnson started spreading rumors that the restaurateur was fighting with his wife and they were on the verge of a divorce. There was zero basis in fact, but the financiers couldn't take the risk of it affecting the opening of the restaurant, so they went in a different direction."

"To the Johnsons?"

"Exactly."

I paused for a second and took in what he'd said.

"Was that rumor spread about you and Gracie?"

"I told you the first time we met that you're a bright guy. Yes, it was."

"This next question is going to hurt."

"You don't have to sugar coat it. I've been through a lot lately. Just lay it on me."

"Did you ever suspect Parker or Caleb Johnson in Gracie's murder?"

He took a sip of his coffee before he responded.

"Yes. I considered it."

"It doesn't sound like you believe it, though."

"They fucked me over, not the other way around. If I'd done to them what they'd done to me, then I think they'd be prime suspects. But if they fucked me over - and killed my wife to boot - then they are true sociopaths."

It was a good point.

I wasn't eliminating them as suspects, but I decided to move on.

"What do you think of Donna Neal?"

"I'm not her biggest fan. She was Gracie's only single friend and always up to no good."

"In what way?"

"Always wanting to have a night on the town. If you're single and want to mingle, I have no problem with that, but don't take my wife out with you. We've built a life together. We have two kids. And then she's out there, acting like she's twenty-five years old again."

"It's not like Donna was the only person she drank with," I said.

"That's true. However, it's different if she's out drinking wine with some big wigs from Walnut Creek. With Donna, they were going to this rinky-dink, honky-tonk bar and drinking Milwaukee's Best or some other shitty beer."

"Donna didn't think you knew about that."

"I know a great many people in this town. You can tell that white trash excuse of a woman that everything gets back to me."

There was genuine anger in Archer's voice. It was the first time he'd shown that side to me and he quickly realized it.

"I'm sorry. I know I'm supposed to be Mr. Level-headed, always sounding like the grieving husband, but some of this shit still pisses me off."

"Be yourself," I said. "I'm sure all your warts are going to come out at trial, so you don't have to sugarcoat them with me."

"Thanks, Quint."

We both took a sip of our coffees which were cooling down quickly in the cold air.

If he thought his wife's relationship with Donna Neal was painful, my next set of questions were going to cut to the bone.

"Do you know who Dickie Faber is?"

"Sure. My wife's shrink."

"Donna Neal thinks they were having an affair."

Archer didn't say anything for several seconds.

"Do you think it's a possibility?" I finally asked.

"Anything is possible. I wouldn't have guessed it was her damn shrink, though."

"Have you ever met him?"

"I don't think so. If so, it was only in passing."

"Did Gracie ever bring up the idea of you guys seeing him together?"

"No. I don't think he was a marriage shrink. Or a marriage counselor. Or whatever they call those."

"Do you know why Gracie was seeing him?"

I quickly realized my mistake.

"Professionally, I mean," I added.

"Why does any woman see a shrink?"

It sounded pretty misogynistic on his end.

"Why does any man see a shrink?" I asked.

"You know what I mean," Archer said. "It could have been a hundred different things."

"Well, which one of those hundred did you think it was?"

I was poking his buttons again and I didn't like the way he was responding. I didn't suddenly flip-flop and now think he was guilty, but I reminded myself I knew very little about the man sitting across from me. I shouldn't just assume he was innocent. He had a motive and was the only person known to be on the premises when Gracie was murdered. Any logical human would know he was a viable suspect.

"I think Gracie feels like she missed part of her childhood. Well, not childhood, per se, but early adulthood. She started dating me at twenty, was married by twenty-two, and was pregnant at twenty-three."

"How could a psychiatrist help her with that?"

"I don't freaking know. By charging her an arm and a leg and letting her talk through her feelings."

Archer was visibly upset at this point.

"You said I could ask you anything," I said.

He took a few seconds to gather himself.

"You're right. I'm sorry. It's just hard talking about my wife drinking beers with Donna and maybe sleeping with her shrink."

"I understand, but I'm just trying to find other suspects to give to Ellie."

"You think Dickie Faber could have killed her?"

"I'm not saying that. He's at least worth investigating."

I was reminded of the letter left on my apartment door. Who had left it? And why?

"I don't know if they were having an affair and I don't know why she started going to him in the first place. I'm sorry."

It seemed odd to me that a husband wouldn't at least ask his wife why she was seeing a psychiatrist.

"How long had she been going to him?"

"I'd guess about a year."

That made more sense. It was after the marriage started crumbling, so there was a pretty strong likelihood Gracie and Archer weren't talking all that much.

I needed to do some more investigating of Dickie Faber. There was not much more Archer could add.

"I met with both of your kids," I said.

"I'm sure Grace was pleasant as always."

"She was, how do I phrase this so as to not offend you? Let's go with combative."

"She's been like that since she was a little girl. I'll bet she said I could have killed Gracie."

"Not in those exact words, but yeah, close enough."

"Oh, Grace. She's always been a contradictory person."

"How do you mean?"

"If you'd been a PI for the prosecution, she'd have said there's no way I could have done it. She always has to argue against someone. She'll be contradictory for no reason."

"Interesting."

"Grace knows I didn't do it. Next time you see her, tell her the sky is blue. Just watch, she'll tell you it's yellow."

The Keats' had such a weird family dynamic. Maybe every family does after a loved one dies, but they were extra odd.

I decided to move on.

"How long have you known Gene Bowman?"

"Probably twenty years. He was a young man and had just opened his business - which was only him at the time - and he'd have business lunches at one of my restaurants. He spent a lot of money and took care of our staff. So I introduced myself one day and we've been friends ever since."

"Did you become a client of his right away?"

"Within that first year. I've been with him this whole time and he's never done me wrong. My murder case proves how good he is. I wanted Ellie Teague and Quint Adler. He helped me secure both."

I hadn't planned on bringing up Ellie, but he'd opened the door.

"How long have you known Ellie?"

"Probably five years. Wyatt Tiller is the other lawyer at her firm and I used him for some civil proceedings. I met Ellie at their office. First, I was struck by her beauty, but then Wyatt told me just how good an attorney she was. And I slowly became friendly with her, never knowing I'd need her at some point down the line."

"Did you ever consider going with someone who had more seasoning? Ellie is pretty young and your life is on the line."

"She's never lost. That was good enough for me."

I was sure Archer would relay every part of this conversation to Ellie, so I didn't want to sound like I was disparaging her.

It was time for some praise.

"Of course. Ellie is very good at her job. You're in good hands. Plus, she's a woman and you'd think that's only going to help considering what you're charged with."

"That's probably true, but it's not the reason I chose her."

There were so many more Ellie-based questions I wanted to ask, but I couldn't risk it.

Hey Archer, do you know why Ellie would want to seduce her private investigator?

That wouldn't have gone over well.

I did think of something that might come in handy.

"What was the bar that Gracie and Donna went to?"

"I think it's called The Cowboy Way."

Holy cheesiness.

"Thanks."

"Anything else?"

"I think we should set up a meeting with Ellie sometime in the next few days. It's easier to discuss strategy if the attorney-of-record is here with us."

"I agree. I'll talk to her and set it up."

Five minutes later, I was driving down Archer's driveway, wondering why Ellie hadn't been there.

Another mind fuck or a legitimate reason?

CHAPTER 13

I was tired of merely conducting interviews.
I felt like I was back writing for *The Walnut Creek Times*.
No, I didn't need the thrill of a life and death struggle with a serial killer, but I needed something besides the question and answer sessions I'd been having.

So, I decided to ratchet things up a little bit.

The Cowboy Way was located in the far corner of a strip mall off of Locust Street near the end of town. It's almost like it was hiding.

If this was Austin or Nashville or a hundred other country-music-loving cities, this bar would have been in the center of town. Walnut Creek was not one of those towns so TCW - as people called it on Yelp - had been relegated to the back of a strip mall.

I ventured in on a Friday night, hoping to catch some information on Gracie Keats.

I'd taken an UBER, knowing this night was going to involve a few drinks. Unlike my visit with Donna Keats, where the beers had come about unexpectedly.

I was wearing a yellow and black flannel shirt - it's the only one I had - along with some brown dress shoes and the biggest belt buckle I had. Which wasn't saying much.

I hoped I passed the eye test. I had a chance as long as they didn't get me out on the dance floor. I wouldn't know line dancing from break-dancing.

To the right of the bar were a stage, all the tables, and a dance floor. To the left, was a long bar where people were saddled up.

I chose the left, knowing bartenders always knew the best gossip. Now, whether you could coax that info from him or her was another question.

The bar was a good fifty feet long with a male bartender on one end and a female bartender on the other. I headed towards the woman. My charm would be more likely to work on her.

"What can I get you, cowboy?" she asked as I grabbed the seat at the very end of the bar.

I wondered if that was her go-to question for every customer.

"I'll take a Bud bottle," I said, sounding like a wannabe Cowboy. All I was missing was a shot of Jack Daniels with my order.

"Bud bottle coming right up."

The bartender was in her mid-30s, but despite her young age, looked like she'd seen it all. She probably had. Working at a bar was like aging in dog years. That doesn't mean it wasn't rewarding or a respectable job. It just aged you dealing with fights, drunks, and bad-tippers. Along with having to be a marriage counselor, shrink, and bartender all at once.

I had a lot of respect for our friends on the other side of the bar.

She set the Bud bottle down in front of me.

"Six bucks," she said.

I gave her a ten and left a two-dollar tip from the change. I wanted to be generous so she kept coming back to me but didn't want to be Captain Obvious and leave her a four-dollar tip.

"Thanks," she said.

"You got it."

I could have introduced myself then, but I was trying to bide my time, wait until we had bonded. If she knew right away that I was asking questions about Gracie Keats, she'd want nothing to do with me. Maybe, if the time was right, she'd be more likely to open up.

So I sat for forty-five minutes and drank two Buds making a little small talk with her when the opportunity presented itself.

At one point, I saw a female on the other end of the bar buy a shot for the male bartender. Some bars don't allow their employees to drink while others feel it encourages camaraderie between employee and client. I was happy to see that The Cowboy Way allowed it. I knew what I had to do.

"Another Bud bottle?" my bartender asked.

"I'm thinking about stepping it up," I said. "But I hate doing shots alone."

I put on my best puppy-dog face.

"I'm in," she said. "What are you having?"

"I'll take a shot of Jack. And you can pour whatever you'd like."

"Two Jacks it is."

She took out the two shot glasses and filled them both up with Jack Daniels.

We both grabbed our respective shots, when I said, "I'm Quint."

"I'm Brittany, but everyone just calls me Britt."

"Nice to meet you, Britt."

"Britt and Quint," she said.

I laughed.

We then took the shots and I told myself not to make a wincing face, despite straight bourbon not being my favorite.

I was going above and beyond for Archer Keats. Time would tell if he deserved it.

"How long have you worked here?" I asked.

A group of four people had walked in. It was obvious they were the band. Once they started playing, it was going to be too loud to talk to Britt. I had to push things a little bit.

"Three years," she said.

"Do you like it?"

She leaned in and whispered.

"Country isn't really my thing, but the cowboys seem to love me."

I was surprised, figuring she'd been a country girl herself.

"I'm not a country guy," I admitted.

"I got that feeling."

"How?"

"We don't see many yellow flannels here. And the way you sternly said 'Bud Bottle' made it seem like you were trying too hard."

"The shot of Jack probably didn't help either."

"I mean, are you going to ask for a steak, extra rare, next?"

I couldn't help but laugh.

"That was my next order."

"So what brings you here?"

A customer came up to order from Britt, so I kept quiet.

I was still on the end seat, which made our conversation as private as it could get.

Luckily, the guy didn't take the empty seat beside me and walked back towards one of the tables.

I decided to come clean. Britt had already realized I was a fraud, at least in my current surroundings.

"I'm a private investigator and I'm trying to find out information on Gracie Keats."

I could tell immediately that she recognized the name.

"I know who she is."

"I heard she liked to have drinks in here from time to time."

"She did."

"Did you ever serve her?"

"Sure have. She had a friend and they'd sit in the two end seats, just where you're sitting now. At least, until the music started, and they'd cut up a rug with some of the cowboys."

"No dancing for this guy."

She laughed.

"No offense, but I don't think you're going to solve her murder by asking questions of me."

"You want to know the truth?" I asked.

"Of course."

"I've been doing boring-ass question and answer sessions with potential witnesses for the last few weeks. I'm sick of it. I wanted to feel like I was actually investigating."

"You wanted three Bud bottles and a shot of Jack."

I laughed.

"That was the added bonus."

"Well, you seem alright, Quint. Not sure exactly how I can help."

"I've known a few bartenders in my day. Even worked a summer bartending gig when I was twenty-three."

"Your point?" she asked, but not in a malicious way.

"Bartenders don't get enough credit for just how insightful they are. I think they take in a lot more information than they let on."

"You're a good brown-noser, Quint."

"That may be true, but I also believe what I said."

"So why don't you just come out and ask me?"

Another patron walked up to the bar.

Please don't sit down next to me!

The bar was starting to fill up and I was sure every bar stool would be taken up soon.

An idea quickly hit me. I grabbed the barstool next to me and propped it up against the bar, a telltale sign that you were saving it for someone.

I figured that would buy me a few minutes.

Britt served the guy and walked back over to me.

It was time to stop beating around the bush.

"I want to know if you ever heard anything from Gracie or her friend Donna that might interest me."

"Was that her friend's name?"

"Yeah. I've met her and I got the impression she likes to gossip."

"That woman is a talker. You got that right."

"Anything you'd like to tell me about."

She eyed me.

"If you're not at a country bar, what's your shot of choice?"

"Probably Jaeger."

"Jagermeister? What are you, twenty-three again?"

"I know, I know. Everyone else starts to hate it after college. I'm still pro-Jaeger."

"Well, I'm a Tequila drinker. Would you like to buy me one more shot?"

"Of course."

She grabbed a bottle of Tequila and a bottle of Jagermeister and poured our respective shots.

We clinked glasses and quickly threw them back.

She leaned closer so as not to be heard.

"So, one night, about two weeks before her death, Gracie was here with that loud friend of hers. Donna. Down on this side of the bar. And her friend was pretty drunk. I mean, so was Gracie, I guess. It's just that Donna was louder. And I remember as clear as day, Donna had both arms in the air. One at her waist and one at her shoulders. She was pretending to be weighing things. And for the next fifteen seconds, she kept saying, 'The shrink or the tennis pro' and would adjust her hands as if giving more weight to one or the other. 'Shrink or the tennis pro.' 'Shrink or the tennis pro.' Gracie was laughing her ass off at first, but as Donna kept doing it, people started looking over. That's when Gracie told her to stop. Vehemently."

Donna had already suggested that Gracie was having an affair with Dickie Faber. And Ellie had mentioned she might be fooling around with her tennis coach, Brad Lacoste. So I guess this news wasn't ground-breaking.

Still, to hear Britt tell it in such detail made it hit home.

Gracie Keats was cheating on Archer with two men.

Whether that was good for his defense was debatable.

Sure, the list of suspects might have grown, but it also gave Archer all the more reason to want his wife dead.

If Britt had heard Gracie and Donna talking about it, how many other people around town knew? Archer had known they came to The Cowboy Way. It wasn't that far-fetched to believe he'd also been told about the little 'shrink and the tennis pro' discussion.

And if he had, I'm sure it would have cut deep.

Having a cheating spouse was bad enough, but knowing they were going around town talking about it would have been completely emasculating.

"Was anyone else paying attention?" I asked.

"At the end, when Donna was getting really loud with it, a few people looked over. And that's when Gracie told her to stop."

"When you found out Gracie had been killed, did you ever consider going to the cops?"

"Not for one second. I'm not a rat. This is a bar and people like to air their dirty laundry. What kind of bartender would you be if you broke that trust?"

I was reminded of Tre who said if people knew he was badmouthing Walnut Creek restaurateurs, he'd be looking for a new job. It was the same with Britt.

"I get your point," I said. "She was dead, though. You're not exactly breaking her trust."

"The authorities arrested her husband a few days later. I just assumed he killed her because he found out she was cheating."

As usual, the general public thought Archer was guilty.

"Is there anything else that Gracie or Donna said that stuck out?"

"Nothing as memorable as what I mentioned. They used to like to comment on the butts of the young guys dancing."

"You said they would get out there and dance."

"Oh yeah. They had enough liquid courage after ordering drinks from me for an hour."

"And you said they came in once a week?"

"Yup. Every Friday night."

"For how long?"

"I'd say for about six months."

"And there's nothing else you can tell me?"

"That's all I got," Britt said.

"I've got one more question. Did Gracie ever come in with a guy?"

"No. I think this place was always a girls' night out with her friend."

"Thanks, Britt."

"You got it, Quint. Now that you got what you came for, will you be heading out?"

When I paused, she pounced.

"In a few minutes, why don't we have one last shot?"

I thanked my lucky stars I'd taken an Uber.

"You're on," I said. "And thanks for everything."

"Next time you want to have a few shots, you know where to find me."

"You'll be seeing me soon."

"And ditch that ugly flannel," she said.

I couldn't help but laugh.

CHAPTER 14

It was another one Advil morning following my night at The Cowboy Way.

I'd ordered an Uber after that last shot with Britt the bartender. If I'd stayed any longer, it was likely going to be a two Advil morning.

I realized I hadn't seen Ellie since our exciting meeting at my office. Or was it regrettable? I couldn't decide and landed on the idea that it might be both.

I called her and asked when we could both meet up with Archer.

"I'll set up something for tomorrow afternoon," she said.

"Text me once you have a time."

"I will. And Quint, we are still going to keep quiet about what happened, correct?"

"Of course," I said.

"Thanks. I'll talk to Archer and get back to you.

The escapades from the night before had my adrenaline flowing. I wasn't meeting with Ellie and Archer until tomorrow, so I decided another "field trip" was in order.

The Walnut Creek Golf and Tennis Club was a posh country club that the Keats belonged to. It's also where Brad Lacoste was the tennis pro.

The name was perfect. Lacoste is the name of a prominent tennis clothing line. I wondered if Brad was part of the family lineage.

I'd made fun of basically everyone's name in the Keats family and Brad "The Tennis Pro" Lacoste was on that level.

I parked my car in the lot and quickly realized it was the most inexpensive one there.

BMW, Mercedes, and Tesla were having their own battle for superiority. My 2017 Toyota Camry wasn't invited to the party.

I'm sure the country club had a bar on-site, but this wasn't going to be a repeat of the previous night. I wasn't going to order three shots and ask the bartender, "So, do you want to spill the beans on Brad Lacoste?"

So I came up with a different plan.

I was wearing tan tennis shorts, a white tennis shirt, and an old pair of Stan Smith tennis shoes that I'd found in the deep recesses of my closet. The outfit was my yellow and black flannel, but for a country club. I had to make it believable that I was a tennis player considering joining the club.

Part of me felt ridiculous, a pseudo-version of Chevy Chase in *Fletch.*

I walked from my car up a slight hill until I arrived at the pro shop. There were tennis rackets and golf clubs scattered throughout the shop. Many were adorned with a red "For Sale" tag. A young lady with a long ponytail was behind the counter.

"How are you?" I asked.

"Good. Can I help you?"

"I just moved to Walnut Creek and am a life-long tennis player. I wanted to know your rates to join the club."

"I'm just the clerk here at the shop. Hold on a second."

She got on her phone and called someone.

"Zach will be with you in a minute. He handles prospective new clients."

A few minutes later, a man in his mid-fifties, with an odd part right down the middle of his hair, approached me. He was strutting and obviously held himself in high esteem. I'm not sure he had a reason to.

"I'm Zach Pemberton, it's a pleasure to meet you."

"I'm Richard," I said, making up a name on the fly.

It's a drawback to being named Quint. It's a name people remember.

"I heard you were inquiring about joining the Walnut Creek Golf and Tennis Club?"

I'd already labeled him a numbskull for his strut. Saying the entire name of the club only furthered that opinion.

Maybe I was getting more judgmental at my ripe old age of forty-two. This clown deserved it, though.

"I was," I said.

"Do you golf, play tennis, or both?"

"I'm more of a tennis player. Are there different membership rates?"

"There sure are. Here, why don't we walk around the club for a minute? The pro shop doesn't reveal the full experience here."

He gave me a big, fake smile and I responded in kind.

We walked outside of the pro shop and he led me up another slight hill.

"If you're only joining for the tennis, obviously it's cheaper than becoming a member of the golf club as well."

"Makes sense. I'm trying to stay in shape, so far now, I'm just here for tennis. Maybe when I get older, I'll pick up golf."

"You won't regret it. Golf is a great sport and the people who play it are all top-notch people. You don't get the riffraff you get in other sports."

Zach gave me the impression of someone who didn't like the rise of Tiger Woods.

Call it a hunch.

"Well, as I said, I'm more of a tennis guy."

"Understood. Understood."

If he was paid on commission, it's no wonder he was pushing me towards golf.

"I'd love to meet your tennis pro as well," I said. "Just to make sure it's what I'm looking for."

"Our pro is a man named Brad Lacoste. He's top-notch all the way."

Top-notch was this jackass's favorite phrase.

"Brad almost made the tour about ten years ago, but a couple of brutal knee injuries prevented that."

"That's too bad. How old a guy is he?"

"Brad is thirty-five."

"Is he here today?"

"He sure is," Zach said and looked down at his expensive watch. "I think he's conducting a lesson right now, but that should be ending in about five minutes. I'll take you down to meet him then."

"Perfect."

"In the meantime, let me tell you about our executive eighteen-hole golf course that was rated one of the best on the west coast from Golf Digest."

You had to hand it to Zach. The guy was relentless.

A few minutes later, we headed down to meet Brad Lacoste.

There were sixteen tennis courts, shaped in a huge square. And off to the side, there was a court that sat on its own. That's where Zach was leading me. I was sure it's where Brad conducted his one-on-one lessons.

I was more interested in a different type of one-on-one. The one he had with Gracie Keats.

When we were twenty feet from the court, two people were stepping off of it.

One was a middle-aged woman in all white. The other was Brad Lacoste.

He was a handsome dude. Tall, thin, and well-tanned. If you imagined a tennis pro, Brad Lacoste probably fit the mold.

"Thanks, Brad," the woman said.

"I'll see you next week, Patty."

As Patty passed us, Zach approached the Walnut Creek Golf and Tennis Club's head pro.

"How are you, Brad?"

"Good to see you, Zach."

"This is Richard and he was thinking about joining our fabulous club. He's an avid tennis player."

"That's great to hear. What level do you play at?"

I knew a little about the tennis rating system and it served me well at the moment.

"I'm a 4.5," I said.

That was the score of a very good amateur tennis player. A touring pro was considered a 7. If he asked me to go out on the court and hit a few, I'd be fucked. I was no 4.5.

"4.5, that's very solid."

"Thanks."

"Where did you used to play?"

I had to talk generally. If I mentioned a specific tennis club, he might call me on my bluff.

"A few different country clubs in Arizona. I moved a lot."

"Are you going to be in Walnut Creek long?"

Zach interjected.

"Our minimum term of service is one year."

Term of service made it sound like I was signing a lease. Which maybe wasn't all that far off.

"That won't be a problem," I said. "How much are lessons?"

"We can talk all about the fees for joining and for lessons when we get back to the pro shop," Zach said. "We don't want to bore Brad with numbers. He's here for his tennis acumen."

"I'm sure Brad can both count and hit tennis balls," I said.

Brad laughed loudly while Zach shrunk back a bit.

"Richard is just busting your balls, Zach."

Zach thought highly of himself, but he was not at the top of the food chain. That was probably Brad Lacoste and whoever the golf pro was.

An awkward silence followed which I decided to break up.

"If I joined the club, how soon could we start lessons?" I asked Brad.

"Not long. I think I'm booked up for the next week or so, but we could fit you in after that."

"Might be a change for you. I'm guessing it's a lot of older ladies that you're giving lessons to."

Brad stared at me, partly offended, partly amused.

"I think I could handle a 4.5," Brad said.

Zach laughed awkwardly.

I decided to play nice.

"I'm sure you could. Zach told me you almost made the tour. Very impressive."

"Thanks. If it weren't for a couple of injuries, you might have seen me out there with Federer, Nadal, and Djokovic."

"That's a bummer," I said.

"It's not so bad here. I get to teach old ladies and 4.5s."

I laughed.

Brad Lacoste knew how to give it back when necessary.

"I'm looking forward to booking my first lesson," I said.

"Shall we go up to the pro shop and iron out the details?" Zach said.

"Sure."

"It was nice to meet you, Richard," Brad said.

"Likewise."

Zach and I then started walking back.

Ten minutes later, after telling Zach that I was in a rush and would be back in a few days to sign the paperwork, I approached my car.

Brad Lacoste was standing in front of it.

"I had a feeling this was your car," he said.

"Oh yeah, how's that?"

"Because P.I.s usually don't make enough to buy Teslas."

I was absolutely floored.

How the fuck did he know who I was?

I decided to play dumb.

"I'm not sure who you think I am."

"Cut the bullshit. I saw your face after you brought down that serial killer."

So much for playing dumb.

"What the fuck are you here for?" he asked menacingly.

He had me asking the same question. What exactly had I hoped to accomplish? If it was to piss off Brad Lacoste, I'd achieved my goal. If it was to learn information about him and Gracie, I'd failed miserably.

It was time to come clean.

"I've been hired by Archer Keats," I said. "And I'm looking for anyone else who might have had a reason to kill his wife."

"And you thought I might?"

"There've been some rumors you were having an affair with her."

There was no one walking towards us, but Brad Lacoste started looking around in fear that someone might.

"Can we talk in your car?" he asked.

"Sure," I said.

I used my fob - yes, even Toyota Camry's have them - and got in the front seat while Brad sat in the passenger seat.

He was now a different man. Fear was in his eyes.

"I had nothing to do with Gracie's death. I promise you. Swear to God. Whatever you need to hear."

"Were you having an affair with her?"

"You're not going to call me to the stand, are you? I'd lose my job for sure. You can't have a tennis pro going around and having sex with his clients. They tend to frown on that type of thing."

"So, you're admitting that it's true?"

His whole body seemed to shrug at once.

"Yes."

"Where?"

"My place. I live alone and she would never risk having me to her place."

"How many times?"

"I don't know. Five. Six, maybe. Less than ten times for sure."

"Over how long a period?"

"Probably four months."

"And when was the last time you had sex with Gracie Keats?"

"About a week before she was killed. Which, just to reiterate, I had nothing to do with. What possible motive could I have?"

It was time to use his words against him.

"Maybe she was going to tell people about the affair and it was going to cost you your job."

He shook his head, realizing I had a good point.

"I love this job. I hope to have it for a long time. But I'd never kill someone to keep it. I'm not a monster."

I believed Brad Lacoste. I can't say I liked the guy - he was too smarmy for me - but he didn't strike me as a cold-blooded killer.

"How did the affair start?"

"She had taken lessons from me for a year or so. We flirted, but that's not uncommon in my profession. One day, she asked where I lived. I knew why and it kind of just went from there."

"If I were you, I'd answer this next question honestly. If not, I'll be back to find out the truth."

"I'll tell you the truth."

"How many other women at the club are you having an affair with?"

"I'd just like to clarify that I'm single and not technically having an affair."

"I'm sure that will make the husbands of the women absolve you."

He shook his head again.

"You're right. And the answer is two other women."

"Do you really love your job? You're not going to be able to keep juggling these women without someone finding out."

"You're already trying to ruin my life. I don't need a lecture also."

"I'm not trying to ruin your life. I want to find out who killed Gracie."

I wondered if Ellie would want to call Brad Lacoste or Dickie Faber to the witness stand. Would the jury just be more apt to think that Archer had a motive to kill his wife?

"Is there anything I can do to prevent this?" Brad asked.

"Not today. But I'm not going to tell Zach or anyone else at the club. It will be up to Archer's attorney whether she decides to put you on the stand."

"Great. Another woman will surely try to bring me down."

"You put yourself in this situation. Stop blaming the women," I said.

He now looked like a scared young man. The menacing, threatening man from a few minutes ago was long gone.

"You're right. I'm sorry."

"Is there anything you can tell me about Gracie? Was she scared in the weeks leading up to her death?"

He thought long and hard about it. I could tell he was trying to remember any nugget that might divert suspicion from him.

"She mentioned how her husband had lost a lot of money during Covid."

"Don't forget who I'm working for."

I immediately disliked what I said. It made it sound like I only wanted to hear information that would potentially exonerate Archer.

"I know."

"Unless you have concrete evidence that Archer had something do with it," I said.

He was shocked by my statement.

"You're not even convinced he's innocent, are you? And yet, you're willing to destroy an innocent man's life like mine?"

His anger returned.

"Watch yourself, Brad," I said. "I'm treating you fairly. As I said, I'm not going to Zach or the Country Club brass and telling them what I know. I'm merely going to give the information I've accrued to Archer's lawyer."

"Can I talk to her before she decides to put me on the stand?"

"If she intends to call you as a witness, you'll definitely be meeting with her beforehand."

Someone approached the car next to mine. And yes, it was a Tesla. Brad Lacoste tried to put his arms over his face as if the people getting in the Tesla had any idea what we were talking about.

"Is there anything else you want to tell me?" I asked.

"She was rich," he said. "Like, really rich. And I certainly wasn't going to be receiving one red cent in her will. Maybe you should be looking for people who would profit from her death."

I hated to admit it, but Brad Lacoste had a point. I was out looking for people she'd been sleeping with when money is one of the oldest motives in the book. Of course, sex and infidelity might have topped that list.

Motive was going to be a problem for Ellie. Archer was the sole beneficiary and he'd lost a good portion of his net worth over the last few years.

Brad Lacoste and Dickie Faber had nothing to gain financially by her death. Although, Brad would have lost his job if Gracie had come forward. And I imagine that psychiatrists might lose their medical licenses if it was proven they were sleeping with their clients.

While it wouldn't have been for the money, Brad and Dickie had their own potential motives.

"I'm looking at all angles," I finally said. "Money. Sex. Revenge. Infidelity."

"If I think of anything else, can I call you? I'd much rather stop this before I have to go meet with Archer's attorney."

I was surprised he called him by his first name.

"Did you know Archer?"

"No. Gracie always called him by his first name so I guess it just kind of stuck."

"I'm surprised she'd talk about him much. Seems like during an affair the last thing you'd want to talk about is your significant other."

"He certainly didn't come up while we were having sex, but sometimes she'd hang around after. And then we'd get to talking."

"And he'd come up?"

"Yeah."

"Did she ever mention she was going to divorce him?"

I sounded like an attorney for the prosecution.

"Not in as many words," he said. "But it was obvious she'd fallen out of love with him."

"Have you ever heard the name Dickie Faber?" I asked.

"No, can't say I have."

That's the answer I expected. I can't imagine Gracie Keats would go around telling guys about other guys she was having affairs with.

I tried to rack my brain for any questions I'd missed.

I took out a business card.

"Here you go," I said. "Call me if you think of anything."

He took a card out as well and handed it over.

"Please have the attorney call me personally and not the club. I'm sure you think I'm some smug asshole, but I don't deserve to lose my job over this."

That was debatable, but I hadn't taken my job to get people fired. Unless they'd done something truly heinous. And in my heart, I didn't think Brad Lacoste had murdered Gracie.

"I'll give her this number," I said.

"Thanks. Is that it?"

"Yeah, we're done here," I said.

Brad Lacoste exited my car and I drove out of the Walnut Creek Golf and Tennis Club. As had become par for the course, I found myself with more questions than answers.

CHAPTER 15

M y meeting with Archer and Ellie took place the next morning.
I knew it was going to be different because Ellie mentioned we'd start talking about potential legal strategy.

As always, Ellie was waiting by the time I arrived. She was a very punctual woman.

There was going to be a fourth for this meeting.

"Quint, this is Cliff Boyd," Ellie said. "He'll be my co-counsel and will be joining us for some of these meetings."

We shook hands.

Cliff Boyd looked to be around seventy-five years old. I'm sure he had accrued some legal knowledge in his years as an attorney, but my guess was Ellie chose him because he looked seasoned.

She was young and the jury might hold that against her. Having an old man as co-counsel might help curtail that.

We convened in the patio area.

It was another relatively chilly day. I know Archer wanted to make the main house seem off-limits because of the death of Gracie, but I was about to say something.

Ellie beat me to it.

"It's freezing out here, Archer. Can't we go into the main house? We don't have to go upstairs."

"Sure, if that's what you guys want," Archer said.

Cliff Boyd and I both nodded.

Archer turned off the stand-up heaters and we made our way inside. There was a long, dining room table that he told us to sit at. We all gathered on one end of it. Ellie and Cliff on one side, Archer and me on the other.

Archer set his hands on the table in front of me and I couldn't help but wonder if they were the hands of a killer. No, they were not scratched up when the authorities brought him in following Gracie's death. But I'd hypothesized that if the knife was used with enough force on the first stab, Gracie wouldn't have been able to defend herself. It would make sense Archer wouldn't have any scratches.

He was still wearing his wedding ring. I had to assume it would be staying on until the trial had finished. The two people sitting across from us would make sure of that. It would be a bad look to be without it once the trial started.

"Quint," Ellie said. "Before we get into the questions of how we are going to defend Archer, why don't you tell us about your last few days and the people you've interviewed?"

I spent the next ten minutes talking about my visits to The Cowboy Way and The Walnut Creek Golf and Tennis Club. All eyes looked on me with keen interest and I was never once interrupted. I felt shitty having to tell Archer that Gracie was having sex with her tennis pro after telling him about Dickie Faber only days earlier. He seemed to take it in stride. Maybe none of this surprised him anymore.

I was close to wrapping it up.

"And that's when Brad Lacoste gave me his business card and I drove off," I said.

"You've been a busy man," Ellie said.

For the twentieth time since I met her, I couldn't tell if there were hidden meanings behind her words.

"Just doing what you and Archer have asked of me."

Cliff Boyd spoke for the first time.

"I know you're not an attorney, Quint, but which of these two men do you think will make a better witness?"

"I guess it depends on what you mean by better," I said. "Dickie Faber is short, unattractive, and has an unlikable quality about him. Brad Lacoste is tall, handsome, and charismatic. So, if you mean who will the jury like more, then Lacoste is obviously the answer. But you guys are trying to get Archer off. For those purposes, I think Dickie Faber is the answer. The jury won't like him and I think they'd be more apt to think he killed Gracie. Lacoste could get a lot of women. It doesn't appear losing Gracie would be that devastating to him. Now, could she have threatened Lacoste about

going public, and knowing he would lose his job, he did something dras-
tic? It's possible, but I don't think that's what happened and I don't think
the jury would buy it, either. If you could only put one on the stand, I'd go
with Dickie Faber."

Archer jumped in.

"Cliff, don't make a joke that Quint should be joining your legal team.
I've already made it."

"Maybe not," Cliff said. "But I'm glad he's on our side."

"This begs another question," Ellie said. "How many other potential
suspects do we want to put on the stand? Is there a point where more
becomes less? If the jury hears about five other suspects, will they start to
tune them out? Would it be better to just throw them one or possibly,
two?"

"I think you're right," Cliff said. "The more suspects we present them
with, the more we sound like we're just fishing. Narrow it down to two.
One is even better. And then go all-in on that suspect."

"Which means we'd need a lot more information on Dickie Faber,"
Ellie said. "Donna Neal and the bartender at The Cowboy Way are hardly
enough to convince people that Dickie could have killed her."

I quickly glanced over at Archer Keats. This had to hurt badly. I'm not
sure I would have remained so composed. On the other hand, these two
men provided him the most likely chance of getting off.

"Do you want me to do some more investigating of Dickie?" I asked.

"Yes," Ellie said. "Try to tail him if you can. See if he goes somewhere
after work that is suspicious. Maybe ask a client of his what he or she
thinks of him?"

I didn't like the sound of that. Then again, I'd confronted Dickie
myself. Asking one of his clients a few questions was no less invasive.

"I can do that," I said.

"Let's look a little more closely at the upcoming trial," Ellie said. "Jury
selection is only three weeks away. Let's talk about the evidence they have
against Archer. Cliff, you want to take this?"

"Sure. So, the prosecution's case is going to be based on three major
things. One, that Archer was the only one on the premises at the time of
Gracie's murder. There were no other footprints found. No other DNA. No
broken windows. No picked locks. You get the picture. They will argue the
person who killed Gracie had a key to the house and the only people who
had that were Archer, A.J., and Grace. With Archer's kids both out of
town, he is the only one who fits the bill. So the police started narrowing in
on him. Now is where it gets tricky. I said there are three major things.
Well, the second and third go together. I think the prosecution is going to

argue for two separate motives. They might not come out and say that, but they will present both. One, that Archer was pissed off because his wife was cheating on him. And two, he wanted her dead because his finances had taken a beating and if Gracie died, he'd inherit her roughly $18 million dollars. They'll also likely claim Gracie was planning on filing for divorce, so Archer was forced to kill her in able to get the money. If not, it would be all Gracie's in the divorce. Now, let's deal with the first part. Does the prosecution want to trot out guy after guy who might have slept with Gracie? Sure, it will give the jury reason to believe Archer would be furious, but as we said, it might also open them up as potential suspects as well. For that reason, I think the prosecution will focus more on the money as Archer's motive. They will trot out financial experts to talk about how much money your businesses lost during Covid, which we've estimated as somewhere between one and two million. They'll focus on your businesses that had to be shut down. And they will also talk about all the money that you borrowed from your wife. And yes, I know you were married, but you had no prenup, so they will use the term borrowing. So you might as well get used to it."

The word 'So' appeared to be Cliff's favorite word.

His voice had gotten a little raspy as he went on. He coughed twice in quick succession.

"Can I get a water, Archer?" he asked.

"Sure. Ellie? Quint? You guys want one?"

We both nodded.

Archer returned with three water bottles. I wondered if he'd restocked the fridge in recent weeks or whether it had remained the same since Gracie had died. Being in this house brought about some odd questions.

"Did you want to finish up, Cliff?" Ellie asked.

"Sure. I didn't have too much more to say. They will beat the jury over the head with the idea that Archer's world was caving in financially. That he was stuck in some corner he couldn't get out of. They'll probably call witnesses who say that Gracie was tired of giving Archer money. We need witnesses that say she had no problem supporting her husband. And Archer, if we have you take the stand, which Ellie and I haven't decided on yet, you'll have to be adamant that the money situation wasn't as bad as they are going to make out."

"It wasn't that bad!" Archer yelled. "I still had money. They were just mostly tied up in my other businesses, so when I needed starter money, I had to go to Gracie. I could have never opened another business and still lived comfortably for the rest of my life."

"Good. You'll have to express that on the stand. But try to avoid yelling. Any semblance of a temper will give the jury reason to consider things we don't want to be considered."

"I know. I won't be like this on the stand."

"I'd start now. It's learned behavior," Cliff said.

I'd originally thought Cliff was only hired to make Ellie look more seasoned. I was mistaken. He was sharp as a tack.

Ellie, never short on opinions, must have felt like she was being left out.

"Archer, I'll need to talk to the financial guys at Gene Bowman's firm. Hopefully, they'll paint a rosier picture of your finances than the prosecution will."

"Everyone at Gene's firm is a team player. They will all paint me in a positive light."

"Good, because they will be crucial. If we can make it look like you were fine financially, the prosecution will have a much tougher time convincing the jury you would kill your wife for money."

"But I didn't kill her," he said.

"While we all know that's true, the prosecution will be saying that you did. So, as Cliff said, you better get used to this."

Archer shook his head back and forth. He was obviously pissed but didn't want to show the anger that Cliff had warned him about.

"Quint, we need to talk about jury selection. I know it won't involve you very much."

"Go right ahead. I'm still interested," I said.

"Cliff, what's your overarching opinion on what type of jury we are looking for?" Ellie asked.

"I'll go down the line. First off, race. This case has nothing to do with race so I don't care if the jury is made of white, black, brown, or turquoise people. This case has a lot to do with class, however. I would try to avoid getting too many poor people on the jury. That may sound harsh, but I do think they might look at Archer as this spoiled millionaire who had it all. Money, looks, a pretty wife, and a great family. And they will be jealous of that, possibly looking for a reason to pin it on him. So, I know you can't pick and choose every juror you want, but I'd use some of our preemptive challenges on people of a lower class. Sure, Walnut Creek is an affluent city, but there are plenty of poorer parts of Contra Costa Country. This will not be a jury made up solely of his Walnut Creek peers."

Cliff took a sip of his water. He was one hell of a talker.

"I'd lean towards having more men on the jury for no other reason than Gracie - a woman - was the victim of such a savage crime. As for age, I tend to think we should shoot for a younger jury. Historically, older juries are more likely to convict. They tend to have more faith in the police. With all the things going on in our country right now, I think younger people have come to distrust the police. And remember, all we need is one to get a hung jury. Maybe we'd get that twenty-seven-year-old kid who can't stand the police and figure they are railroading Archer."

"They are railroading me," he said.

"Hey, Archer, we're all on the same team," Ellie said. "You don't have to interject each time we speak as the prosecution or the police."

It was a rough rebuttal.

"I get it, Ellie, but it's hard to just sit here and take this."

"If you can't handle this, how are you going to handle a trial?" she asked rhetorically.

As with many rhetorical questions, no one knew how to respond for several seconds. Cliff finally spoke.

"So, I would lean towards men, younger people, and maybe people of a higher economic stature."

"I think you're overlooking one thing, Cliff," I said.

"I doubt you've worked many legal cases, but let's hear it."

He gave me a slight sneer.

"The people who distrust the police most are often people of color. So, while I agree that race means nothing in Gracie's actual death, if you're trying to get jurors who might think Archer is being railroaded by the police, then race could be a factor."

"It's a great point, Quint," Ellie said.

"Maybe, you're right," Cliff said. "But do you think some poor Hispanic or black kid is going to give a shit about some wealthy, white restaurateur?"

"I didn't say anything about being poor," I said.

Cliff's face lost its color very quickly.

"I'm sorry. You're right."

I could have followed up on it but saw no reason to embarrass him. I kept quiet.

"Why don't we hold off on the jury talk," Ellie said. "The truth is, we need to look at each potential juror as his or her own little case study. We can't just look for all young people. Or all men."

"Are we going to have a jury selection expert?" Archer asked.

"We can," Ellie said. "It's going to cost you, obviously."

"Shit, I'll pay for one just so we don't have to have this conversation."

We all laughed and it served as a nice respite.

"Alright, to be continued on the jury front," Ellie said.

I spoke next.

"Do you mind if I ask you a few questions, Archer?"

"Go ahead, Quint."

"How do you think the killer got into the main house?"

"I don't know."

"Do you have any guesses?"

"I haven't come up with a good answer. Maybe he was a lock-picker."

"The cops found no sign of forced entry."

"Maybe he could pick a lock without it making it appear as if he did."

"I imagine that theory will be shot down by a prosecution witness."

Archer and I were having a two-person conversation as Ellie and Cliff looked on.

"What do you want me to say, Quint?"

"I want an alternative that your lawyers can present to the jury. If there are only three people who have keys - and your kids are off-limits - then how do we explain how the killer got in?"

"I don't know. Maybe Gracie gave a key to one of the guys she was cheating with."

"See, now we're getting somewhere. You could give me your key and I could hit up some local locksmiths and see if that key had been replicated in the weeks leading up to Gracie's death."

I saw Ellie nod in deference to my idea. Cliff spoke up.

"Another solid idea, Quint."

"Thanks, " I said, but quickly moved on. "Archer, did you ever lose your key in the last several months? Or have it go missing for an extended period of time? Even if that was just a few hours."

"No, not that I can think of."

"When Gracie relegated you to the guest house, did you keep the main house key on your keychain?"

Ellie continued to look at me with reverence. As if I was asking all the right questions.

"I did. I never took it off. It would have been admitting defeat and I'd always hoped Gracie would allow me to return to the main house. And our bed."

"Did you ever lend the key to anyone else?"

"No."

"I know you don't like questions about them, but did either of your kids ever lose their keys?"

"Not that I know of."

"And did either Grace or A.J. have any friends who might have hated Gracie?"

Archer shook his head. He was pissed again.

"A.J. and Grace have nothing to do with this."

"You didn't answer my question."

"No, none of their friends hated Gracie. No one hated Gracie."

"Someone did," I said.

The temperature in the room had picked up and it was all my fault.

"Yes, I guess someone did," Archer admitted. "But it wasn't my kids or friends of my kids."

I wondered why Archer and seemingly everyone else wanted to keep his kids out of it. The logical answer was that no one wants to involve their kids, but it felt like more than just that.

Was there something Archer was trying to shield his kids from?

Did it have anything to do with Grace being a complete she-devil when I'd met with her?

Archer was already on edge, so I figured this wasn't the time to keep pushing his buttons. I'd planned on meeting with Grace and A.J. one more time so I could broach the subject then.

"I'm sorry, Archer, but we have to consider every possibility."

I sounded like one of his defense attorneys.

"Quint is right," Cliff said. "Luckily for you Archer, I don't think the prosecution will focus on your kids too much."

"Finally some good news, "Archer said. "But why?"

"Because they are convinced that you murdered Gracie."

The logical - but unexpected - answer elicited a few more seconds of silence.

"Well, this conversation has gone off the rails," Ellie said. "But it has been productive. I think we should reconvene in a few days. In the meantime, Quint, you said you'd do a little more investigating of Dickie Faber."

"Sure."

"Have you interviewed everyone from my initial list?"

"Everyone except Archer's next-door neighbor."

"Vic Parsons," Archer said.

"Do you think he'd be home right now?" I asked.

"Probably. Vic is retired, a widower, and in his 80s. Good chance he's home."

"Does he like you?" I asked.

"Yeah, we always got along."

"I was kind of curious why he was on the list, Ellie."

"He's the only real neighbor. After this house, there are a hundred yards until the next home. So, if anyone saw anything on the night in question, it would be Vic Parsons."

"I'm sure the police interviewed him and asked him that."

"Humor me, Quint," Ellie said. "He's an old man. Maybe he'll remember having seen something."

"Or forget what he really saw."

"You're impossible," she said, a smile on her face.

I almost gave a biting comeback, but smartly kept it to myself.

"Fine, I'll go interview Mr. Parsons after this," I said.

"Thank you, Quint," Ellie said, a hint of sarcasm in her voice.

Our meeting disbanded a few minutes later with a promise to all meet again soon.

CHAPTER 16

Vic Parson's home was only fifty yards or so from the Keats' driveway.

The problem is that Vic Parsons was in his eighties. Fifty yards might have been more like a quarter-mile to him. Plus, Gracie's time of death was set between midnight and two a.m.

I wasn't putting much stock in the old man having seen something relevant.

"Can I help you?" Vic Parsons asked as he opened the door.

He was wearing a robe that showed quite a bit of chest hair. He was also rocking some green Crocs. I had a feeling Vic Parsons had said "Fuck it" long ago.

And who could blame him?

Widowed. Retired. Old.

I hoped to live to the point where I didn't give a shit what anyone thought.

I think I was partially jealous of Vic Parsons.

"I've been hired by Archer Keats to help in his defense."

There was no need to lie.

"Are you an attorney?"

"No, a private investigator."

"Okay. What's the investigation about?"

Vic didn't appear to be all there.

"I want to know if you saw anything on the night Gracie Keats was killed."

"Didn't it happen late at night?"

"Yes. Between midnight and two a.m. they think."

"That's right. I think I talked to the cops after it happened. You'll have to excuse me if I don't remember every detail. I'm eighty-seven years old."

"You don't look it," I said.

"No, I didn't look out my window," he said, misunderstanding my comment. "I was asleep."

This was going nowhere, so I tried a Hail Mary.

"Too much to hope for. I told my associates there was no way an eighty-something-year-old guy would have seen anything."

He bristled. I'd gotten under his skin.

"Well, no, not that night."

"But another night?"

"Yes."

My pulse accelerated ever so slightly.

"What did you see, Mr. Parsons?"

"I saw a guy going into Gracie's house."

"When?"

"I don't know. Two or three days before she died."

"What time?"

"Maybe eight p.m. or so."

"It wasn't Archer walking towards the guest house?"

"It wasn't him."

"What makes you so sure?"

"Because the person walked from the street. Whenever Mr. Keats was arriving, he'd park his car up on their driveway."

Brad Lacoste was tall and Dickie Faber was short.

"Was the guy short or tall?"

"Just kind of average, I guess."

So much for that.

"And just to be clear, this wasn't the night Gracie was killed?"

"No, as I said, it was a week before."

This was going nowhere. A minute earlier, Vic Parsons had said it was two or three days before Gracie's murder. Now it was a week. This guy's best days were behind him.

"Thanks for your time, Mr. Parsons."

I bid adieu a few seconds later.

I arrived home and took my usual seat on the couch, but not before throwing on *A Love Supreme* by John Coltrane.

I leaned back on the couch, kicked my legs up on the coffee table, and began to think about the case.

I'd now met with everyone on Ellie's original list.

Was I any closer to knowing who killed Gracie Keats?

No.

But that didn't mean I hadn't made progress.

I'd learned a hundred things since taking the case. Whether any of them held the key to solving Gracie's murder was yet to be determined.

I decided to take a quick roll call of the ones I found most intriguing.

The list had to start with Dickie Faber. I probably knew the least about him of anyone.

And yet, if I had to put odds on who was the killer, he'd be right near the top. I hated to admit it, but Archer probably still held the top spot. That didn't mean I thought he did it. He just remained the most likely.

If this was a pie chart, Archer might inhabit 25% of it. Dickie Faber 20% of it. Brad Lacoste 15% of it. And on down the list.

Ellie wanted me to follow Dickie around. It wasn't a bad idea.

The case against Brad Lacoste was pretty straightforward. For him to be the killer, Gracie would have threatened to go public with their affair and Lacoste feared it would have cost him his job. It seemed pretty far-fetched. Plus, he didn't strike me as the jealous boyfriend type, especially since he was dating other women on the side. I'd definitely overestimated the probability that Brad had done it. Giving him 15% of the pie chart was far too much. He was down at more like 3%.

For obvious reasons, I hadn't focused much on A.J. and Grace Keats as potential murderers. They both had alibis on the night in question. A.J. was two hundred miles away in Lake Tahoe as verified by his roommate. And Grace was getting drunk in Napa and had the bar tab to prove it. More than that, thinking that one of them killed their mother was morbid as all hell. Lastly, if Archer found out I was making inquiries into his children, I'd be getting a quick pink slip.

But still, I couldn't rule them out. I put them at 2% each on my make-believe pie chart.

There were some other periphery characters like Gene Bowman or Parker and Caleb Johnson. I wasn't ruling them out - I wasn't ruling anyone out - but they occupied a very small slice of my pie chart.

Let's say they were at 1%.

The last person I had to consider was Ellie Teague. She probably didn't even belong on my mock list, but something had rubbed me wrong since I'd first met her. I'd constantly felt she was holding something back.

The fact that she'd flirted with me from day one and then initiated us having sex had given me pause.

It wasn't that I hadn't been with beautiful women - I certainly had - but it had rarely been so easy. A little flirting, a Dickie joke here and there, and then she's grabbing my dick? I knew I wasn't that irresistible.

Maybe there was another reason.

Ellie was a month from trying a monumental case, surely the most important of her life. Maybe she thought if she had the P.I. under her thumb, there would be no last-minute surprises.

It wasn't inconceivable.

If that were the case, was she sleeping with Archer too? How about Cliff Boyd?

I laughed, in spite of myself. Ellie wasn't banging Cliff Boyd.

I also put Ellie at around 1% on my pie chart of which I'd only allocated about 40%. The unused portion was reserved for people I'd never met. I saw it as a distinct possibility that I hadn't yet come across the man who murdered Gracie. Or the woman.

I was dizzy.

My head was overworked. It was like an engine that was revving at six thousand revolutions a minute.

I got up off my couch, walked to the kitchen, and poured myself a glass of wine.

I told myself no more thinking about the case for the rest of the night.

Easier said than done, obviously.

I took a big sip of the Cabernet I'd poured.

It didn't help.

Seconds later, Gracie's murder was back on my mind.

CHAPTER 17

The next day began slowly.

Unlike my previous case, there weren't loads of police reports to read over in my spare time. The initial police report for Gracie's murder was only a few inches thick. None of the discovery handed over by the District Attorney was all that interesting either. I guess that's what you get in a he said/she said case.

They were going to limit their witnesses and make it out as if Archer was the lone suspect. They had a motive, and Archer had the means to have committed it. That was enough from their vantage point.

While I had my doubts whether Archer had committed the murder, there was still a good chance he could be convicted. He was fighting an uphill battle.

Once 4:30 p.m. hit, I decided to scope out Dickie Faber's office, in hopes of following him around. I wasn't sure where exactly I hoped he'd lead me, but I didn't have many options at this point.

I arrived a few minutes before five and less than fifteen minutes later, Dickie was leaving his office. I recognized his car from our last visit and had parked far enough away so he wouldn't be able to see me.

He was wearing an ugly, poorly-fitting suit and his goatee was unkempt. I had no idea what Gracie Keats had seen in him.

He pulled out of the parking lot and I followed, careful to keep my distance. He took two lefts and a right before getting on Highway 680 East, heading towards Pleasant Hill and Concord.

Five minutes later, he exited on Willow Pass Road and I did the same, continuing to keep my distance. My car blended in with the best of them and I was happy I didn't have a red Tesla like the one that Dickie Faber drove. At least, not at that moment.

He took a right on Diamond Boulevard and drove down about a mile before he pulled into a small, horseshoe driveway and a nice, but unspectacular, home. I was expecting more from a psychiatrist, but maybe I mistakenly thought they all charged five hundred dollars an hour. The truth was, I really didn't know what most psychiatrists charged, nor what Faber himself charged.

I was slowly driving by as he got out of his car and approached the front door. There was no other car in the driveway and I wondered if Faber lived alone.

"Now fucking what?" I asked myself.

And as I sat there, gliding by the Faber home, I came up with a brilliant idea.

At least, I thought so.

I pulled over a block down the road and googled "Dickie Faber Yelp."

Sure enough, there were fifteen reviews for his psychiatry practice. Twelve five-star reviews and three one-star reviews. That didn't really surprise me. So many reviews - much like our polarizing society these days - are all or nothing. You either loved something or hated it. Subtlety was gone. The middle ground was a lost art.

I wasn't concerned with the five-star ratings. I wanted someone who hated Dickie Faber. Someone who would be willing to dish the dirt on him, if there was any to uncover.

One of the one-star reviews was left by a man, one by a woman, and one by someone named G. Smith without any picture.

The woman, Jan Goddard, left a very short review, but when I saw it, I knew she'd be the one to talk to.

It read: *"If you're a woman, I beg of you, don't go see Dr. Faber."*

I realized how few times I'd actually referred to him as Dr. Faber. The name Dickie had been too fun to make fun of, I guess.

I clicked the "Send Message" box next to Jan Goddard on Yelp. I had always seen this option, but this was the first time I'd ever used it.

My response:

"Hello, Mrs. Goddard, I'd love to talk to you about Dr. Faber when you have the opportunity. My number is 925-555-9257. Thanks."

I decided against leaving my name.

I started my car back up and headed home, hoping I'd be receiving a text from Jan Goddard at some point in the next day or two.

~

That text came later that night.

At nine p.m. to be exact.

She was suspicious to begin with and I had to tread lightly. I came up with the lie that a few other women had complained about Dr. Faber and I was a personal investigator doing some research. There was enough truth in there that I didn't feel too guilty.

Mrs. Goddard agreed to meet me the next morning.

CHAPTER 18

Jan Goddard looked to be between thirty-five and forty-five.
She was an attractive woman despite her dour expression. I wondered if that had something to do with Dickie Faber.

Mrs. Goddard was wearing jeans, a white t-shirt, and a denim jacket.

"Thanks for agreeing to meet me, Mrs. Goddard. "I'm Quint Adler."

There was no point in lying since we were meeting at my office. I just hoped she didn't recognize my name. Nothing seemed to register when I said it.

"You're welcome," she said.

"Why don't we go inside?"

She followed me inside and I knew I had to tread lightly. She was scared - I wasn't sure about what yet - but if I pushed things, I was sure she'd make her exit a quick one.

So I decided to move slowly.

I led her to my office and had her take a seat. I asked her if she'd like anything to drink, which she politely declined.

"Why did you ask to meet with me?" she said sheepishly.

"Well, as I said, there's been a few other women who have brought Dr. Faber to my attention."

I made sure to refer to him by doctor. This had to sound official.

"What are they alleging?" she asked.

I figured it was likely something sexual. Not only because of how she was acting but because Gracie had an affair with him as well.

"They've both said that Dr. Faber acted inappropriately."

I decided to talk in generalities, hoping that would get Mrs. Goddard to open up.

"In what way?" she asked.

She was no dummy. I had to tell her what I had first.

"One is saying that Dr. Faber touched her at ill-suited times. They didn't have sex, but it was very uncomfortable for her."

"And the other woman?"

"She said that Dr. Faber came on to her and because he was the doctor and in power, she didn't know how to say no."

She looked like she had the weight of the world on her shoulders.

"Mine was a combination of both."

"Would you care to elaborate?"

"Like the first girl, he'd touch a shoulder or a thigh the first few times I went to see him. It felt weird, but I'd liked our sessions, so I just let it go."

"And it continued?"

"He stopped for a few sessions. He's a smart guy and could probably tell that I didn't like it."

"And he recommenced it at some point?"

"Yeah, after five or six sessions. At this point, I was becoming pretty reliant on him. He was very good at his job, and I'll be honest, I'm pretty fucked up. So when he touched my shoulder again, I didn't protest or say anything. I don't know, maybe I was even starting to fall for him. Not because he was some handsome man, but because I was becoming so dependent on his help."

"When did it escalate?"

"It was probably like the tenth session or so. I think he knew I was wrapped around his finger by that point. So, when I didn't protest about his shoulder touching or grazing the top of my butt, he kissed me."

I could tell she was about to cry. I felt terrible for Jan Goddard. I certainly hadn't expected this when I set up this meeting, although I probably should have.

"Did you kiss him back?" I asked.

"Yeah, I guess I did. Again, it wasn't because I really liked him. It's just that he had all the power, just like your second woman said."

"What happened after you guys kissed?"

"We had sex."

"In his office?"

"Yes."

"Does he have a secretary or anything?"

I'd seen the outside but obviously hadn't set foot in the office yet.

"No. It's just him. He greets you at his door like he's the friendliest guy in the world. I think I now know why he doesn't have a secretary."

I didn't have one either, but for wholly different reasons.

"Did you continue having sex?"

"Yes. After that, it was basically every session."

"Did you ever tell him that you wanted him to stop?"

"No. In my own screwed-up way, I needed him. I was worried that if I asked him to stop, he'd tell me I couldn't see him anymore. And this may be hard to understand, but my sessions were going great. I didn't want to stop seeing him. At least, not at that time."

"What changed?"

"I think over time I started to realize just how wrong this was. I don't care how good a psychiatrist Dr. Faber was, he shouldn't be sleeping with his patients. And I could and should have known better myself."

"Don't blame yourself," I said. "As you've mentioned, he was the guy with all the power. He's the doctor. This is on him, not you."

"Thank you," she said and then started weeping.

I wanted to put my arm on her shoulder and comfort her, but after all she told me, I knew that wasn't the proper gesture.

Fuck, Dr. Dickie Faber!

I didn't know if he killed Gracie Keats, but I was sure looking forward to him sweating on the witness stand if it got that far. I wanted to embarrass him for what he'd done to Jan Goddard. And probably others. Maybe I could get his medical license revoked.

Jan slowly stopped crying and she asked for a tissue. I grabbed a box and pushed them across to her.

"Just remember, you're not at fault. He's the asshole and deserves to pay!"

"Thank you," she said for the second straight time.

"What happened when you told him it was over?"

"He said that if I told anyone we'd had sex, he'd inform everyone of my problems. And that was not an option for me. I'd have lost my job and my friendships."

I really wanted to ask her what those problems were. I decided against it. This woman had come to me on her own free will and opened up more than I ever could have imagined. Whatever her problems were, they didn't really matter. Dickie Faber had betrayed her trust regardless.

"I'm very sorry you had to go through this," I said.

"Thank you," she said once again.

She grabbed a Kleenex and blew into it.

I decided against telling her why I'd really brought her to my office. I felt guilty as shit over it.

No, it was nothing on the level of Dickie Faber, but I'd betrayed her trust a little bit.

"Is there anything else you want to add?" I asked.

"Not that I can think of right now."

I hated what I asked next, but I had to know.

"If this ever goes to trial, would you be willing to testify against Dr. Faber?"

"I don't know. I just don't know."

She was about to cry again, so I decided to stop it there.

"You're a strong woman, Mrs. Goddard. I'm so sorry for all you've been through. Is it okay if we keep in touch?"

"Sure, that's okay," she said, barely audible.

I rose from my chair and we walked out of my office together. She buried her face into my chest before she left, the tears having returned.

As she started to drive away, I was the one with a tear in my eye.

I headed back into my office, trying to absorb all the information I'd just been given.

It only furthered my opinion that Dickie Faber was an untrustworthy asshole.

This was far different than Gracie Keats, however. Gracie had seemingly enjoyed being with Dickie. I couldn't know for sure, but if Donna Neal is yelling "the tennis pro or the shrink" at a bar, it can't be all that bad.

Maybe, Gracie soured on Dickie just like Mrs. Goddard had, and that's when things went wrong.

No matter what happened at Archer's trial, I wanted Dickie Faber to pay. Jan Goddard was a really nice lady who looked to be a shell of herself now. And that was his doing.

My next order of business was to conduct secondary interviews with A.J. and Grace.

It proved unnecessary.

"Hey, Quint."

"What's up, Ellie?"

"We're going to do another sit-down tomorrow. Are you up for it?"

"Sure."

"The Keats children will be there as well."

"Are we meeting at Archer's house?"

"No, we're going to start making this more official as we head towards the trial. We'll be meeting at my firm. Tomorrow at 11:00."

I hated still considering Ellie a suspect in one form or another. I wanted to clear the air with us.

"I'll be there. Listen, Ellie…"

"I know what you're going to say. Can we talk about this some other time? I'm about to interview the testator and the executor of Gracie's will. They are crucial and I don't want to be worrying about my careless actions."

She'd read my mind. Not that it should have been that big of a surprise.

"Alright, but I really do want to talk about it."

"Soon," she said sternly.

I spent the night going back over the initial police report.

No DNA. No sign of forced entry.

If Dr. Dickie Faber had really committed the murder - or, even Brad Lacoste - they probably would have needed the key. I doubted "the tennis pro or the shrink" were expert lock-breakers.

Which reminded me of something I'd told Ellie, Archer, and Cliff on our last visit. I'd go and check local locksmiths to see if they'd duplicated a key that matched Archer's house key.

I called Ellie back.

"What is it that you need, Quint?"

It was a dismissive way to answer the phone and I didn't like it.

"Ask Archer if I can swing by his house tomorrow morning at eight a.m. to pick up his house key."

"I'll make sure he's there."

"Thanks."

She hung up on her end.

Maybe the pressure of the upcoming trial was starting to get to Ellie. Better than some of the alternatives I'd been conjuring up.

CHAPTER 19

I woke up the next morning, knowing it was going to be a long day.

I cooked myself an omelet with ham, cheese, sautéed onions, and mushrooms. I also had two sides of toast and a few slices of bacon.

Who knew if I was going to eat again before the afternoon so I made breakfast count.

At 7:30, after a long shower, I changed into some khakis and a clean, white dress shirt. I wanted to look the part today. Not for the locksmiths, but with the trial fast approaching, I decided to look nice for the two attorneys and the Keats family.

I headed out at 7:52 a.m., my apartment being less than ten minutes from the Keats' family home.

⁓

"Hello, Quint."

How many times had I heard that over the last several weeks? Meetings. Interviews. Gatherings. Get-Togethers. That's all I'd been doing.

Archer was wearing some acid-washed jeans and a light blue sweater. His wavy hair gave the impression that he hadn't showered yet.

"Do you have that key, Archer?"

He handed it over.

"I'll bring it to the meeting in a few hours."

I turned to go.

"Why the rush?"

"I'd like to hit as many of these locksmiths as I can."

"Give me ten minutes," Archer said.

I had no idea what he had in mind, but I was intrigued.

"Sure."

We walked back towards his house. The main one. I wondered if the charade of having to use the courtyard each and every time was now over.

He led me to the kitchen and had me sit down at a little nook that must have served as their breakfast spot back in happier times.

He didn't ask me if I'd like anything to drink. This was going to be brief and to the point.

"Do you think I'm innocent?" he asked.

"I think the proper phrase is not-guilty," I said, trying to lighten the mood.

"That's legal jargon," he said. "I'm asking if you think I'm innocent."

I gave the question the proper time it deserved.

"In my heart, I don't think you killed your wife," I said. "But I can't say that with the utmost certainty."

That answer seemed to satisfy him, despite my addendum.

"I want to know the people working for me don't think that I'm a sociopath. I didn't leave my guest house, walk up the stairs, and stab my wife twenty-seven times. I'm not a murderer. Maybe I wasn't always the best husband or father, but I still loved Gracie. I didn't kill her."

Archer was convincing. I tended to think it's because he was innocent, but as I'd laid out to him, I couldn't be positive. One thing I did know for sure; he'd come across well with a jury. If I was one of the attorneys of record, I'd have no issues throwing him on the witness stand. I know in most criminal cases it's not advisable, but I bet Archer would handle himself just fine.

We'd see if Ellie and Cliff thought the same.

"Like I said, Archer, I don't think you did it."

"Thanks, Quint. That means more than you know."

He started to get up.

"That's it?" I asked.

"Anything else, we can bring up at our meeting in a few hours. I just wanted to hear that from you."

"Alright," I said.

It was an odd moment, the two of us sitting there talking about whether I thought he'd murdered his wife. I understood it from his end. He wanted people who worked for him to believe in his innocence. For me, it was just awkward.

"See you soon, Archer."

And with that, I headed towards the front door.

~

The first locksmith I hit up, Lock-it-Up, was a mere half-mile from Archer's home.

The man behind the desk was weathered, his face resembling an old catcher's mitt. He gave a slight head nod as I walked towards him, but nothing approached a smile.

"Hows can I helps ya?" he said, butchering the English language in the process.

"I have a weird request," I said.

"I've heard it all. Nothing going to surprise me."

I took out my P.I.'s license and showed it to him.

"I'm investigating the murder of a woman and trying to find out if her house key may have been duplicated in the last several months."

"I takes it back. That is a weird request."

"I told you," I said and smiled, trying to get him on my good side.

"Does you have the initial key in question?"

"I do."

I presented him with the key. He spent about thirty seconds examining it.

"I hates to tell you, mister, but you're shits out of luck."

He continued to use plurals when unnecessary, but I resisted pointing that out.

"Why is that?" I asked.

"Because these types of keys are dimes a dozen."

"You get a lot of these?"

"I'd say I got probably ten to fifteen keys that looked just like that. And I'm only talkings about yesterday."

"How about looking up an order by name?"

"Now that's something I can do."

"Great. Can you check if Gracie Keats made a duplicate of a key?"

I looked to see if the name hit home. It didn't.

"Gracie. Is that G-R-A-C-E-E?"

I almost laughed, but to be honest, Gracie sounded just like Grace with an extra E on the end.

I realized I might as well ask for the whole family.

"Actually, I'm searching for anyone in the Keats family. Can you see if that last name comes up at all?"

"Sure cans," he said. "Give me a few minutes."

He disappeared into the back of the small little shop, reemerging a short time later.

"You said Keats, like K-E-A-T-S?"

"Yes, that's correct."

"Sorry, we don't got none."

Sadly, this guy wasn't using a double negative to inform me they did actually have one.

"Was there a name that was close?"

I didn't entirely trust this man's spelling and hoped maybe he'd made a mistake.

"There was a Keating."

I decided to take a flyer.

"What was the first name on that one?"

"Rachel."

So much for that.

"Actually, can you try two more names for me?"

"Okay," he said.

"Brad Lacoste and Dickie Faber."

Two minutes later, I got my answer. A negative for both.

"Could you tell me all of the other locksmiths in Walnut Creek?"

"Sure cans," he said.

~

An hour later, I'd visited the other three locksmiths in Walnut Creek.

They'd all been as successful as my visit to Lock-It-Up, which is to say, not at all.

Everyone reiterated that this type of key was nothing special.

They all checked orders for the last names Keats, Faber, and Lacoste. No luck.

I left the last locksmith, wondering if I should check out ones in other cities.

I decided it was a dead-end and I could spend my time better elsewhere.

~

I arrived at Ellie's law firm a few minutes after eleven.

One of the two receptionists escorted me to the conference room in the back. It's where I'd first met Ellie which felt like three months ago, even though it was closer to three weeks.

Archer, Ellie, Cliff, Grace, and A.J. were sitting there waiting for me. I felt like a young child chastised for being late.

"Long time no see, Quint," Archer said.

I smiled and gave him his house key back.

"This key wasn't duplicated at any locksmith in Walnut Creek," I said.

"It was worth a try, Quint," Ellie said. "Not every one of your ideas is going to pan out. Even good ones like that."

"Thanks," I said.

"Take a seat."

I was still the only one standing. I sat next to the two Keats children, with Archer and his two attorneys facing us.

"Thanks to everyone for coming here today," Ellie said. "A.J. and Grace, I know you've got lives to live, so I appreciate this."

Grace nodded. A.J. said, "Of course."

"Why don't we structure this one like our last meeting. Quint, first you can tell us all you've learned in the last few days. And then we'll talk strategy. Keep in mind, jury selection is a little more than two weeks away. This is approaching fast. Quint, you've got the floor."

I started by telling them of my visit to Vic Parsons and how he wouldn't have been a reliable witness even if he had any information to share. Which he hadn't.

Next, I told them of my following Dickie Faber home, and nothing coming of it.

They were expecting another disappointment when I dropped the bomb about Jan Goddard.

Finally, I reiterated what I'd told them about the locksmiths. None of them seemed to care as they were all still focused on Jan Goddard.

"Tell me more about Ms.Goddard," Cliff Boyd said.

"I'd never met her before obviously, but I think this affair really affected her. She spoke with utter disdain of Dickie Faber. I imagine she's half the woman she used to be."

"And she said Dr. Faber initiated the sex?" Cliff said.

He'd opted to go with his official name. Maybe I was being childish by still referring to him as Dickie.

"Dr. Faber initiated the touching and the kissing. She said she was a willing participant in the sex, but she was wary of the power he held over her. I imagine it's similar to many workplaces examples of sexual harassment where the employee is afraid to stand up to her superior."

"Or his," Ellie said.

"Indeed. My fault," I said.

"You said this happened for weeks?" Cliff asked.

"Yes."

"That will make it harder for Ms.Goddard to prove Faber was at fault. If they'd had sex once and she went screaming to the authorities - or the medical board - then her story would hold more weight. Is Ms.Goddard married?"

Shit!

I had forgotten to ask.

"I don't know," I admitted. "I have her number and can find out easily."

Ellie had let Cliff ask most of the questions of me, but decided to jump in.

"Did you tell her who you were?"

"Sort of," I said.

"What does that mean?"

"I told her I was a P.I. investigating two other women's issues with Dr. Faber."

"But you mentioned nothing of Archer or this case?"

"No. I was afraid she'd clam up and refuse to meet me."

"I understand where you were coming from, Quint, but you have to be more upfront with our prospective witnesses. If we call Ms.Goddard to the stand and then the prosecution is able to show that your interview with her was under less than truthful circumstances, the jury will hold it against us."

Ellie may have been right, but I felt like the schoolboy being admonished again.

"This is my first time working on a prospective trial. Maybe you should have told me that beforehand," I said.

I sounded pissed. Probably because I was.

Ellie looked at Cliff, who gave her a look telling her to calm down.

She was lecturing me on ethics and standards when she had sex with her private investigator. An extreme example of the pot calling the kettle black.

I couldn't drop that bomb obviously. I'd be fired immediately and likely so would Ellie.

"I'm sorry," Ellie finally said. "I should have told you that."

"Apology accepted," I said, knowing it was an apology she didn't want to make.

She glared at me. I smiled.

"Kids, can't you behave?" Archer said. "Let's not forget what we're here for."

"Archer is right," Cliff said. "Time is of the essence. Let's stop with these unproductive pissing contests."

Ellie extended her hand. I shook it.

"Good," Cliff said. "Now, we can talk more about Ms.Goddard next time, but let's hit on some of our strategies at trial. Let's start with you, Grace and A.J."

They'd stayed silent while Ellie and I butted heads.

"We're here for our Dad," A.J. said. "Whatever you need us to do."

"Yeah, we are," Grace said.

She seemed to be a changed young woman. Gone was the vigor with which she'd treated me the first time.

"Grace, let's start with you. We're going to need you to be a lot more gregarious while you're on the stand."

"I'm not exactly the gregarious type."

Maybe I'd jumped the gun.

"Fine, but you're going to have to do better than speaking with a monotone. We're calling you and A.J. to the stand so that the jury can understand your father is a good man. You will both be crucially important."

"Just tell me what to say," Grace said.

"We'll be going over the questions I'm going to ask you," Ellie said. "But you really should try and have a better attitude about this going forward."

Grace didn't like being called out.

"You just fought with Quint and now you want to fight with me," she said.

There was that vigor she'd been missing.

"I'm not trying to fight with you. I'm explaining just how crucial your testimony is. If you and A.J. don't show the jury how lovable your father is, they'll start believing that maybe Archer is capable of what he's been charged with."

"We'll do the best we can," A.J. said quickly. I think he was trying to beat his sister to a response, knowing hers wasn't going to be as pleasant.

"Good. Thank you, A.J." Ellie said. "Now, I'd like to talk about a few things that I've found out. I've talked to the testator and the executor of Gracie's will. Archer is the sole heir to the money. That's going to be a problem for us because it's one of the oldest motives in the world. We will argue, rightfully, that Archer never would kill his wife when he was the only other one on the property. He'd be asking to get arrested for his wife's murder. We'll also have our own financial experts who will try to paint a rosy picture."

I'd been told that things weren't all that bad financially. I had a feeling I'd been misled.

"Was it not rosy?" I asked.

Archer decided to speak for himself.

"My debts were more than I realized. A few of my businesses were in danger of going under. And several others were in serious debt."

"It doesn't matter," Ellie said. "Archer didn't kill Gracie and they can't prove it, anyway."

Those last two statements almost seemed at odds with each other.

Archer didn't kill Gracie. They can't prove it, anyway.

Which one was it? Was he innocent or they just couldn't prove it?

I held my tongue.

"I don't care if I was twenty million dollars in debt. I loved Gracie and never, ever, ever could have done that to her."

I looked at the expressions of his children. A.J. nodded along with his father. Grace, with another slight show of compassion, smiled softly at Archer.

"The truth is, this is not a very complicated case," Cliff said. "The prosecution will be laying out the fact that there is no evidence of anyone entering Gracie's house. No broken window. No picked lock. They'll say that Archer had more reason to kill Gracie than anyone else. Those will be the two things they focus on the most. It's hard for us to refute either of them. We have no evidence that anyone else entered Gracie's house and Archer was indeed suffering some financial difficulties."

"I know you're getting to something, but what exactly?" Archer asked.

"In a roundabout way, I'm trying to tell you that the witnesses will be of the utmost importance in this case. More so than in most criminal cases. This may come down to being a popularity contest which is why witnesses, including A.J. and Grace, will be so important. Whichever side paints the more convincing picture of you will likely win this case. There's no DNA. No smoking gun. So whether the jury likes you or not is tantamount."

"And that's why we need to get all of our witnesses prepared," Ellie said. "Grace and A.J., give me a few times over the next few weeks where you can set aside an hour to talk to me."

They both nodded.

"Quint, who are some other character witnesses you think we should call?"

"I think Gene Bowman would present a good side of Archer. Plus, he's someone the jury would like."

"Anyone, to avoid?"

Grace was the first person who came to mind, but I couldn't come out and say that.

"Parker and Caleb Johnson. They hate Archer."

"That hate goes two ways," Archer said. "So you no longer consider them suspects, Quint?"

"It's a hard sell to the jury. They were rich assholes, but nothing to suggest they would kill your wife. Dr. Faber - or even Brad Lacoste - would have more believable motives."

Ellie turned to me.

"Quint, talk to Donna Neal again. The way you described her makes me suspect she has more to say. Maybe we'll get a gem like Dr. Faber had threatened Gracie. Or Gracie told Brad Lacoste she was going public with their affair."

"I'll talk to her."

"Also, try to keep in touch with Jan Goddard, but don't be pushy. Maybe subtly mention that you are working for Archer's defense and judge her reaction. If you explain that Dr. Faber is a suspect, she might be more willing to testify."

"Sure. Anything else?"

"Maybe talk to another client or two of Dr. Faber's. Try to keep it to former clients, if possible. We don't want him finding out and feeling like we're closing in. At least, not yet."

"Gotcha," I said.

No one spoke for several seconds. Ellie broke the silence.

"We'll try to do this every few days leading up to jury selection. This is going to be an exciting few weeks leading up to the trial."

Ellie was wrong. The next two weeks ended out being boring as shit.

The trial? Now that was a different story.

PART TWO: THE TRIAL

CHAPTER 20

The next sixteen days slowly meandered by.

I kept doing my job, including second interviews with Donna Neal and Gene Bowman. I followed Dickie Faber a few times to no avail. I found out he was unmarried and lived alone.

The fact that he wasn't technically cheating didn't absolve him in my book. He was still taking advantage of his clients by using his dominant position.

As Ellie had asked, I'd kept in touch with Jan Goddard. She seemed to like talking to me. I felt like a shoulder to cry on during some of our text exchanges. A week before the trial was set to begin, I explained in full what was going on and apologized for misleading her. She forgave me and claimed she was willing to testify if the defense felt they needed her.

$\approx$

The big change leading up to the trial was the amount of media coverage. It began to occupy the first slot on most local news.

My former newspaper, *The Walnut Creek Times,* ran article after article about Gracie Keats's murder. My old boss, Tom Butler, had reached out to me. I told him I couldn't comment since I was involved in the case. He understood and threw out the idea of doing a post-trial interview with the paper. I told him I'd do what I could. Tom was a friend and I still loved the guys and gals at the paper, so I'd try to make it up to them after the trial.

My mother called every day and asked about the case.

I had a feeling that her demographic - older, widowed women - were particularly infatuated with the case. Especially those living around Walnut Creek. Archer Keats had been a pretty well-known name. Imagining him on trial for his wife's murder certainly had some intrigue.

None of the news segments ever mentioned that Gracie was having two affairs, so the general public still viewed her as this angelic figure. I hoped that would change.

Fuck!

I was pissed at myself. I'd started thinking like Ellie, viewing Gracie as an impediment to getting Archer acquitted. She was a woman who died a savage death and I should have more compassion for her.

I reprimanded myself.

As for Archer, I could sense his nervousness start to ratchet up as he approached his day in court.

He wasn't the only one. I was feeling it too and I wasn't the one facing life in prison.

A few days before the trial was set to begin, Ellie got the witness list. She wanted me to find out what I could on a guy named Kirk Stroud. He was a construction worker in Concord, and despite meeting him - I was brushed off - and talking to a few of his co-workers, I couldn't find any connection to Archer.

We knew almost everyone else on the prosecution's witness list, so it bothered me that I couldn't discover why they would call this seemingly random construction worker.

Archer said he didn't know the man so he couldn't be all that important.

I didn't have much time to focus on it, because before I knew it, they'd selected a jury and the trial was set to begin.

I'd missed Archer's arrest, his arraignment, the preliminary hearing, and all of the other pre-trial court appearances.

Those were for the lawyers.

Now that the actual trial was here, I was all-in.

The mano a mano of us versus the prosecution was set to begin.

And I had to admit it. I was excited.

Walnut Creek is in Contra Costa County, but the biggest criminal courthouse in the county is the Contra Costa Superior Court in Martinez. It was located fifteen miles east of Walnut Creek and sat within a few miles of The Delta, the largest estuary on the West Coast.

The trial was originally supposed to take place at the AF Bray Court

Building, but with all the attention it was getting, they decided to transfer it to the Civil Courthouse across the street.

The change was merely for logistical purposes. This was still very much a criminal case.

The Civil Courthouse had six huge white columns surrounding the front doors. When you think of old Greek architecture, this courthouse fits the bill. To me, it resembled the Parthenon. At least, the front facade did.

Inside was more like your average courthouse. Very few windows. Muggy. Impersonal.

I'd been there several times while working some small trials for *The Walnut Creek Times*. This case would be different. There was no doubt about that.

~

The trial began on a Monday.

I'd come once during the previous week to watch jury selection, but Ellie and Cliff had hired an expert and I was persona-non-grata. Maybe that's going too far. I was more persona-non-needed.

I wondered if that was going to be the case going forward. After all, the trial was about to commence and one thing I was not was an attorney. As a P.I. I'd done my job investigating as we led up to the trial. Now it was time for the legal experts to take over.

That being said, they still wanted me at the trial every day. Maybe I'd discover a contradictory statement from a witness. Or catch something our lawyers missed.

I remember in my first discussion with Gene Bowman telling him I didn't want to go to court every day. I'd been wrong. I was now looking forward to seeing the spectacle.

And hopefully, that ended with our client being acquitted.

~

I parked in the closest lot at 8:40 that morning.

As I walked toward the courthouse, there were six or seven news trucks sitting outside on the street.

Two women looked to be live on the air, the sprawling courthouse serving as a backdrop.

I guess I shouldn't have been surprised with the local coverage it had been getting. At least I didn't see CNN, Fox, or Court TV. This hadn't become national news. At least, not yet.

I walked up the steps, trying not to make eye contact with anyone. I'd been a local celebrity a few different times and the last thing I wanted was for one of the newsmen or women to recognize me.

I wasn't an important part of this case and would hate if my presence became an angle for some member of the media.

There were probably fifteen police officers standing at the entrance to the courthouse. They'd known this was going to be a media circus.

I approached the metal detector.

"Take your wallet, your keys, your belt, and your cellphone out," a massive police officer said. "Set them on the tray and then pick them up after you walk through the metal detector."

I did as instructed. No one had to worry about their wallet being stolen as you waited to walk through. Cops were everywhere.

I got through unscathed and made my way to Department 22, which had been assigned the case.

The judge's name was the Honorable Vicky Kilgore.

Ellie had told me most lawyers perceived her as being advantageous for the prosecution. Not what we wanted.

Kilgore was in her sixties and from the lone day I'd spent watching jury selection, it was obvious she had an acid tongue. She'd admonished both Ellie and the district attorney trying the case, Will McNair.

McNair was younger than me, somewhere in his mid-thirties. He was handsome, cocky, and the cameras loved him. When it came to murder trials, most news outlets liked to focus on the defendant and the defense. It was almost always more interesting. Not when Will McNair was trying a case.

He'd be outside of the courthouse answering every question from the gathered media. He usually became the story. And I honestly couldn't remember him ever losing a case.

There were always rumors that he was eyeing political office. If you'd ever seen Will McNair interviewed, this wouldn't surprise you one bit.

Everyone knew he had loftier ambitions than being a district attorney.

I approached Department 22 and saw Grace and A.J. standing outside of the doors, along with fifty other people. Gene Bowman waved in my direction. I also saw Donna Neal at the far end of the room. I'm sure there were others I was missing.

Ellie and Cliff were likely already inside, going over pre-trial instructions.

"How are you guys doing?" I asked Grace and A.J.

"As well as can be expected," A.J. said.

Grace surprised me with her answer.

"I'm sorry for being a witch when I first met you. I saw you and Ellie as the bad guys, but I know you're just trying to get my father off."

"Don't worry about it," I said. "We're all on the same team now."

Five minutes later, the doors opened and everyone made their way in. This was a large courtroom, but I wasn't sure it was going to hold everyone.

Grace, A.J., and I made our way to the left side, where the defense sat. We took our seats in the first row, sitting behind Archer, Ellie, and Cliff who were at the defense table in front of us. Archer turned around and tried to smile when he saw his kids approach.

"Hi, guys."

"Hi, Dad," they both said.

Archer was wearing a dark suit with an unmemorable gray tie. I wondered if that was Ellie's doing. I could see her telling Archer not to stand out with some bright tie.

"You're the grieving husband. Suits with dark ties and no smiling at the table."

Or, at least, that's how I imagined the conversation going.

Ellie nodded in my direction. I responded in kind.

Gene Bowman sat in the row behind us. As did a few people I recognized from his firm.

I turned around, curious where Donna Neal was going to sit. She was sitting in the second row, behind the prosecution table.

Was this a sign that she thought Archer did it? I couldn't be sure, but this didn't bode well.

In the row in front of her, I recognized a few pictures I'd seen of Gracie's parents. This had to be excruciating for them.

I hated the fact that we were divided along Archer/Gracie lines. Especially since I didn't think Archer had committed the crime.

I turned around one more time and noticed there were no cameras in the courthouse. My guess was that Judge Kilgore had made that decision.

The door shut loudly behind me and then a bailiff stood up near the front of the courtroom.

"All rise for the Honorable Vicky Kilgore."

The courtroom stood up in unison.

The judge took her seat at the head of the room. I know they call it the bench, but it was more like a throne.

"Welcome everyone to the case of the State of California versus Archer Keats. The charge is murder in the first degree. I'd like to get something out of the way first. You may notice that there are no cameras here inside the courtroom. That was my decision. My courtroom will not be made into some madhouse. I understand this is a high-profile case, but this will not become a kangaroo court. If I hear people talking during opening statements or while a witness is testifying, you will be removed. I'm fair, but I'm strict. Abide by the rules of my courtroom or suffer the consequences."

Judge Kilgore was undeniably tough. I imagined most female judges had to be or risk men trying to run all over them. It was obvious that no one was going to be running over Vicky Kilgore. She ran the show.

"As I said, we are here for the case of California vs. Archer Keats. He is represented by Ms. Ellie Teague and the prosecution is being led by Mr. Will McNair. We selected a jury last week and we'll be commencing the trial momentarily. First, I'd like to address our jury and give you my instructions."

As Judge Kilgore gave her jury instructions, I looked around the room. There was no Dickie Faber or Brad Lacoste. No surprise there. As I continued scanning the room, there was a face I was shocked to see. Tre Larson. He gave me a naval salute and I responded in kind. I wondered if he was here because we were friendly or because he knew this case was going to be huge for the Walnut Creek hospitality business. One of their own was on trial for murder.

I'm sure I'd be talking to Tre during the first recess.

Judge Kilgore had finished her instructions to the jury.

"Without further ado, Mr. McNair, if you'd like to make your opening statement."

Will McNair methodically stood up from his chair. He first looked back out at the people assembled in the room. Next, he looked over at Archer Keats, followed by a slight nod to the judge.

He then slowly walked towards the jury box and set his eyes upon them. He was a handsome guy and was no doubt using that to his advantage. It wouldn't have surprised me if he was holding eye contact with a few of the female jurors.

"Ladies and Gentleman, my name is Will McNair and I'm going to be trying the case against Archer Keats. The same Archer Keats who seems like a good family man. A man about town. There's a good chance that some of you have eaten at his restaurants. Da Vinci's was a personal favorite of mine. They had a Veal Marsala to die for."

Will McNair paused. He was soaking up all the eyes on the room being on him. He was a Grade-A ham and I actually meant that as a compliment. He knew how to take control of the room.

"The garlic bread was top-notch also. Maybe the best Italian restaurant in the East Bay. And Cilantros was one of my favorite Mexican restaurants this side of San Francisco. Their homemade salsa would make even the best Mexican chef blush. And don't forget about Xiao's. I couldn't get enough of their lemon chicken or their pork potstickers. The perfect Chinese food. Loved me some Xiao's."

I glanced around. Everyone had the oddest expressions. No one knew where this opening statement was going.

"That's three of Mr. Keats twenty-one restaurants. And you know what they all have in common besides having excellent food?"

Will McNair paused for dramatic effect. I knew this wouldn't be the last time.

"They were all going under. They all had serious financial problems. Safe to say, none of them was going to be around in six months or a year. And those weren't the only ones. Bobby's Burgers. The Grill. Fresh Fish Daily. All of them were on their way to going bankrupt. And soon."

People's expressions had turned to slight admiration. Will McNair had them right where he wanted them.

"But you know what wasn't going under? What was strong and only getting stronger? Gracie Keats' finances. She inherited twenty million dollars when she was a young woman. Don't hold that against her. A lot of people inherit money. They don't deserve to get stabbed twenty-seven times because of it."

McNair paused again.

"We'll get back to that. Gracie still had eighteen and a half million dollars at the time of her murder. Do you know where the other one and a half million went? To her husband's failing businesses. To Da Vinci's. To Cilantros. To Xiao's. But that wasn't enough for Archer Keats. He knew that many more of his businesses were on the path to failure. And he started to get the idea that his wife wasn't going to be his loanshark for much longer. So, on December 22nd, in the hours after midnight, he savagely killed his wife, two days before their children were coming home to visit for Christmas Eve. We will get into just how brutal the actual murder was, but committing this so close to the holidays is a crime on its own."

McNair turned away from the jury and made sure that the judge and the audience all got a look at him.

"Now, we have to talk about the murder itself. Gracie Keats was stabbed not once, not twice, not three times, but twenty-seven times. I've been a DA for six years now and I've never had a case with a victim stabbed that many times. This is probably the most horrific murder I've ever been asked to prosecute. As if it can't get any worse, the perpetrator, who we believe to be Archer Keats, kept the knife protruding from Gracie's heart. That's right, she had a knife through her heart. The murderer stabbed her so many times that the tissue covering her heart, and basically the entire breastplate, had been diminished to nothing. Surely, Gracie Keats was dead at this point, but which stab killed her? The 4th? The 10th? The 22nd? There's no question that she suffered a pain none of us ever want to imagine. And the killer leaving the knife protruding from her chest shows what a sociopath he is."

Will McNair paused for probably the fifth time and this one was welcomed by everyone in the courtroom. The details of Gracie's murder were too much to handle. I saw a few people crying on the prosecutor's side of the aisle. Archer himself had his head buried in his hands. It probably wasn't advisable, but in the moment, I think the jury would understand.

I even saw a gigantic bailiff wipe something from his eye.

Part of me felt that Will McNair could rest his case right then and there. His opening had been that devastating.

I had to remind myself that this was a long trial. Many twists and turns were sure to come. And the way things had started, Archer Keats was going to need them.

McNair continued.

"Ladies and Gentlemen, I apologize for the graphic details. But they are tantamount to this case and you'll be hearing them from time to time. The prosecution will show beyond a reasonable doubt that Archer Keats was going broke. Furthermore, we have witnesses who will testify that Gracie had told Archer that she no longer was going to lend him money. Worse yet, she was going to ask for a divorce."

There was a noticeable reaction in the courtroom. Grace, who was next to me, put her head in her hands as her father had done earlier. A.J. looked straight ahead and didn't say a thing. He was pretty mild-mannered, but I imagine he was seething underneath.

The divorce news was a mic drop.

Sure, Ellie, Cliff, and I knew they weren't getting along, and Archer had long been sleeping in the guest house, but Archer never said Gracie was going to divorce him. I wondered who was going to be their star witness that would testify to that. My money was on Donna Neal.

I wished I could see Ellie's reaction.

Would this change her opening statement?

As everyone took a second to gather themselves, Will McNair looked ready to continue.

"One more piece of information that is relevant," he said. "The Keats' had signed a prenuptial agreement. In a divorce, Archer would get none of that money. But if Gracie died, he was the beneficiary and would inherit 18.5 million dollars. He could go on living the good life. So Archer had two options. Get divorced and be a broke, in-debt, has-been restaurateur. Or do something about it. And he did..."

Will McNair paused for the last time. And I knew what he was going to say next.

"Twenty-seven times!"

He backed away from the jury and returned to the prosecution's table on the right side of the courtroom. No, I wasn't an attorney, but it was a great opening statement. Bordering on superb.

"And for the defense, Ms.Teague," Judge Kilgore said.

Ellie was next and she had a tough act to follow.

She stood up from her table, nodded at the judge, and walked over to the far right where the jury was seated. She was wearing a navy blue pantsuit with a white blouse underneath. Her hair was in a bun and her beauty was understated. In a situation like this, I imagined she didn't want to emphasize her great looks.

This was a time to show off her brains.

"Hello, Ladies and Gentleman. There's been a long-running misconception in our society over the years. We are taught to believe that women are the emotional ones and men are the more rational. That's not always the case. That opening by Mr. McNair proves it. He relied on emotion, passion, sentiment, and other supposedly feminine attributes.

Not me. I believe in science and real-life evidence. And here's a fact that Mr. McNair failed to mention. There is zero evidence that Archer Keats killed his wife. Zero. And all the sentimentality and emotion that he bestowed upon us isn't going to change that.

Sorry to break that to you, Mr. McNair."

The courtroom was in awe of what was transpiring in front of them. Some people laughed at Ellie's ridiculing of the DA. Others weren't as impressed. Judge Kilgore was definitely in the latter. She looked furious.

"Settle down, everyone," she yelled and pounded her gavel.

"Ms. Teague, I'd watch yourself. You're a minute into trying this case."

Maybe the judge didn't like it, but I did. Ellie had stood up to Will McNair, who had delivered a home run opening statement. This let the jury know this wasn't going to be a first-round knockout. Ellie was here to fight.

And her point was well taken. Will McNair had relied heavily on emotion, emphasizing the way Gracie died over and over. Ellie was saying that did nothing to help prove his case.

If I were Ellie, I'd have considered stopping right there. She'd made her point. On the other hand, she'd just been admonished by the judge. That wasn't a good look. Maybe it was better that she continued.

And she did.

"I'm sorry, your honor. Maybe my emotions got the best of me."

I laughed out loud, along with a few others.

Ellie had brought the whole emotion thing back onto her. It was funny, even if the judge didn't think so.

"Strike two," Judge Kilgore said.

"Speaking of baseball," Ellie said, showing off her razor-sharp brain. "Archer's son A.J. played the sport growing up and Archer attended just about every game. His daughter Grace was a dancer and he rarely missed any of those, either. He was a great father. And also a loving, supportive husband. I acknowledge that he's had some financial difficulties the last few years. And yes, his wife did give him some money to help support his businesses. But for over twenty years he'd supported his family. He opened twenty-one restaurants which is a pretty amazing feat. During that time, he never asked to borrow one red cent from Gracie. Things changed when Covid hit, and yes, many of his businesses suffered. But this wasn't some plan to fleece his wife. It was a worldwide pandemic that affected millions. Small-business owners more than most. And yes, Archer owned twenty-one restaurants, but each of those is a small business of its own."

Ellie was making some decent points but was starting to ramble. She'd have been better off keeping it short and sweet.

"Archer Keats didn't kill his wife. I've known this man for several years and it's not in his DNA. You shouldn't take my word for it, but you should ask yourself this question. Why would a man kill his wife if they were the only two people on the premises? He'd absolutely have known that he'd be the primary suspect. It just doesn't make any sense. You can call Archer a lot of things, but dumb isn't one of them. He's a brilliant man, a great father, and was an awesome husband."

Ellie was losing steam and repeating herself. The courtroom could sense it.

She looked in my direction. I quickly tried to think of a way to relay that to her. I subtly pointed down at my wrist - as if a watch was there - and hoped she gathered that I was telling her to wrap it up.

She'd been predominantly standing in front of the jury. She took a few steps back and was now in the center of the courtroom.

"I'd like to ask for one thing before I finish up here. I'm going to be presenting some evidence that paints Gracie Keats in a bad light. This is not to be gratuitous. Gracie suffered an unimaginable death and I don't mean to besmirch her. I promise there will be an endgame to it, but I'm sure you will hate me at the time I present that evidence. So, back to the favor, I ask. Please, I beg of you, hold that against me all you want, but not against my client. If you're able to look at all that evidence without preju- dice, you'll come to the inevitable conclusion that Archer Keats is not guilty of killing his wife Gracie. Thank you."

Ellie's opening statement had been a disjointed affair, but I thought she'd ended on a high note. Telling the jury to hold it against her and not her client was smart.

Ellie walked back to the defense's desk and as soon as she sat, Judge Kilgore spoke.

"Ladies and Gentlemen of the jury, you got off easy. I've seen murder cases where the opening statements took hours. Why don't we all take a fifteen-minute break and when we get back, the prosecution can call their first witness."

CHAPTER 21

After the judge excused us, everyone in the courtroom rose to their feet and headed towards the exit.

Ellie turned around and spoke to me and the Keats children.

"There's a little bench at the far end of this hall. I'll meet you guys there."

~

"Thoughts on the opening statements?" Ellie asked once we'd all gathered together.

People were milling around the hall, but we were at the far end and had a certain degree of privacy.

"He was good, you were better," Grace said.

I wasn't sure I agreed, but I was fine with her saying it.

"Quint? Any thoughts?"

"I think it's obvious that the prosecution will be using her inheritance as the motive. I'm guessing they will harp very little on Gracie's cheating and how that might have served as a motive."

"I agree," Cliff Boyd said.

"I'm not sure the judge loved you," A.J. said.

His father agreed.

"A.J. is right. Do you think you should tone it down a little bit, Ellie?"

"Judge Kilgore is known for being biased towards prosecutors, so that may have clouded my judgment coming in. I'll watch it from here on in."

"That's all I'm asking."

"What did you think the audience thought of the opening statements?" Ellie asked.

In reality, it shouldn't matter what the audience thought. Only the jury would determine Archer's guilt or innocence. However, there are inevitable oohs and ahhs from the crowd that could have an impact on the jury. So, I get where Ellie was coming from.

"I think they were impressed with both of them," I said. "Your line telling McNair that emotion wasn't going to change the evidence went over very well."

"And the jury?"

"It's hard to read their faces from where we're sitting."

For a confident woman, Ellie seemed very interested in my feedback on what others thought of her. I guess I couldn't blame her.

"I know they like that handsome fuck, Will McNair. Maybe we should have chosen all men on the jury for that reason alone."

Cliff Boyd laughed, but I wonder if Ellie had a point. Could a handsome man - or a beautiful woman - potentially affect the jury. Or more specifically, affect one juror, because that's all you needed in a criminal case. It might sound outlandish, but I'm sure there were examples of it happening.

Grace decided to chime in.

"Why don't you eye-fuck some of the male jurors?"

There were a few laughs and a stern rebuttal from Archer.

"Grace, watch your language."

That elicited another few laughs. Here Archer was, on trial for his life, and he was worried that his daughter had dropped an f-bomb.

"I should probably head back soon," Ellie said. "Thank you all for being here. It's nice to know we've got some people on our side."

That jogged my memory.

"Donna Neal was sitting behind the prosecution table," I said.

"Was she really?"

"Yeah. I worry that she might be the witness to testify that Gracie was going to ask for a divorce."

Once again Grace winced and A.J. remained stoic. It was hard to overstate how tough this must have been on them.

"She never mentioned it when you talked to her?"

"No. Not once. She talked about a range of other things, even fed me two beers, but never mentioned that Gracie wanted a divorce."

I quickly realized it was right after my meeting with Donna that I'd had sex with Ellie. I wished I'd left out the part about having beers.

"We'll use that against her when we cross-examine her."

"What, her having beers?" Cliff said, tongue firmly in cheek.

"No, you sarcastic clown. Her not having mentioned the possible divorce to Quint."

There was a weird playfulness to our conversation. It didn't fit the seriousness of Archer's situation.

"Okay, this time I really am headed back," Ellie said.

She, Archer, and Cliff walked back toward Department 22.

I remained with the two Keats children. I felt like, without my knowledge, I'd been appointed as their trial guardian for the time being. Trial having two meanings in this case.

"Will we know when they reconvene?" Grace asked.

"Yeah," I said. "The bailiff will yell it from outside the courtroom."

"How do you think it's going so far?"

It appeared that Grace was changing before my eyes. The general unpleasantness was gone. Seeing her father on trial surely brought about that change.

A.J. was quieter, maybe taking it all in on the first day.

Cliff came running back down in our direction.

"Quint, can I talk to you?"

"Sure."

We walked twenty feet or so away from Grace and A.J.

"What is it?" I asked.

"The prosecution's first witness is one of the cops who arrived at the scene. He's going to be describing what they saw. It's going to make McNair's description look like a picnic. That's going to be followed by a DNA expert and a forensic pathologist. It will only get worse."

"And you want me to discourage Grace and A.J. from being there?"

"Actually, it was Archer's suggestion."

"I'll try."

"Thanks," Cliff said.

∼

I walked back over to Grace and A.J.

"What is it?" she asked.

"The prosecution's first witness is one of the police officers who came upon your mother's body. The following two are crime scene experts. All they are going to talk about is your mother's murder, including details you don't want to hear. Your father thinks it would be better if you're not there."

"But…" Grace said.

"Dad is right," A.J. said. "We don't need to hear the particulars."

He put his arm around his sister. She didn't seem to want any part of it.

"Let's go do something else for a few hours."

"Fine."

The two of them headed towards the elevator. I gave them both a tap on the shoulder as they left.

～

As I walked back towards the courtroom, I saw Tre Larson.

"The courtroom makes good theater," he said.

"It certainly does," I admitted. "What was the last movie or book that took place in a courtroom you didn't enjoy?"

"Been a long time. Are you able to enjoy it or is it too close to home?"

"I wouldn't choose enjoy as the word to describe it. It's downright riveting. I'll give you that."

"And we're only an hour in."

"I know. Do you plan on staying for the entire trial?"

"You know when I usually work," Tre said. "Nights. So I'll be here for quite a bit of it. How long will this last?"

"It will be done before you know it. A week or ten days, I'd say."

"Really?"

"People see trials like O.J. or Casey Anthony or Scott Peterson and they take weeks or months. But most murder trials don't last nearly that long. And I hate to say it since I'm working it, but this isn't exactly the most complicated trial."

"Yeah, it's kind of a he said/she said, if only Gracie Keats could still talk."

"That's morbid, Tre."

"Doesn't mean it's not true. Hey, will I see you out again soon?"

"We could meet up Friday night. I've got to be on my A-game during the week."

"You didn't tell me the defense attorney was downright gorgeous."

Down the line, maybe I'd tell Tre what happened between Ellie and me, but it certainly wasn't going to be here and now.

"Very smart woman too. Cutthroat. Someone you'd want on your side if you were in court."

"Yeah, she was impressive. So was that DA McNair, though."

"He's a hot dog."

"Being good at your job and being a hot dog aren't mutually exclusive, you know."

"I know, Tre. I've seen you pour drinks now and then. You add that little flair to it."

Tre laughed.

"Well, let's grab those drinks on Friday then. Although, I won't be pouring them. The perks of being management."

"You've come a long way from the Rooftop bar."

Tre laughed.

"That's for sure."

"Hey, I'm going to head in. Thanks for showing me solidarity."

"Don't pat yourself on the back. I came for the theater of it all."

I laughed and we both walked towards the courtroom.

CHAPTER 22

"The Prosecution may call their first witness," Judge Kilgore said.

"The State calls Officer Kyle Stringer," Will McNair declared.

From the seats behind McNair, Officer Kyle Stringer emerged. He was a good 6'4" with wide shoulders. He's not the type of police officer you wanted to fuck with.

He was wearing his police blues as he walked and sat down on the witness stand.

Judge Kilgore looked in his direction.

"Do you solemnly swear that the testimony you are about to give shall be the truth and nothing but the truth?"

"I do," he said.

Weddings and courthouses. The two times that you have to say, 'I do.'

Will McNair approached the witness, glancing at the jury box on the way there.

"Officer Stringer, what is your profession?"

"I'm a Walnut Creek police officer."

"And what happened on the morning of December 23rd of last year?"

"Me and my partner, Dave Donnegal, were called to a house. Some man had called 9-1-1 asking for the police."

"Was that man Archer Keats?"

"Yes."

"Can you describe what you saw when you first arrived?"

"Mr. Keats was standing in the driveway when we got there. He told us that his wife had been murdered and that she was in her bed upstairs in the main house."

"The main house?"

"Yes, Mr. Keats made sure to tell us that he was living in the guest house at the time."

Will McNair had obviously trained Officer Stringer well. He was making it look like Archer was setting up his alibi. That he no longer lived in the main house.

"What happened next?"

"Mr. Keats led us in and we walked up the stairwell. At this point, we didn't know just how gruesome the murder was going to be."

"Describe what you saw."

"When we arrived at the top of the stairs, we got a look into the bedroom since the doors were opened wide. We could immediately see that something was coming out of the deceased's chest."

There were a few groans from the crowd.

"And then you walked closer?"

"Yes. We walked into the room and saw the knife protruding from Gracie Keats."

"From her heart, correct?"

"Yes. It was the most heinous thing I've ever seen."

"Where was the skin that protects the human heart?"

"She'd been stabbed so many times that it had turned into mush. I guess that's the only way I can describe it."

"That must have been terrible?"

"It was brutal."

"What position was she lying in?"

"She was on her back on the right side of the bed."

"Was she clothed?"

"Yes. She had a white nightgown on. Or, at least, it had been white."

We heard a jurist audibly gasp.

"Were there any signs of rape?"

"Not from where we stood. She was clothed, as I said."

"So what happened next?"

"We called in for homicide detectives, a crime scene unit, DNA expert, a coroner, and things of that nature."

"If you're not a homicide detective, do you know why you were initially called to the scene?"

"From what I understand, the defendant just told 9-1-1 to send someone quickly. We didn't know at the time that it was a homicide."

"How long until the homicide detectives arrived?"

"I'd say ten minutes or so."

"And in that time were you with the defendant, Mr. Keats?"

"Yes. After the carnage we saw in the bedroom, we decided to walk back downstairs and wait."

"Why was that?"

"I didn't want to risk damaging the crime scene so we decided to vacate the bedroom."

"While you waited for the detectives, how did Mr. Keats appear to you?"

"Honestly, he seemed robotic. He wasn't crying. I know if that was my wife, I'd have been acting differently."

"Objection, your honor," Ellie said.

"Sustained," Judge Kilgore said. "Let's keep your testimony to what you saw, Officer Stringer."

"Yes, your honor."

Will McNair stepped closer to the witness.

"To you, did he seem broken up about his wife's savage murder?"

"Not as much as I would have guessed."

"No more questions, your honor," McNair said.

Judge Kilgore looked towards the defense table.

"Ms. Teague, your chance for cross."

Ellie stood up, pushed down the creases on her pantsuit, and approached the witness. She stood on the left of the witness, in front of the judge. My assumption was that Ellie knew both the jury and the witness could see her from that angle. If she went to the right side of the witness, she'd be blocking members of the jury.

"Officer Stringer, I've only got a few questions for you."

"Alright."

"Did you see any scratches or marks on Mr. Keats?"

"No."

"Did you see anything that would suggest Mr. Keats had been in a life or death struggle?"

"No, but maybe if he stabbed her quickly..."

"Your honor," Ellie said.

"Officer Stringer, please just answer the questions at hand. No need to give your personal opinion."

Ellie's eyes went from the judge back to the witness.

"I'll ask again..."

"No, he didn't look like he'd been in a fight."

Officer Stringer had interrupted Ellie while also sounding perturbed. It was a bad look for the prosecution since he was their witness.

"Isn't it true that when the homicide detectives got there, you escorted Mr. Keats back to his guest house?"

"Yes, that's true."

"Did you see anything in that house to suggest he'd committed a murder?"

"There were bloodstains out in the courtyard."

"That's not what I asked, Officer Stringer. Those could have been left by anybody. I'll ask you again. Although I'll admit, I'm getting tired of repeating my questions."

The judge rolled her eyes, but let Ellie continue.

"Was there anything in the guest house - where Mr. Keats had been living - to suggest that he'd committed a murder?"

"No."

"Was there a bloody pair of pants?"

"No."

"Was there a bloody shirt?"

"No."

"How about a bloody glove?"

"No."

"Any bloody socks?"

Will McNair stood up.

"Your honor!" he yelled.

"Ms. Teague," Judge Kilgore said. "I think we've got the point."

Archer gave Cliff a slight elbow on the table in front of us.

"This will be my final question, Officer Stringer. Was there anything at all that suggested my client had killed someone? Anything?"

"No."

"No more questions," Ellie said.

As she walked back towards the defense table, you could tell that Ellie had gotten her mojo back.

∼

The next two witnesses didn't carry the intrigue of Officer Stringer or the two opening statements.

The first was a forensic pathologist who described how Gracie Keats died. As if the whole courtroom didn't know. The witness couldn't narrow down exactly when Gracie Keats died, but he said it was likely from the first several stabs.

This was an important piece of information for the prosecution. The longer it took for Gracie to die, the more likely Archer Keats would have had some scratches or marks on him. Which he had none of.

The forensic pathologist also talked about all the damage that would have to occur along the way to enable you to stab someone through the heart. I quickly glanced around the courtroom and could tell that people didn't enjoy hearing it. Still, it showed how grizzly the murder was, which hypothetically would help the prosecution. This murder seemed personal and what's more personal than a husband and wife relationship?

The second witness was a DNA expert and he testified that there was no DNA found at the scene. This included on the stairs, in the courtyard, or on the door. The prosecution tried to steer that towards meaning it couldn't have been some random perpetrator of the crime.

The forensic pathologist and DNA expert took much longer than the Walnut Creek police officer and the two opening statements.

Boring science questions had to be asked and repeated several times. That's what made it so tedious.

Ellie asked very few follow-up questions. She'd made an impression against Officer Stringer and knew she wasn't going to play gotcha on one of the science-based witnesses.

It was 3:30 p.m. by the time the DNA expert left the stand.

Judge Kilgore spoke.

"I think we'll call it a day. Thanks, everyone. We'll reconvene tomorrow morning at nine a.m. Court is dismissed."

And she brought her gavel down with unnecessary force.

Seven of us met at Ellie's law firm an hour later.

Archer, his two children, myself, Ellie, Cliff, and Gene Bowman were wrapped around the giant table in the conference room.

Ellie stood up.

"It was a long first day," she said. "I don't know if there was a winner. Keep in mind that the prosecution calls their witnesses to start, so you just want to tread water. They didn't get a first-round knockout so I'm alright with how today went."

"You were excellent," Gene Bowman said.

"Thanks, Gene. I'd rather not talk about myself, though. I invited everyone here to see if they have any questions. I don't want you guys to be surprised by anything that happens. I've laid my cards on the table and want you to see everything we've got."

"I've got a general question," A.J. Keats said. "What will this week look like? Will the prosecution rest by week's end?"

"If I had to guess, they'll put on their case till at least Thursday. Possibly Friday or into next week. A lot of it depends on the judge. I've had judges who will call it a day at two p.m. and others who are sticklers to make it till five. Judge Kilgore called it at 3:30 today, so who knows."

"Is she rooting for the prosecution?" Grace asked.

"She's not rooting for anyone, Grace."

"It seemed like she was favoring the other side."

"Now, that's a different question. As I told you guys before the trial, Judge Kilgore is generally seen as being a prosecution-friendly judge."

"That's all I was saying."

"Then yes, you're right, Grace."

"How are you feeling, Archer? After all, it's you who's got everything to lose. We're all just talking heads."

"I thought you did well today, Ellie. I'm not going to get my hopes up. I know this trial could go either way."

I hadn't said a word up to this point.

"Have you thought more about whether you're going to put Archer on the stand?" I asked.

Cliff took the question.

"Ellie and I have been weighing the pros and cons. A lot depends on how well the prosecution makes its case. If they stink up the joint, we'll be less likely to put Archer on. If they knock it out of the park, we might be forced to," Cliff said, using another sports-related analogy.

His answer was well-stated and I agreed with all of it. Calling the defendant to testify was like having a trump card that could go badly. You only wanted to use it if you were sure it would help.

"Will you call Dr. Faber to the stand?" A.J. asked.

"Almost certainly."

"How about Jan Goddard?"

"Almost certainly, as well. Like Cliff just said, we like to keep our options open. If the prosecution is absolutely terrible and doesn't prove their case at all, why make public an affair that Gracie was having? That might give the jury more reason to think Archer did it."

"With all due respect, Ellie," Gene Bowman said. "Will McNair is not going to be terrible. He's a considerable adversary and I'd take him seriously."

"Who said I'm not taking him seriously?"

"You've mentioned twice what would happen if the prosecution fails to make their case. We should assume they are going to. Will McNair doesn't lose often."

"With all due respect, Gene," Ellie said, repeating his earlier words. "I'm taking Will McNair very seriously. I'm also not committing to who I'm putting on the stand until after the prosecution has rested. Do you understand that part?"

Things were getting heated.

"Yeah, I get that part," Gene said.

Everyone took a few seconds to chill out.

"When will Donna Neal testify?" A.J. asked.

"If she is indeed the witness who will say that Gracie was going to ask for a divorce, then I imagine she will be one of their last. You won't see her till later this week at the earliest."

"Speaking of which, Quint, have you found anything more about this Kirk Stroud guy?"

"I haven't. Talked to probably eight of his co-workers. Supposedly an intense dude, but nothing else stands out."

"We had work done on our garage about a year ago," Archer said. "It's possible he was one of the guys. But I still don't know what he'd say. I mean, I hate to ponder this, but maybe Gracie had brought a guy back and this Stroud guy saw something. I honestly don't know what else it could be."

"You didn't tell any of the construction workers anything relevant?" Cliff asked.

"Relevant to this case? Absolutely not. This was almost a year ago."

"If you're not worried, then I'll try not to be," Cliff said.

"What's on deck for tomorrow?" Grace asked, changing the subject.

"Don't take this the wrong way, because every witness matters, but it's going to be a relatively boring day. They are calling three or four different financial experts. All of whom will testify to how royally screwed Archer was financially. They will say that companies in debt were going to go under. That companies doing alright were heading towards debt. They will make it seem like the end of the world for Archer."

"Is there anything you can do to mitigate them?" I asked.

"Not a whole lot," Ellie said. "You can ask Gene about that. I've talked to the people in his office doing the finances. It's not going to be a good look tomorrow, but that doesn't mean I'm not prepared. I have all of Gene's employees' estimations on each particular company and if these experts get out of line, I'll be there to correct them."

It was a part of the case I was barely familiar with, but it was obvious how much work Ellie had done. And that wasn't easy work, slogging through financial records. She deserved credit for that. I'm glad I had nothing to do with it.

"That sounds time-consuming," Grace said.

"You have nooooooo idea," Ellie said, accentuating the word no.

Grace smiled.

It made me wonder if many legal teams and families had this level of camaraderie. We were probably smiling - and even laughing sometimes -

more than we should, considering the circumstances. Oddly, I imagined this wasn't that rare. It's almost like when a loved one is in the hospital. When you're in the waiting room, you try to enjoy each other as much as possible, maybe make some jokes, knowing it's the best way to cope. That's how these meetings felt.

"Are there any more questions?" Cliff asked. "If not, Ellie and I should start working on our cross-examinations for tomorrow."

No one said anything, so Cliff stood up, signaling the meeting was over.

There were a few handshakes and hugs and a few minutes later, I was on my way back to my apartment.

I arrived home and as I started to turn my key, I looked up at my door.

Who had left the note to investigate Dickie Faber?

I never had figured that out. Or, if I was being self-critical, I hadn't spent too much time thinking about it. I probably should have. It had led me to what we now considered a viable suspect in Gracie's death.

I walked into my apartment, and as had become custom, threw on some jazz and started contemplating things.

Who would know about Gracie and Dr. Faber?

Donna Neal, obviously. Had Archer known before I told him? Did I tell him before the note was left on my door? I couldn't remember, because my mind was going in fifty different ways.

Did Archer's kids know Gracie was having an affair with Dr. Faber? Or Brad Lacoste?

The note had been left while I had my first meeting with Grace, so she would have known I was at my office.

And like I'd said, it's pretty easy to find out someone's address these days.

Grace was a possibility for those reasons.

I didn't know what to think. Just another mystery in this crazy case.

Just be happy you received the damn letter!

My interior monologue always seemed to play devil's advocate.

Sure, I was glad I received it, but I didn't like not knowing why.

Should I ask Grace tomorrow, point-blank?

I'd think about it.

I kicked my shoes off, changed out of the clothes I'd worn to court, put on some basketball shorts and a t-shirt, and returned to the couch.

I felt like there was something I was missing.

Not a specific thing that would break the case, but an overriding theme that was eluding me.

I tried to rack my brain. To no avail.

I don't think it was working at full capacity.

What was I overlooking?

CHAPTER 23

Like Ellie had predicted, Tuesday turned out to be a boring day in court.

It was filled with financial experts, accountants, and talks about business models.

If they'd set up a hammock in court, I could have taken a nap.

And yet, I knew that it was a crucial day for the prosecution. They did a good job showing that Archer was in dire straits financially. As many as half of his businesses were in serious danger of folding.

I glanced at the jury a few times, curious if they were bored.

To me, they looked more disinterested, but what the hell did I know?

Once again, I'd sat with A.J. and Grace in the first row behind the defendant's table of Archer, Ellie, and Cliff.

There was no need to have the Keats children avoid court on this day. Still, it must not have been easy to hear that your father's businesses were failing.

And I couldn't help but wonder if that led to them second-guessing their father's guilt or innocence? They were in such a tough spot. I felt for them. I'd come around on Grace as well. She'd been the snotty little brat the first day I'd met her, but had been engaging ever since. Maybe I'd been too quick to chastise her. Who was I to judge someone who'd just lost her mother and was awaiting the trial of her father?

A.J. seemed quite interested in hearing about his father's finances. I wonder if he regretted not going into business with him? Did he think things would have been different if he'd been there to help his father out?

Will McNair was once again stellar, laying out Archer's financial problems in a way that the layman could understand. Ellie couldn't do much but made a few objections that Judge Kilgore upheld. I guess that's a good thing in the long run.

Mercifully, the day ended around 4:45, with the judge banging the gavel and telling everyone assembled that she'd see them tomorrow.

As we left the courtroom, Ellie leaned into me and said, "Tomorrow will be more exciting, that's for sure."

~

That night at home, in lieu of jazz music, I decided to watch the local news to get a read on what they were saying.

At 6:00 p.m., I threw on KTVU, Channel 2 in the Bay Area. There was an older white woman and a young black guy co-anchoring.

"Hi, this is Julie Haverty along with Curtis Grady. We know you have a lot of options for your news and we're happy you chose us."

The camera switched to Curtis Grady.

"It was another interesting day in the trial of Archer Keats, accused in the horrific murder of his wife, Gracie. The prosecution called five different witnesses who all testified that Archer Keats was indeed in financial straits. The well-known restaurateur had as many as half of his businesses expected to go under. Our very own Bob McKenzie was there in the courtroom. We'll go to Bob now."

They cut to Bob McKenzie, a fifty-something with gray hair and a potbelly.

"Thanks, Curtis. Yeah, most people I talked to said it was a great day for the prosecution. The DA, Will McNair, made a point of emphasizing just how dire the defendant's business woes were. In fact, it was so one-sided today that we barely heard from Ellie Teague, Archer Keats's lead defense attorney. Ms. Teague had been so fiery yesterday and had received rave reviews from the legal community, but today she was mostly an afterthought. I caught up with Jim Sullivan, one of the most well-regarded criminal defense attorneys in San Francisco history for his thoughts."

The camera cut to Jim Sullivan, a distinctive-looking man in his mid-seventies.

"I think Will McNair did a nice job today, but to be honest, you'd expect that. The prosecution is playing offense right now. They should look better on days like these. I've heard some people say Ellie Teague was quiet today. What exactly was she supposed to do? Go head to head with some financial wizard about the likelihood of a business going under? No, she shouldn't. She's smart to bide her time and play defense, waiting for her time to pounce once the prosecution rests. So yes, Will McNair was good today, but that's hardly news. It would have been news if the prosecution hadn't done its job."

The camera cut back to Bob McKenzie.

"Wise words there from Jim Sullivan, who often goes against the grain. Sure, Will McNair dominated the court today, but that's to be expected. He seems to be more interested in what Ellie Teague will do once it's the defense's turn to call their witnesses."

Cut to Julie Haverty asking a question.

"When do we think that might be, Bob?"

"From what we've gathered, the prosecution could rest as early as Thursday or Friday."

"That's very soon."

"It sure is. As I've mentioned before, there's a whole lot of intrigue in this case from the general public. In legal circles, they are saying this case isn't all that captivating. I take issue with that. I've covered many high-profile cases and whenever they say it's going to be a ho-hum trial, it never is. I'd bet dollars to donuts something unexpected happens soon."

Curtis Grady spoke next.

"And we're glad we have you there to cover it, Bob."

"Glad to be here, Curtis. Take care, Julie."

They cut back to the two in the studio.

"There's no one better in the business at covering trials," Julie Haverty said.

"McKenzie has seen it all," Curtis said.

"I'm going to tell him you called him old."

Curtis laughed and I turned off the T.V.

A few thoughts flooded my mind.

Why is the local news so cheesy? Do they always have to end every segment on some corny joke?

My mind then focused on the trial itself.

Were we actually headed towards something unexpected? And what could that possibly be?

CHAPTER 24

"Come to order," Judge Kilgore said.

It was the third day of the trial and the courtroom remained packed.

Walking up to the courthouse that morning, I'd noticed even more news vans parked in front. There were probably fifty people from the media assembled near the front entrance. I recognized a few, including both Bob McKenzie and Jim Sullivan from last night's news.

As Judge Kilgore called everyone to order, I heard some people making noise in the back of the courtroom.

"If you can't keep it down, I suggest you leave and catch the updates on tonight's news," the judge said.

Sure, it was directed at the people making noise, but I think she was subtly rueing having this trial on the news every night.

"Mr. McNair, you can call your first witness."

Will McNair was wearing a dark blue suit with a yellow tie. He was dressed impeccably, as he had been each day.

"The prosecution calls Natalie Slater."

A woman emerged from behind the prosecution desk, strutting towards the witness stand. She was dressed in a pair of white pants and a beige top. She was wearing bright red lipstick and her hair looked like she'd just come from the salon.

Judging by her appearance, I think Natalie Slater was looking forward to this moment and intended to look her best. I sensed some theatrics headed our way.

Ellie had told us that today was going to be a day of character witnesses who were either friendly with Gracie, didn't like Archer, or both. Will McNair had structured his witnesses so that he'd have the same type of witnesses appear one after another.

It probably made things easier for the jury. He'd gotten the DNA/forensics out of the way on the first day and the financial experts out of the way on the second.

Judge Kilgore swore in Natalie Slater and told McNair he could continue.

"Thanks for appearing here today, Natalie."

"It's my pleasure!" she said with too much aplomb.

"You were friends with Gracie Keats, weren't you?"

"I sure was."

"How did you meet?"

"My oldest boy was the same age as her son. And they played sports together. You know how it is. You kind of just become friends with their parents."

When one sentence would have done the trick, Ms.Slater used four.

"So, we're saying roughly fifteen years or more?"

"Yeah, that's about right. I'd say seventeen, maybe eighteen. My Justin is twenty-three and so is her son."

"Were the two sons close?"

"No, they didn't really become friends, but Gracie and I sure were close."

I looked over at A.J., wondering if it felt odd to be referenced in open court.

"What would you and Gracie do socially?"

"Well, she'd always give me invites to those great parties they threw. Restaurant grand openings. A bar having its ten-year anniversary. Those types of things."

"I've heard Gracie was the life of the party."

"She was. Then again, so was I."

She twirled her hair as she said it and a few people in the audience laughed. It was hard to tell if they were laughing at her or with her. Her testimony was performance art to Natalie Slater.

"Would you and your husband ever double date with the Keats?"

"Yeah, we did for years and years and years."

"And this stopped at some point?"

"Yeah. I'd say about eighteen months ago."

"Do you know why?"

"Of course. Gracie told me."

"What was her reason?"

"She said that she and Archer were going through some things."

"Did she say what kind of things?"

"She didn't have to."

"What do you mean by that?"

"It was obvious they were either fighting or worse."

"Worse?"

"Like getting separated or something."

"Did Gracie ever tell you that?"

"No, but some of the other mothers I knew told me that Gracie had put Archer in the guest house. Should have been called the dog house if you asked me."

She laughed at her own joke but wasn't joined by anyone else.

"Did you stay close with Gracie through this?"

"Oh, sure. We were always going to be tight."

"What type of things would you do?"

"We'd have coffee together. Things like that."

I thought Natalie Slater was starting to falter.

"And you said Gracie never told you that she was getting a separation?"

Ellie stood up.

"Objection. Asked and answered."

"Sustained. Mr. McNair, you did already ask that."

Ellie sat back down.

"From your discussions with her, did Gracie seem happy with her marriage?"

"Oh, no sir. It was obvious to me that she wasn't. She used to love hosting those restaurant openings I talked about. And those were drying up. I guess, kind of like Archer's finances."

"Objection, your honor," Ellie yelled.

"Sustained," Judge Kilgore said. "Let's answer the questions at hand, okay, Ms.Slater."

"You're the boss, judge."

There were some laughs in the courtroom after that. Judge Kilgore almost managed to look amused.

Will McNair was not amused. His witness was going off the rails.

"Let's get back to Archer," he said. "Did you ever see him argue with his wife?"

"Oh, yeah. Pretty much at any of their functions."

"Do you know why?"

"Well, he'd probably say it's because Gracie had one too many glasses of wine, but I don't think that was it. I think he was jealous."

"Why would he be jealous?"

"Because these were his restaurant openings and Gracie would always steal the show. She was much more entertaining than him and people gravitated more towards her. That must have made people," Ms.Slater paused, realizing she was walking into another objection. "That made me think that he was jealous of her."

"Did he ever touch her that you saw?"

"I saw him grab her arm several times. And I don't mean in a loving way. In a fierce, forceful way."

Will McNair paused for a minute. My guess was he was debating whether to ask any more questions. This witness was a wild card and he could have ended on a relatively high note.

"I'm going to ask one last question, Ms.Slater."

"Okay."

"Who do you think killed Gracie Keats?"

Natalie Slater pointed at Archer Keats.

"That man right there. Archer Keats. The defendant."

"Thank you. No more questions."

Will McNair walked back to the prosecution's table and said, "Your witness" in Ellie's direction.

Ellie walked towards the witness stand, taking her usual position, facing both the witness and the jury.

"How are you doing, Ms. Slater?"

"Good, thanks."

"Are you enjoying your time as a witness?"

"Yes."

"I thought so."

My eyes went to the judge. She looked as if she wanted to laugh.

"Now you said you were great friends with Gracie, correct?"

"Oh, yeah. We were thick as thieves."

"You testified earlier that some friends told you that Gracie and Archer might be living in separate houses."

"Yeah, that's right. Why?"

The question at the end made Ms. Slater appear nervous. This was no longer friendly fire. She was now under cross-examination.

"I'm wondering why, if you and Gracie were so tight, you had to hear that from someone else?"

Natalie Slater looked around, not sure what to say.

"Well, I don't know. You know how sometimes when you're really close to someone, they are the hardest ones to tell?"

"If you say so," Ellie said. "Did Gracie ever tell you herself that they lived in separate houses?"

"No, I guess not."

"And this had been going on for some time, correct?"

"Yeah, I guess so."

The once verbose witness was now responding with terse, one-sentence replies.

"You've now used the word guess in your last two answers. That seems pretty appropriate for you, Ms. Slater. A whole lot of guesses during this testimony."

Will McNair stood up.

"Objection, your honor."

"Sustained."

Ellie managed to smile.

"No more questions," she said.

Will McNair next called a set of sisters back to back. Pamela and Bunny Arden. Donna Neal had mentioned them when I'd met with her, stating they were close friends with Gracie.

They turned out to be pretty blah witnesses. They testified to all the great qualities Gracie possessed while reiterating that her marriage was on the rocks. They were pretty one-toned and unexciting, but I guess they did their job. They made Gracie come to life. They helped personalize her when the first two days were just DNA, forensics, and tedious financial charts. Maybe most importantly, the Ardens weren't blowhards like Natalie Slater. The jury must have, at least, appreciated that, despite them being a cure for insomnia.

Donna Neal had told me that Gracie was friendly with the Arden sisters, but she much preferred going out with her. Judging by their performances on the witness stand, I can't say I blamed Gracie.

I don't think the Arden sisters were the line dancing, beer-drinking types.

I'd covered quite a few cases in my days as a journalist, but what really hit home this time was the starts and stops. A fifteen-minute break here, a late jurist there. A judge's warnings here, a sidebar for the lawyers there.

It wasn't as continuous as the cases you'd see on Law & Order, which obviously was just the Hollywood version of the law. The real thing wasn't as exciting, but it was authentic. I'm sure attorneys watched Law & Order and just shook their heads.

~

The afternoon was more of the same. Character witnesses for Gracie Keats, but none dropped the bomb that she was going to divorce Archer.

Cliff seemed to revel in that when court ended for the day.

"Still nothing about Gracie asking for a divorce," he said.

There were about seven of us huddling outside of the courtroom. The judge had ended the day a few minutes before. Since we were the last ones to leave, we held our conversation feet from the courtroom door.

"It's coming," Ellie said. "Will McNair mentioned it in his opening. You can be sure we'll be hearing about it at some point."

"I don't think it's the end-all, be-all that everyone seems to think," I said.

"Why?"

"Not necessarily for the reasons you want to hear."

"Try me."

"The prosecution has proven that Archer was going through some serious financial hardship. And we've basically conceded that the marriage was on the rocks, with Archer living in the guest house for almost a year."

"And…"

"My point is that if Donna Neal - or someone else- says that Gracie was going to ask for a divorce, what's the damn difference? They already know he was borrowing money and had been emasculated by being sent to the guest house. I think that might be enough to convict."

I could tell immediately that Archer didn't like me using the word emasculated.

"I hope you're wrong."

"There's a positive spin to put in," I said.

A bailiff exited the courtroom and I stayed quiet until he was out of view.

"This will sound odd, but because I think jurors could convict without the divorce testimony, it won't have the same effect when they hear it. It won't be a moment where the jurists all say, "Well, now I'm convinced!"

Ellie put a finger up to her mouth.

"So your logic is that they've already heard enough to convict Archer and that's a good thing?"

"Well, we haven't played our best card yet."

"And what's that, Quint?"

"It's you, Ellie. It's your defense. It's throwing them, Brad Lacoste. And Dickie Faber. And Jan Goddard. And these two making their father sound like the best human on earth."

I nodded in A.J. and Grace's direction as I did.

"Thanks. I guess," Ellie said.

"No pressure," Archer retorted.

He'd been getting quieter the last few days. I had no doubt he was starting to think about the inevitable moment they read the verdict. It could be as soon as a week away and I couldn't imagine the pressure. The nerves. The sense of helplessness.

"I don't think they've proved shit," A.J. said. "What, some forensic dorks and some financial geeks. What does that prove?"

"The problem, A.J., is that this is not your normal case," Ellie said.

"How so?"

"While we always hear about being innocent until proven guilty, I think those have flipped in this case. Because Archer was the only person on the premises, it's almost like he's considered guilty and we have to prove him innocent. I'm not saying it's right, but I do believe it to be true. That's why getting the jury - at least one of them - to think that Dickie Faber could have committed the murder is so important."

She made a great point. In this case, it was on the defense to prove Archer didn't do it.

"I guess you're right," A.J. said.

For about the tenth time, I marveled at how well Grace and A.J. were holding up. I understand pulling for your father to be acquitted, but how can you not be thinking about your mother the whole darn time?

They were stoic when most kids would be a wreck.

"So, what's tomorrow going to look like?" Grace asked.

"Incredibly, they will likely be resting their case tomorrow. They have Donna Neal first and then …"

"That's good, right?" Grace asked.

"I'm not sure. If Donna Neal is their big witness and she's going to say Gracie was asking for a divorce, why not end with her?"

"Maybe Quint was right and the DA realizes she's not the grand finale he'd hoped for."

"Thank you, Grace," I said.

"Maybe, but I'm just a little uneasy," Ellie said. "Quint, nothing more on Kirk Stroud?"

"I've contacted his construction company, trying to find out if they fixed the garage at Archer's house. They haven't gotten back to me. I'm getting stonewalled."

"I smell a rat," Cliff said.

Grace jumped in again.

"If the prosecution ends tomorrow, will Grace and I testify on Friday?"

"Yes, probably. There's always the chance the judge could push us to Monday, but my guess is we'll be starting on Friday."

"But not tomorrow, right?"

"No. I don't care what time Will McNair ends. The judge will at least allow us the night to get our witnesses ready to testify. You seem nervous, Grace."

She looked oddly at Ellie.

"Wouldn't you be?"

"Yes. Yes, I would. I'm sorry."

"Why don't we end on that," Cliff said. "Quint, I want you to reach out to Jan Goddard. She won't get called until at least Monday, but just let her know it's fast approaching."

"I will."

"There's no chance she's going to back out, is there?"

"No, I think we've got a pretty nice understanding of each other now. She knows I won't steer her wrong."

"That's good to hear. And that bartender from The Cowboy Way?"

"Britt. She's looking forward to testifying."

"Well, let's hope that Donna Neal makes a few fibs tomorrow and Britt can point them out when we call her."

With that, we all went our separate ways.

I stopped at Taco Bell on my way home. Banana bread for lunch just wasn't going to cut it.

When I arrived back, I bit into my first taco and, as always, thought about the case.

And just how tedious it had been. Who would have thought that a high-profile murder case could be boring?

But for the most part, that's what it had been.

I thought back to Bob McKenzie's line:

I'd bet dollars to donuts something unexpected happens in the days to come.

CHAPTER 25

As I was approaching the courthouse on Thursday morning, a reporter recognized me.

"Quint Adler?" she asked.

I quickly ran past her, entered the courthouse, and got in line for the metal detector.

The media was getting bigger by the day and the last thing I wanted was to somehow be mentioned on the five o'clock news.

After passing through the metal detector, I made my way to Department 22 and took my usual seat in the first row behind the defense table.

I turned around and saw Gene Bowman a row behind us.

Still no Dickie Faber or Brad Lacoste.

I'm sure they were scared to death to appear in court. Their affairs would go public, although I could tell Ellie was waffling about whether to put Lacoste on the stand. One, there was very little likelihood that he killed Gracie. Two, the more potential suspects you threw at the jury, the less meaningful each one was. I think Ellie was putting most of her eggs in the Dickie Faber basket.

The bailiff introduced the judge and we all rose to our feet as she took her seat on the bench/throne.

"Hello, everyone. This trial is moving at breakneck speed and I'd like to thank everyone for keeping it moving. We expect that the prosecution may rest later today. When that happens, we will take the rest of the day off and reconvene tomorrow at nine a.m. for the defense's first witnesses.

Now that we've got that out of the way, Mr. McNair, you may call your first witness."

"The prosecution calls Donna Neal."

Donna stood up from the second row on the prosecution's side of the courtroom. She was dressed in a fancy, navy blue dress. You could probably argue she was overdressed for court, but I thought she looked sophisticated and classy. It certainly wasn't the country-western vibe I'd got when I first met her.

Judge Kilgore ran her through the witness edict.

"Can you state your name for the record?" Will McNair asked.

"Donna Neal."

"And where do you reside, Ms. Neal?"

"Walnut Creek."

"And you were friends with Gracie Keats?"

"I'd go so far as to say we were best friends."

"That's nice to hear. How long had you known each other?"

"We'd met about fifteen years ago."

The testimony had started almost identically to Natalie Slater's.

"Did you have kids her age?"

"No, Mr. McNair. I've never been married and don't have any kids."

So far, so good for Donna Neal. She was handling herself well. Not that I was rooting for her.

"Then why do you think you and Ms. Keats got along so well?"

Most women were referred to as Ms. in the courtroom, but I wondered if Will McNair intentionally used it in Gracie Keats's case. She had been married and Mrs. would have fit, but maybe he wanted to emphasize they weren't exactly living like a married couple when she was killed.

That, or maybe I was just overthinking things. It was known to happen.

"I think that's exactly why we got along so well. I was single when she had a million married friends. With her other friends, they probably just talked about their kids all day. With me, she could talk about anything."

"What would that usually entail?"

"Men. Fashion. TV shows. Men."

"You said men twice, surely that wasn't a mistake."

"We liked to talk about men. What's wrong with that?"

"Even though she was married?"

Will McNair knew that Ellie was going to bring up Gracie's cheating, so he wanted to nip it in the bud. It would sound better coming from a prosecution witness.

"Yes," Donna Neal. "Even though she was married."

"Are you just talking about men in general?"

"And some specific men."

"Are you saying that Gracie Keats was having an affair?"

"Yes, she was."

There was an audible gasp from the courtroom. Keep in mind, Gracie's affair had not been reported on the local news.

"I won't have you mention names, Donna. I think that would be pretty sleazy."

"Me too."

This was so obviously coordinated and yet it was genius as well. Now, Ellie would look like the sleazy one when she mentioned Dickie Faber or called him to the stand.

"So in general terms, what can you tell me?

"There were two guys that she was sleeping with off and on. I think she was excited by both of them for different reasons."

"Do you know if Archer knew about these?"

"I'm sure he must have known."

"Objection. Calls for Speculation," Ellie yelled but remained seated.

"Sustained."

I couldn't remember many objections that Judge Kilgore had overruled. Probably because Ellie and Will McNair were making them judiciously.

"I'll put it like this," Donna Neal said. "I have a big mouth and I'd bring up these two guys when we were out on the town. Archer knew a lot of people. I'm sure it got back to him."

This time, Ellie stood up.

"I object again, your honor."

"Sustained."

Judge Kilgore turned to Donna Neal.

"Ms. Neal, please don't make a conjecture about what the defendant did or didn't know."

"Okay. I'm sorry."

While it wasn't a good look to have the judge chastise your witness, I still think Will McNair came out the winner here. If the jury didn't believe that Archer killed his wife over money, now they had revenge or jealousy as a possible motive.

"You mentioned that you guys would go out on the town. Where would you go?"

"It depends. If Archer and Gracie were hosting something, we'd be at some nice restaurant. I preferred the other times when it was just us. We'd go to this place called The Cowboy Way which was more my style."

It was the first time that Donna had shown off that country-western vibe I'd gotten so much of.

"And it would just be you two?"

"Yeah. No one else went to that bar but us."

"I'm sure you two had lots of talks."

"Oh, yeah," Donna said and then laughed.

I knew it was a harbinger of what was to come.

"Anything you'd like to mention."

"Mostly the things I'd mentioned earlier. Sometimes we'd talk about the cowboys at the bar at the time."

"Did you ever talk about Archer?"

"Of course."

"What would Gracie say?"

"She'd just be down on their marriage."

"Had she been saying that for a long time?"

"Yes. It was almost two years ago that Gracie started bringing it up."

"Before that point, did you think she was happily married?"

I expected an objection from Ellie, but none came.

"I think so. She never mentioned any problems."

"Do you know when Archer started borrowing money from Gracie?"

"Around two years ago."

This was an expert class by Will McNair on how to guide a witness.

"Was money the main reason they fought?"

"Yes. And I think some of the passion was gone."

"From their sex life?"

"Yes. After twenty years, things must get stale. That's why I never got married."

There were a few quiet chuckles from the audience. I could tell Will McNair didn't like it, being the first time Donna had kind of gone out on her own. He didn't want a repeat of Natalie Slater.

"Do you think that's why she began having these two affairs?"

"Yeah, probably. Maybe she was also getting back at Archer for borrowing all that money from her."

"Objection," Ellie yelled.

"Sustained."

"Watch yourself, Ms. Neal," Judge Kilgore said.

"Okay. Sorry," Donna said.

Will McNair did a quick circle from in front of the witness stand, over to the jury, and then facing the gathered audience, looking over at Ellie, then the judge, and finally, back to Donna Neal.

I knew we were about to get the culmination of her testimony.

"Did Gracie ever talk to you about her future with Archer?"

"Sure. Many times."

"And what would she say?"

"Early on when he started borrowing money, she was still optimistic. When it kept happening, she became less and less optimistic."

"How about in the last few months of her life?

"Very pessimistic. She knew her marriage was going to last."

"Did she tell you that directly?"

"Yes."

A few groans from the audience.

"When?"

"About two weeks before her death. We were at the Cowboy Way and about three drinks in when she leaned in and told me."

"Told you what, exactly?"

"She told me she was going to tell Archer and the kids that she wanted a divorce."

A few more groans from the audience. I was shocked by the kids comment. Neither one had ever mentioned it. Then again, Donna Neal may well have been full of shit. She'd never mentioned any of this to me.

"And this was two weeks before her death?"

"Yes."

"You're sure?"

"I'm positive. I remember the moment vividly."

"Anything else, Ms. Neal?"

"Yeah. Right after that, she said, '*He's going to be livid. I fear for my safety.*'"

The groans from the audience reached a fevered pitch.

The line sounded made up. Something you designed in a lab. '*I fear for my safety*' rang generic to me.

"Thanks for your time, Ms. Neal. I have no more questions."

Will McNair took his customary strut as he walked back to the prosecution table. He must have felt like he'd nailed it. He wasn't wrong. It was devastating testimony, regardless of whether it was true.

"Your witness," he said to Ellie as he sat down.

Ellie rose up. She was wearing a light blue pantsuit with a white blouse. I'd seen Ellie be a knockout in various outfits. I don't think pantsuits would have been her first choice, but there weren't many options for women in court.

She took her usual position when interviewing a witness.

"Ms. Neal, do you remember meeting with my P.I., Mr. Adler?"

Here we go.

At least she used my last name. People knew the name Quint. My last name? Not so much.

"Sure, I remember."

"Did you mention to him that Gracie was asking for a divorce?"

"No."

"Why not?" Ellie said forcefully.

"Because he was working for the defense."

"What does that mean? You only tell the truth if you're talking to one side?"

That body blow connected.

I remember thinking after beers with Donna and then sex with Ellie that somehow they'd planned this together. I didn't think that now. Ellie did not like the woman in front of her.

"No. I just..."

"You just what?"

"I just thought that information was too important to share at the time."

"So you knew you wanted to wait until the trial to drop that on us?"

"I don't think I knew when I was going to drop it."

"When you met with my P.I., do you remember cracking open a couple of beers?"

"Yes."

"What time was that at?"

"It was in the a.m."

"Do you regularly crack open beers in the a.m.?"

"Not regularly."

"Sometimes?"

"Yeah, sometimes, I guess."

Ellie had Donna reeling.

"What time of night did Gracie tell you that she was going to ask Archer for a divorce?"

"It was probably nine p.m."

"Did you start drinking in the a.m. on that day?"

Donna Neal gave Ellie a brutal stare down. If looks could kill, Ellie would have been meeting her maker.

"I don't remember."

Ellie paused, allowing Donna's answer to sink into the jury.

"You said you were best friends with Gracie, correct?"

"Yeah, that's right."

"How many times in the last few years did you go to Gracie's house?"

"None."

"I'm sorry, did you say none?"

"You know I did," Donna snapped back.

"Isn't that odd?"

"Gracie said that Archer didn't like me very much."

"Hmmm. That helps explain a few things."

This time Will McNair rose from his seat.

"Objection, your honor."

"Sustained. Is there a question there, Ms. Teague?"

"Did you like Archer Keats, Ms. Neal?"

"No."

"And did you lie to my private investigator?"

"I didn't tell him the whole truth."

"Are you telling us the whole truth today?"

"Yeah."

"How can we be sure?" Ellie said rhetorically.

When there was no response, she said, "I have no more questions for this witness."

I'd lamented how boring this case had been, but the last ten minutes had been lightning, thunder, and fireworks. All rolled into one.

It was fantastic theater.

"Let's take a twenty-minute recess," Judge Kilgore said. "I think we could all use it."

CHAPTER 26

W e all met at our usual spot at the end of the hall.
"Your cross was excellent," Cliff said.
"Yeah, but so was her original testimony."
"We can always call Quint as a witness to rebut her testimony."
Great. Just what I wanted.
"Let's wait and see if that's necessary," Ellie said.
"One more witness for them, right?" Grace asked.
"Yeah. Kirk Stroud, the construction worker. We're going in pretty blind on this one, but your father said we have nothing to worry about."
But there was something to worry about.
Will McNair called him as his final witness for a reason.
We just had no idea what that was.

Twenty minutes later, Kirk Stroud was being called to the stand.
I'd met him briefly before, but his intensity seemed to stand out this time.
He was around fifty years old, completely bald, with a nasty scar on the left side of his chin. He walked slowly towards the witness stand, moving his arms as much as his legs. This wasn't a guy to be fucked with, that much was obvious.
I started to feel even more uneasiness.
What was it that I'd missed?

Judge Kilgore swore him in.

"State your name for the record," Will McNair said.

"Kirk Stroud."

"And where do you live, Mr. Stroud?"

"In Antioch, but I work out of Concord."

"What is your profession?"

"I work for Lancaster Construction."

"Lot of tough people in your type of work?'

"Sure is."

"Are you one of those tough guys?"

"Yeah, I'd say that's fair."

"Have you ever been in jail?"

"Once."

Jesus, how had I missed that? Ellie turned around and glared at me.

Luckily for us, Will McNair brought it up. He probably assumed we already knew and better him than us to bring it to the jury's attention.

"What happened?"

"I beat a guy to an inch of his life."

"How long did you spend in jail?"

"Only a few months."

"Why is that?"

"He had a knife. I only had my fists."

A few murmurs came from the audience.

Will McNair was doing a good job showing how ominous Mr. Stroud was. To what end, I wasn't sure yet.

"Did people know you were a tough guy?"

"Sure."

"I'd like to ask you about December 14th of last year."

"Alright."

"You got off work and a man approached you, is that correct?"

"Yeah, but not out in public for everyone to see. We were working a job in Walnut Creek and he was waiting for me when I arrived at my car, which was down the block from the worksite."

"Can you describe what happened next?"

"He asked me if I'd like to make a lot of money. At first, I thought he was some fruitcake."

There were groans from the audience.

"Sorry, homosexual," Kirk Stroud said, alienating the courtroom even further. "But then I realized that he was there to talk business. He asked if we could talk in my car so we wouldn't be seen. I agreed."

"Then what happened?"

"We got in the car and I could tell he was tip-toeing around what he wanted to ask, so finally I told him to just ask it."

"And what did he ask?"

"He asked me if I would murder his wife for $50,000."

There was madness in the courtroom for the seconds that followed. It was like an earthquake had just hit. Which, for us on Archer Keats team, it pretty much had.

"Settle down, everyone," Judge Kilgore yelled as she slammed her gavel. "Settle down!"

It was a good minute until people did so

Will McNair rode it out, knowing the reaction was exactly what he'd intended.

"How did you respond?" he finally asked.

"I said '*Hell no!*' He pleaded with me a few more times, but I said he must be crazy. I may be a tough guy, but I ain't no killer."

"What happened after that?"

"I realized I recognized the man."

"From what?"

"From a construction job we'd done about a year ago. We elongated a garage and some guys re-surfaced their driveway. It was only like a three or four-day job."

"And where was this job?"

"In Walnut Creek."

"And who was the guy you recognized?"

Kirk Stroud pointed at Archer.

"The defendant, Archer Keats."

There were more shrieks and moans, but not from me. It had been where this was headed.

"The defendant in this trial, Archer Keats, asked you to kill his wife on December 14th of last year?"

"Yes."

"You're positive?"

"1000% percent. There's not a single doubt in my mind."

"Thank you, Mr. Stroud. Your witness, Ms. Teague."

More than anything, I wanted to see both Archer and Ellie's reaction at that moment, but sitting behind them, that wasn't possible.

"No questions for this witness," Ellie said, her voice barely audible.

She probably figured she'd just make it worse.

"The prosecution rests," Will McNair said.

A silence came over the courtroom that I wasn't expecting.

"We are recessed until tomorrow morning at nine a.m. The defense will start its case then. We are adjourned," Judge Kilgore said and pounded down the gavel.

It was then that Ellie and Archer turned around.

Ellie appeared shell-shocked and Archer looked like a ghost.

No one said a word.

We all exited the courtroom together, everyone continuing to stay silent.

A.J. looked like he wanted to say something, but held back. He and Grace had been staying with Archer during the trial. I couldn't imagine what it was going to be like at their house tonight. It gave me goosebumps just thinking about it.

I imagine that Ellie felt deceived by Archer. She was also probably pissed at me for not finding out more about Kirk Stroud.

In my defense, there was absolutely zero chance I was ever going to find out the information he testified to.

We kept walking and waiting for Archer to say something. Anything.

He finally did, mere seconds from us walking outside the courthouse. He knew what was waiting for him. Cameras flashing and microphones being shoved into his face.

Archer led A.J., Grace, Cliff, Ellie, and myself into a little alcove just before you exited the courthouse.

"I'm going to say this one time and one time only. That guy on the stand is full of shit. Not one thing that he said was true. Okay, maybe he worked at our house, but all the rest are lies. I never, ever, ever talked to anyone about killing Gracie. I'm as flabbergasted as any of you."

Ellie had finally gathered the courage to talk.

"We can talk about this later, and I'm sure we will. A.J. and Grace, I need to meet with you tonight. You're going on the stand tomorrow. Quint, I don't care if you come to court or not. I want you to find out everything you can on Kirk Stroud."

"Alright," I said.

"This trial isn't over," Ellie said.

I'm not sure any of us believed that.

CHAPTER 27

I took Ellie's advice and didn't go to court the following morning.

I went to the offices of Lancaster Construction at nine a.m. sharp.

No one would talk to me about Kirk Stroud. I'm assuming they'd all heard his testimony and either by their own choice or by someone above them, vowed not to talk.

I waited in the parking lot until someone dressed in construction gear headed towards the office.

"Excuse me," I said. "Someone from Lancaster left a circular saw at my house and I wanted to return it. Do you know what sites they are on right now?"

"I know we've got one going on Civic Drive in Walnut Creek. And I'm working at a house on Clayton Road out in Concord."

"Do you have the address on that one?"

"2626 Clayton."

"Thank you."

"You got it."

I headed to 2626 Clayton Road first, hoping to be finished before he got back there.

Once I arrived, I approached around twenty different people.

Not a single one was willing to talk about Kirk Stroud.

As I was leaving the site, the guy from the corporate office was walking up.

"Did you return that saw?" he asked.

"No one here claimed it."

He looked down and saw I wasn't carrying anything. He began to get suspicious.

"Do you happen to know Kirk Stroud?" I asked.

Now he was more than just suspicious. He knew what I was doing.

"Get the hell out of here!" he yelled.

A few of his co-workers looked in my direction and started walking my way.

It was time I got out of there.

The construction site off of Civic Drive in Walnut Creek was equally as unreceptive.

I got a few 'nos', a few 'hell nos', and even a 'fuck no.'

It was obvious that Mr. Stroud's testimony had spread through Lancaster Construction.

And no one was going to talk to me.

Despite hitting three different spots and talking to probably forty people, it was still only 11:50 a.m. I wouldn't make it to the Contra Costa Superior Court by the standard noon break, so I decided I'd grab some lunch and make it there for the one p.m. restart.

The morning had been a total waste.

I'd gone home before I grabbed lunch and it caused me to be late. I didn't get to the courthouse until about 1:15.

For the first time, I walked into the courtroom while they were in session. I got several irritated glances in my direction. I quietly inched towards the first row. I looked up and Grace was on the stand and Ellie was in front of her.

"No more questions," Ellie said.

Shit, I'd missed her whole testimony in only fifteen minutes.

"No questions for this witness," Will McNair said.

I leaned over to A.J.

"How did she do," I whispered.

"She was a little nervous."

Grace walked back and took a seat next to me in the first row. Archer turned around and glared at his daughter. She must have been really poor.

"The defense next calls A.J. Keats," Ellie said.

A.J. walked past me and his sister, making his way to the witness stand.

"How was it?" I whispered to Grace.

She looked genuinely scared.

"I was terrible," Grace said. "Everyone knows it."

For a brief second, the unlikeable woman from our first meeting had returned.

"I'm sure you weren't that bad," I said.

She didn't respond.

A.J. was sworn in and Ellie asked her first question.

"State your name for the record."

"Archer Archibald Keats the second."

I remember how much I'd despised the name when I first heard it, but I'd come around on A.J.

"But everybody calls me A.J." he added.

"And you are Archer's son, correct?"

"Yes."

"As well as being Gracie's son."

"That's right."

A.J. was hard to get a read on. He was usually polite, but he was never exactly the life of the party. His testimony was only three questions old, but he didn't seem all that into it. He may well have been nervous, but I was unimpressed thus far.

"What can you tell us about your mother?"

"She was a great woman. We miss her every day. She really held our family together."

"And your father?"

"My father didn't kill my mother. He loved her. Everyone loved her, to be honest. She was larger than life. A true titan."

A.J. was laying it on a little thick.

"Did you know that your parents were going to get divorced?"

My eyes shot towards Grace. I wanted to see her reaction.

"No, my mother never told us that."

Grace's face seemed to slightly harden. As if she knew I was looking at her to gauge her reaction.

Or was I just crazy? Maybe I was reading into something that wasn't there.

As I always told myself, go with your gut.

And I thought Grace's reaction gave something away.

Did A.J. and Grace know their parents were getting a divorce? And if so, why did Archer lie this entire time about it? Worse yet, if Archer was lying about that, what else was he lying about?

"Can you describe how you found out about your mother's death? I'm sorry, I know this is tough."

"I was in Tahoe and got a call from my father."

"Do you know what time that was at?"

"I'm guessing like ten a.m. or so. He was at the police station at that point. I don't think he had time to call us before then. I know he called 9-1-1 and then the police got there. I'm sure he was swamped and under enormous pressure."

"What were your initial feelings?"

"I just remember thinking this can't be true. I was going to be seeing her in a few days for Christmas Eve."

"Did your family always get together for the holidays?"

"Of course. We all loved each other."

"Now, I'd like to talk about your father."

"Okay."

"Did he love your mother?"

"Of course he did."

"Would you call it a happy marriage?"

"Yes. That doesn't mean they didn't fight, but c'mon, doesn't every married couple?"

"Most do, A.J. Did your father spoil your mother?"

"Oh, yeah. He'd buy her flowers all the time. Bought her a new car for one of her birthdays years ago. And whenever he opened a new restaurant, he kind of let my mother be the face of it."

"Did she like that?"

"She loved it. Hosting those grand openings was a big deal to her. And honestly, it seemed like she'd go to that restaurant every night for the next two weeks, soaking in all the new business."

"It sounds like they were a good pair."

This was more like it.

"They were. He was more the business side and my mother was probably better at the social aspect of it."

"That's nice to hear. I'm now going to ask you a tough question, A.J."

"Alright."

"Did you ever suspect your father had killed your mother?"

"No, of course not."

"Not even with Kirk Stroud's testimony yesterday?"

"It was shocking, but no, that didn't change my mind. My dad is not guilty."

They'd deviated off course again. Why was Ellie asking about Kirk Stroud? But then I realized I did know why. To soften the blow of Stroud's testimony. To show that the people close to Archer still loved him. And still believed he was innocent. Despite the ramblings of an ex-con construction worker.

"You love your father, don't you?"

"Of course I do. He was an awesome family man. "

"Did you drive down from Tahoe when you heard the news?"

"Yeah."

"How long does that take?"

"About three hours."

"And was your father still at the police station?"

"No, he was home by then."

"I assume the main house was considered a crime scene."

"Yeah. Grace came down from Napa and we all got a hotel that night."

"Because it was too tough to stay at your parents' house?"

"Exactly. It had been less than twenty-four hours since my mother had been killed."

"How was your father during the time at the hotel?"

"Devastated, obviously. Grace and I would have tried to comfort him more, but we were in shambles ourselves."

My guess was this was meant to contradict Officer Stringer who said Archer hadn't shown proper grieving. Whatever that means.

"I'm sure you were. Just a few more questions, A.J."

"Okay."

"You know your father didn't kill your mother, don't you?"

"Yeah."

"And how do you know that?"

"Because he loved her. I know everyone's been talking about his financial problems, but he still loved my mother. In fact, he was still hoping to get back together. He didn't want her dead. He wanted more of her in his life."

"I have no more questions for this witness."

It was a strong ending to an up-and-down testimony.

"No questions," Will McNair said.

McNair likely thought this had not been the greatest testimony. Also, you're just going to look bad if you badgered A.J. He'd lost his mother and his father was on trial. Going after him would be a bad look. It's the same reason he hadn't cross-examined Grace.

A.J. exited the witness stand and came and sat next to his sister.

～

The next two hours were like watching sands in an hourglass.

Interesting for about two seconds and then boring as hell.

Ellie called a restaurateur, a bartender, and a waitress, all of whom had worked at one of Archer's restaurants. They all testified that he was a great boss and treated everyone fairly.

Like Will McNair before her, Ellie had specifically called the same type of witnesses for one day. In this case, character witnesses. A.J., Grace, and three others all testified to how good of a man Archer Keats was.

Mercifully, at a few minutes after four, Judge Kilgore called it a day. Or, in this case, a weekend.

I was happy to have the first week in the books.

What had generally been a repetitive week had been turned on its head by Kirk Stroud. Luckily, we started playing offense next week, today merely being a warmup.

Dr. Dickie Faber. Jan Goddard. Brad Lacoste.

All three were on the docket for Monday.

Things were about to ratchet up a little bit.

We had a meeting at Ellie's firm on Friday night, where we covered many of the same bases that we always did.

I could tell everyone was disappointed in Grace's testimony. She looked like she wanted to bury herself in a hole. I wanted to know what went down, but Ellie didn't focus on her testimony for long. Probably for the best. I could tell she wasn't taking it well.

Friday night, I went out with Tre and had a few drinks. I told him the trial was off-limits and he understood. We had a nice time, but I called it early. I didn't want to feel the after-effects the following morning, even if I had nothing to do on that Saturday.

Saturday came and went without even a call from Ellie.

I called Lancaster Construction a few times, but the secretary refused to talk to me once I mentioned Kirk Stroud.

I read the police report again, just to feel I was being productive.

I went to sleep at nine p.m. on Saturday. This weekend was moving slowly as hell.

Monday couldn't come fast enough.

CHAPTER 28

I woke up early on Sunday morning.

Instead of using my Keurig or French Press, I decided to go out and grab a coffee. I walked the quarter-mile to Tellus, my favorite local coffee shop, and ordered my usual order, a half-caff Americano.

Everyone always asked me why I ordered half-caffs and I explained to them with the amount of coffee I drank, I'd be bouncing off the walls if I was always fully caffeinated. People seemed to enjoy my explanation, imagining me amped on caffeine.

I was dressed in flip-flops, shorts, and a t-shirt and got a few curious looks. Sure, it was March now, but it was still pretty cold early in the morning. People must have thought I was crazy.

Maybe I was rebelling from having to wear nice clothes to court for the last week. I'd always preferred dressing casually, anyway. Give me flip-flops over a suit any day of the week.

I had half of my coffee at Tellus, said hello to some of the regulars I'd come to know, and then headed back towards my place. A breeze quickly kicked up and gosh darn it, those people were right. I was cold.

I arrived back at my apartment and after finishing the coffee, decided to make myself a scramble. On this day it was eggs, three types of cheeses - Cheddar, Jack, and Goat - sausage, and a green pepper. It would serve as both the color and the vegetable.

As I finished making the scramble and scooped it onto my plate, the phone rang.

Nice freaking timing!

I had planned on letting it go straight to voicemail, but then I saw it was Ellie.

"Hello?"

"Are you sitting down, Quint?"

It was quickly apparent this was something serious.

"Just tell me what it is, Ellie. Did they find something incriminating against Archer?"

"Not exactly. What they found was the body of Jan Goddard."

"What?"

"She was murdered."

My heart sunk.

"Holy shit. How terrible."

"It sure is."

"Who killed her?"

"The police have no idea."

I hoped with all my heart that it had nothing to do with this case. It was me who'd brought her in, and I'd share at least some of the blame.

"What can you tell me about it?"

"You're not going to like it."

"Just tell me, Ellie!" I snapped.

"She was stabbed multiple times. And the knife was left there, protruding from her heart."

At that point, I did go and sit down. I thought I might lose my balance if not. I was flooded with so many emotions, none of them good.

"Who found her?" I asked.

"I guess she was supposed to meet a friend yesterday morning. And she never showed. They did a welfare check late last night and found her. They think she was killed Friday night."

"I don't know what to say. This is fucking horrible."

"It's a tragedy, no doubt. Now, Quint, can I say something and you won't get pissed off?"

"I can't promise that, but go ahead."

"Archer has an ankle bracelet tracking his every move. He has been at his house all weekend. He didn't kill Jan Goddard."

The implications were massive.

"What does this mean exactly?"

"I'm not sure yet. I guess, hypothetically, Judge Kilgore could toss the case, but I don't think she will. She'll wait to see what happens with Jan Goddard's murder investigation."

"Will they postpone the trial?"

"My guess is they'll ask for a delay. Maybe a few days. Maybe a week. Who knows? I guess we'll find out tomorrow morning."

"Everyone knew she was testifying tomorrow, right?"

"Everyone involved with the defense and everyone involved with the prosecution."

"Have you talked to the police?'

"Yes."

"And did you tell them about…"

Ellie interrupted me.

"Yes, I told them about Dr. Faber."

"And?"

"And I imagine they are paying him a visit right now."

"This is freaking crazy."

"Yeah, it is."

"Jan Goddard was a very nice woman. Damaged, but sweet. I feel heartbroken."

"She was a sweet woman. Remember, I'd met with her two times to prep her as a witness. I feel as bad as you, Quint."

"I brought her into this case."

"You never could have known this was going to happen. Don't beat yourself up over this."

"That doesn't mean I won't."

She didn't respond, knowing I had to deal with it on my own terms.

"Do you think Dickie Faber could have done this?" I asked.

"He had the most to lose by her testimony."

"Unquestionably."

"Will you allow me to make a leap?" Ellie asked.

"Sure."

"If Dickie Faber did kill Gracie Keats because she was going to expose their relationship and he'd lose his license to practice psychiatry, would he have any reservations about killing Jan Goddard for the same reason?"

What Ellie said made perfect sense.

"No."

"I agree," she said unnecessarily. She'd brought it up, after all.

"Does Archer know?" I asked.

"Yeah. I called him right before you."

"What does he think?"

"He knows it's good for him personally, but he's not going to celebrate a woman's death."

"Yeah," I said, having nothing to add.

"Listen, Quint. I have a few other people I have to tell. Can we talk later?"

"Of course. Thanks for calling, Ellie."

"I'll be in touch."

I laid the phone down and my thoughts turned to Jan Goddard.

~

Two hours later, Ellie called back.

"Any news?" I asked.

"If I hadn't said it last time, I'd tell you to sit down again."

"Just tell me."

"The police went to Dickie Faber's house. He wasn't there. They tried his cell phone. It went straight to voicemail."

"Jesus."

"Exactly. Do you think this is some odd coincidence and Faber just happens to have his phone off until eleven in the morning?"

"No, I don't."

"You know what that means, right?" Ellie asked.

"Dickie Faber is on the run?"

"Exactly."

"This is fucking nuts," I said.

"Right again."

"I'm guessing there's going to be a little more media at the courthouse tomorrow."

"I'd say that's a fair assumption."

"I don't know what else to say. I guess I'll just see you tomorrow."

"See you then, Quint."

~

I threw on the news at five p.m. that night.

The lead story was the death of Jan Goddard. They mentioned that she'd been stabbed through the heart and had been scheduled to testify on Monday in the Archer Keats murder trial.

What had already been a well-covered trial was now going to the next level.

CHAPTER 29

Yes, I'd been expecting quite a bit more media on Monday morning. Nothing could have prepared me for the onslaught that greeted me.

When I exited the parking garage, there were dozens of media members live on the air. Literally, dozens. This went on for at least a quarter-mile, leading up to the entrance of the courthouse.

As I walked that stretch, I also noticed news vans from CNN, Fox, and Court TV. Just as I was fearful of. The case had gone national.

If there was even a case anymore.

It was impossible to know what Judge Kilgore was going to rule.

On one hand, it looked as if whoever had killed Gracie had struck again. On the other hand, the prosecution's last witness had testified that Archer tried to hire him to murder his wife.

As I finally bypassed all of the media members and entered the courthouse, I knew I'd find out soon.

I approached Department 22 and there was no way everyone was going to get in. The crowd was twice as big as it had been the previous week. I saw Ellie near the front and approached her. She was standing with Archer and Cliff.

I nodded at them.

"Good thing you're on time, Quint," she said. "The bailiffs aren't going to be able to let everyone in."

"Where are the kids? And Gene Bowman?"

"They just texted me and are headed here now."

"Do you have any idea what's going to happen today?"

"Nothing I'd put money on."

"How are you holding up, Archer?" I asked.

"I'm numb to the whole thing. These last two days have been a roller coaster."

I felt for the man. Each day that passed, I thought it less likely he'd killed his wife.

The Kirk Stroud testimony was obviously a problem, but something stank about him as a witness. Would Archer just randomly approach a construction worker who'd worked at his house a year earlier? It seemed unlikely. Still, the testimony was on record. Without it, I think Judge Kilgore would likely have called a mistrial at this point.

Three minutes later, A.J., Grace, and Gene all arrived together.

Five minutes after that, the doors to Department 22 opened.

We were right near the entrance and were among the first people to get in. I was curious to see what the bailiffs did once it filled up.

Within two minutes of opening the doors, the courtroom was full and the bailiffs started to push people back into the hallway. People were shouting that they'd been there the whole trial. The bailiffs didn't care and continued pushing them back. It was wild.

What made this even odder was that there was going to be no testimony today. They'd all come for what was likely a minute or two of the judge talking.

The massive bailiff who'd been here since day one yelled from near the front of the courtroom.

"Ladies and Gentlemen, please stand for the Honorable Vicky Kilgore."

Vicky Kilgore walked in and took her seat on the "bench." Chair. Seat. Throne. Bench. I didn't know what to call it.

The audience fell silent. Everyone was on pins and needles. I imagine Archer Keats felt it more than anyone.

"As I'm sure all of you know by now, Jan Goddard, a defense witness who was scheduled to testify today, was murdered on Friday night. She was stabbed several times and the knife was left protruding through her heart."

I was expecting gasps and moans, but everyone stayed quiet. They were transfixed by the words of Judge Kilgore.

"Obviously, this leaves me in an extremely difficult position. The defense would surely argue that we should toss the case. That this murder, which was not committed by Archer Keats, proves that he didn't kill his wife and the real murderer is still out there. And still at it.

The prosecution would rightfully point out that only four days ago, they had a witness testify that Mr. Keats tried to pay him to murder his wife. And they'd argue that throwing the case out would be a miscarriage of justice.

This may come as a surprise for those who know me, but I can see both sides. And I sympathize with both Ms. Teague and Mr. McNair.

I've thought long and hard about this and here's what I've come up with."

You honestly could have heard a pin drop.

"I'm going to temporarily pause the State of California versus Archer Keats. We can't move forward when one of the defense witnesses was just murdered in the same exact manner as Gracie Keats. There are too many questions to be answered. Now, if we find out that her death is somehow unrelated, then we will resume the trial. If, on the other hand, they arrest someone who also had reason to kill Gracie Keats, I will consider dropping the case entirely. We are at a standstill for the moment."

Still complete silence from the crowd.

"So, I'm putting this trial on a one-week hiatus. We will meet back here at 9:00 a.m. next Monday and I'll reassess. Ms. Teague, make sure to have your witnesses ready to testify. If I decide to restart the trial, I don't want you unprepared and making excuses. Is that understood?"

"Yes, your honor," Ellie said.

"That goes for you as well, Mr. McNair. Is that understood?"

"Yes, your honor."

"The last thing I'd like to say is to the jury."

Judge Kilgore turned to her left to face the jury.

"When you were assigned to this case, you agreed not to talk to anyone else about this trial. That's especially important in a case that has caught the public eye. And now, with the death of Ms. Goddard, there's only going to be more media coverage. So I implore you, please don't talk to anyone else about this case. That includes this coming week while we're on a hiatus. Is that understood?"

A few nods and a few audible "Yeses" were heard.

"I don't have much more to say," Judge Kilgore said. "This is new to me as well. I think I'm being as fair to both the defense and prosecution as I can be. With that, I'll see you next Monday, and court is dismissed."

She banged her gavel.

There was no mad rush to leave the courtroom. People remained for over a minute. You could tell they wanted more.

If you thought of it in a carnal sense, there'd been so much foreplay leading up to this morning, and then the judge spoke for two minutes and it was over. People felt let down. Unsatisfied.

Finally, a few bailiffs started telling people they had to go. Being near the defense table had always given us a few extra minutes, so I knew we had time.

Ellie turned around and faced us.

"Is this good news?" A.J. asked.

"I'd have preferred a mistrial," Ellie said. "This isn't bad, though. If whoever killed Ms. Goddard is caught, there's a very good chance the charges will be dropped. Especially if it's Dickie Faber."

"What if they don't catch the killer?" Grace asked.

"Well, you heard Judge Kilgore. We'll be meeting here next Monday."

"Ellie, what do you think the judge will do if no one was arrested in Jan's death?" I asked.

I was still referring to Jan by her first name. I felt tremendous guilt for bringing her into the case, despite Ellie's telling me it wasn't my fault.

"I fear that the judge will decide to reconvene the case."

"How can she?"

"She can because of the Kirk Stroud testimony. That was a game-changer."

Ellie turned to me.

"Quint, I'd like you to go rogue for the rest of this week. You don't need to come to our usual meetings. What I'd like is for you to show off those P.I. skills in regard to Goddard's murder and finding more about Kirk Stroud. See what you can dig up. You've got a week."

I actually liked the sound of that. While I'd enjoyed parts of the trial, it wasn't what I'd signed up for in being a P.I. Getting back out there and doing some investigating just felt right.

"I'm up for that," I said.

"Great," Ellie said. "If you learn something, let us know. Besides that, you're on your own."

"Got it."

No one spoke for ten seconds.

And then Ellie smiled.

"Well, what are you waiting for? Get to it!"

I headed toward the exit of the courthouse, knowing I wouldn't be back for six days.

If at all.

PART THREE: THE PERFECT MURDER (S)

CHAPTER 30

W ord travels fast these days, there's no doubt about that.
So when I walked out of the courtroom and some news anchors were already reading Judge Kilgore's statement word for word, I shouldn't have been surprised.

I wasn't going to miss the hoopla outside of the courtroom. Especially because it was only going to get worse if the trial had continued.

I arrived at my car without anyone recognizing me and headed home.

Technically, I was supposed to be looking into Kirk Stroud and learning more about Jan's death, but I spent that morning on my couch, watching the local news. And then the national news. Sure enough, it was the lead story on every news station in the country.

It probably said something about the media that I wanted nothing to do with them when I was walking out of the courthouse, but now that I was in the comfort of my own place, I couldn't get enough of it.

Or, maybe it said more about me.

The captions on the bottom of the news stations were fascinating.

A few of them read:

"Is Archer Keats actually innocent?"

"Who is Dr. Dickie Faber?"

"Where is Dr. Dickie Faber?"

"Who was Jan Goddard?"

And the cheesiest of all:
"Is there a Dickie on the run?"

~

Reports were that Jan Goddard was stabbed upwards of ten times. For around the fourth time in twenty-four hours, I bowed my head and said a slight prayer for her. I wasn't a very religious guy, but I didn't know what else to do in times of tragedy, so I'd often default to praying.

Although it was getting more unlikely by the minute, I was still holding out hope her death was not related to the Archer Keats case.

I was in an odd position. If Dickie Faber had indeed killed her, then he'd almost assuredly killed Gracie Keats as well. And if that were the case, Archer would go free.

That would be a good thing for me and the reason I was hired. To get Archer acquitted. Or in this potential scenario, the case gets dropped.

However, if Dickie did kill Jan Goddard, that meant Jan was dead because I reached out to her.

I'd have regrets for years to come.

But, Archer would be free.

I didn't know what to think.

~

I called Lancaster Construction and tried to get an answer regarding Kirk Stroud. Nothing worked. Like each time I'd tried it, the secretaries or employees gave me the stiff arm.

I know Ellie and Cliff had been all excited about me going rogue, but I wasn't sure there was all that much I could do.

Monday turned into a wasted day. Unless you count watching the news for hours upon hours as a win.

On the eight o'clock news, they announced that Dickie Faber still hadn't been found and the police had put out an APB on him.

One news anchor said, "Dr. Dickie Faber is now wanted by the Pleasant Hill police for the murder of Jan Goddard. Will it be long until the Walnut Creek police want to question him about the murder of Gracie Keats?"

It was amazing how much things had changed.

~

I woke up Tuesday morning and headed toward my office.

I ordered an Americano at the neighboring Starbucks and took a sip as I opened my office door.

The answering machine had a bright red light flashing. It was so rare that I received a message, the flashing light kind of shocked me. I set my coffee down and pressed the button.

"If you want to know the truth about Jan Goddard's murder, meet me at Walden Park in Walnut Creek at two p.m. today. If I see any signs of even a single police officer, you'll never see me again."

And with that, the message ended.

I was floored. Who the hell was that?

My first guess was Dickie Faber. I'd only talked to him for a minute or so, but the voice resembled his. Could I be sure? No.

I didn't know who else it might be.

Unless proved otherwise, I was going to assume it was Dickie Faber.

Do I call the police? He was now a person of interest, so it was understandable if that's the route I took.

If I see any signs of a police officer, you'll never see me again.

I believed the voice when it said that.

I had to ask myself if I was at risk. I didn't think so.

Sure, there was a chance that Dickie Faber - if that's who this was - had killed two people. However, Walden Park was a big, open set of land with bike paths and kids' jungle gyms. It's not where you'd invite someone to commit a murder. Especially not at two p.m.

Maybe I was a maniac, but I wasn't going to call the cops.

I would be at Walden Park.

I considered calling Ellie or someone non-police-related. I even pondered calling my old friend Paddy Roark, who was a guy you wanted on your side when shit went down.

In the end, I decided to go alone.

I'd returned to my place and at 1:50, I started the five-minute drive to Walden Park.

Without a gun - it wasn't easy for Bay Area P.I.'s to get one - I parked my car and headed towards Walden Park.

Most people would have thought I was crazy.

And maybe I was.

I'd entered from the west end. There was a basketball court and a children's playground on this side. There were also more people and it seemed a much safer place to meet.

I scanned some of the faces as I entered Walden Park. None registered. I knew Dickie Faber's face, but if it was someone else, I didn't know what to expect. I'd probably have to wait until he approached me.

I continued to walk slowly, but after a few minutes, I passed the playground and was walking on a concrete path towards the other side of the park. There were a few couples lying on the grass and looking up at the sun, but nothing caught my attention.

Another minute passed as I meandered down the path, moving at turtle-like speed.

It was then that I saw a man, standing by himself, in the far-right corner of the park.

I couldn't make out the face from this far away, but I had a sneaking suspicion I was looking at Dickie Faber.

I could have picked up my phone at that point and called 9-1-1, but I wasn't going to. He'd trusted me enough to call. I was going to trust him enough to listen.

That didn't mean I'd forgotten what he'd done to Jan Goddard.

And I was only talking about her as a client.

If he'd actually murdered her, I wanted to tear him from limb to limb.

The man looked in my direction but didn't take a step. It was going to be my obligation to get to him. I picked up the pace, leaving the turtle behind. I exited the concrete path and started on the grass towards him.

Two minutes later, I was fifty yards from the man. And I'd been right. It was Dickie Faber.

He had strategically placed himself in the far corner, and the closest people were a hundred yards away. We could talk in peace.

Dickie was wearing jeans, a dark-colored jacket, and an Irish tweed hat.

When I got within twenty feet, he spoke.

"Thank you for coming," he said.

I didn't answer. I wasn't going to say "you're welcome" to a potential murderer.

"First off, let me get this out of the way," he said. "I didn't kill either Jan Goddard or Gracie Keats."

"Then why don't you turn yourself in?"

"I'm not an idiot. I know the whole world has already convicted me of Jan's murder."

"If you didn't kill her, then who did?"

"We'll get to that."

He'd said as much on the phone, but it still surprised me when I heard it.

Did he know who killed Jan? Or was he bluffing?

We were a good five to six feet from each other, but I was still on guard, despite his profession of innocence. What else was he going to say?

"Do me a favor?" I asked. "Lift your jacket up. Show me there is no knife under there. Or a gun."

He did as I asked.

"And open up your pant pockets."

He could have hypothetically had a small gun or knife in them.

There was nothing. Only a pair of keys.

"No wallet or cell phone?"

"Wallet is in my back pocket. Not risking the cops tracing my cell."

"Turn around, please."

He did so quickly and I could see the wallet, but there was nothing else. Dickie Faber wasn't armed.

"I don't have a weapon on me," he said.

"I believe you. Now, you said you know who killed Jan Goddard?"

"I said we'll get there."

"Then start at the beginning," I said.

"Alright."

He glanced over both of my shoulders to make sure no one was coming. When he felt safe, he continued.

"I admit to having affairs with Gracie Keats and Jan Goddard. I didn't kill either one of them, though. Not that you'll believe me, but I'd swear on fifty Bibles if you had them here. I met Jan about four years ago and I behaved abhorrently. I used my dominance to seduce her. And I've regretted it ever since. Gracie was different. She actually liked me and initiated our romance.

When things ended poorly with Jan, I was always expecting a knock on my door. Either the police or someone from a medical board telling me my license had been pulled. Somehow, it never came.

I vowed not to treat another client like I'd treated Jan. And I didn't. Once again, you probably won't believe me, but it's true.

Fast forward a few years and Gracie came along. I liked her from the start. She was long-legged and beautiful. She'd tell me about her problems with her husband. And it made me look like the good guy because I'd just sit there and listen. I think that's part of the reason she fell for me. We know it's not my looks."

I wanted to interrupt and ask a few questions, but he was giving away so much information, I thought better of it.

"I think it was about our fifth session when Gracie came over and grabbed my shoulders. The opposite of how it happened with Jan, where I instigated it. Gracie and I had sex right there in my office. At this point, I knew who Archer Keats was. He was an important guy and everyone around town knew him, so meeting up with Gracie in public wasn't advisable. Even getting a crappy little motel had its own risks. So we continued having sex at my office. And it wasn't always during our sessions. Sometimes she'd come over when I had a break between clients."

"The thing I was going to say when I testified - the thing that defense attorney didn't seem to consider - was that Gracie and I never stopped sleeping with each other. We didn't have some bad parting of ways. We were still friendly when she died. And still having sex. I had no reason to kill her. Let me ask you a question. Was Archer's attorney going to paint me as a scorned lover?"

I felt like telling the truth was advantageous. It would make him more likely to do the same.

"Partly," I said. "But she was also going to say you were afraid you'd lose your medical license if she went public with the affair."

"As I said, we hadn't stopped having sex. I was never in fear of losing my job with regard to Gracie. Jan was different. She probably could have argued that I'd coerced her into it. Gracie never could have said that with a straight face."

"When was the last time you slept with Gracie?"

"About five days before she was murdered."

Everything in me wanted to hate Dickie Faber.

But I had to admit it, I believed he was telling me the truth.

And that meant the killer was still out there.

"Did Gracie tell you she was getting a divorce?"

"Yes."

"Was it to be with you?"

"No, I don't think so. We might have continued having sex for a while, but I'm sure she would have traded me in at some point."

"Do you know who Brad Lacoste is?"

"No, I don't. Who is that?"

My intuition told me to keep telling the truth.

"Gracie was having an affair with him too."

He looked hurt, but not crushed.

"I guess I should have expected that. If she could cheat on Archer, she could certainly cheat on me."

"You said Gracie told you she was getting a divorce. Do you know if she had told Archer?"

I believed Archer when he said Gracie never told him she wanted a divorce. My opinion of Archer's guilt or innocence hinged a lot on Dickie's response.

"Gracie told me she was going to tell Archer and the kids, but I don't know if she ever did."

That was hardly conclusive.

"Describe the last time you saw her?"

"As I said, it was about five days before she was murdered. We had sex. We usually saw each other around twice a week, but remember, she was killed right before Christmas. We agreed it was too risky around the holidays, so that's why we weren't seeing each other until after Christmas. And by then, it was too late.."

"Why didn't you go public with your affair after she was killed?"

"Why? To get shamed publicly for something that was consensual? To potentially become a suspect in something I had nothing to do with? Give me one good reason."

I struggled to think of any.

"So it wouldn't have come to this," I finally said.

He didn't really have an answer to that.

"Shall we get to the crux of why I invited you here?"

"In a second. First, I want to know, why me?"

"When you confronted me at my office, I did a little research. You've got quite the résumé. I was impressed."

I nodded.

"And again and again, people said that you had morals. And a back-bone. So, I was willing to brush aside our first meeting as you merely trying to find out information in the Gracie Keats murder."

"That's all I've been trying to do."

"I believe you. Now listen, if I could go to the cops, I would, but I'm afraid they'd just arrest me. So I'm stuck with you. And I'm hoping you won't do me wrong."

"If you turned yourself in right after hearing of Jan's death you wouldn't have been arrested. You might have been a suspect, but if you didn't do it, they would have had no reason to hold you."

"That's where you're wrong."

He stared at me. His diminutive stature and haphazard goatee made him so odd-looking. I didn't know what Gracie Keats saw in him. I imagine it went well beyond looks. As Dickie had said, maybe just sitting and listening to Gracie did the trick.

I told myself to focus. He was ready to drop something important.

"Please tell me why I'm wrong," I said.

"I got a call on Saturday morning around seven a.m. On my main phone. I'm paraphrasing, but the voice said something like this: *'Jan Goddard is dead. She was stabbed through the heart. Just like Gracie Keats, who you were having an affair with also. You will naturally be the #1 suspect. And just to make sure they come knocking at your door, I left some of your DNA at the crime scene. How did I do that? I broke into your house with a piece of flypaper and rubbed it all over your doorknob, refrigerator door handle, and your bedroom door handle. Then I rubbed the flypaper all over Ms. Goddard's body. And her door. They are coming for you. And it will be an open and shut case. This phone will be turned off forever. Don't call back. You have one chance and that is to flee. They probably won't find her body for at least twenty-four hours, so now is your chance. It's that or be on trial for murder. With your DNA at the scene.'* And then the caller hung up."

I was speechless. If this were true - and I tended to think it was - it threw this case for the biggest loop imaginable.

The killer was still out there and he was a true sociopath.

I had a million questions and didn't know where to start.

"Did you recognize the voice?"

"No," Dickie Faber said. "And I think he was talking through a cloth or something. It was hard to make out exactly."

"Was it a male?"

"Yeah, I'm pretty darn sure."

"Did you think about calling the cops after the phone call?"

"With my DNA on Jan Goddard? No thanks."

"So what did you do next?"

"I grabbed some cash I keep at the house and left. I checked into a seedy hotel in Antioch under a fake name. Paid with cash. And I've been wondering what to do ever since. At some point, I remembered you. And hoped I could trust you to meet with me and hear me out, while not calling the cops."

"Well, I've held up to that end of the bargain."

"Thank you."

"You're welcome," I said, marking the first time I'd responded to one of his pleasantries.

"So, I ask you, Quint. Are you ready to find out who called me? I saw on the news that the trial is suspended for a week. So you have the time. And if you help me out, you'll be chasing the real killer. Not confronting some psychiatrist outside of his office."

I ignored that last dig.

"Are you safe at the motel you're staying at?"

"I think so."

"Is your car on the premises?"

"I parked it a few blocks down."

"Then you're not safe. They are probably looking for your license plate."

"How will I get around?"

"You won't. Not until you allow me to do my thing."

"I'm listening."

I was about to take a huge leap into the abyss.

"Did you drive here today?"

"Yes."

"You'll leave your car here. I'll drive you to your hotel. On the way, I will pick up a burner phone for you. If you still have your own phone, power it down right now."

"I already told you I'm not carrying it. I'm not that dumb."

What I said next was shocked even myself.

"Here's what's going to happen. I'm going to set up a meeting with the people I've been working with. That includes Archer, his son A.J., Gene Bowman, and an older attorney named Cliff. Also Ellie and Grace. I'll subtly record our conversation and then send it to you. Let me know if you recognize the voice that called you."

"You're brilliant."

"I'm a turncoat to the people I'm working with."

"No, you're not. I hate to ask, but why are you doing this for me?"

"Because I believe you. And more than anything else - even loyalty - I care about the truth."

"Thank you, Quint. I have hope for the first time since Saturday morning."

"Let's get out of here. Keep your head down when I'm driving. We don't need some hero spotting you in my car. Your face has been all over the news."

"I know. Thank you so much for this."

"Let's go," I said.

I went to a small-time cell phone store and picked up a burner phone.

I pre-paid for the minutes.

I was afraid to know how many people picked up burner phones for less than savory reasons.

As I dropped off Dickie Faber at his motel, I thought of something.

"What's your house phone number?" I asked.

"925-555-0702."

"I'll be in touch."

CHAPTER 31

I arrived back to my apartment, dread and excitement running through my body in equal measures.

I first called Ellie and asked to be part of their next meeting. She said they were meeting the following morning at her office at ten a.m. I said I'd be there.

Next, I called an old friend. Paddy Roark.

I'd met him and his boss, the legendary San Francisco bookie Dennis McCarthy, when I was investigating my father's murder. We'd remained friends to this day.

"Hello?"

"Paddy, this is Quint."

"Quint, how the fuck are you?"

"I'm good. Got myself embroiled in something once again."

"I'd expect nothing less. What is it?"

"Have you been following the Archer Keats murder case?"

"I sure have. You're involved in that?"

"Yeah, The defense hired me as their P.I."

"Looks like you're on the winning team. No way that judge reconvenes that trial with another woman killed in the same way."

"We'll see," I said, not wanting to give away too much.

"I know this isn't a courtesy call, so what can I do for you, Quint?"

"Do you still have friends who work for the phone company?"

"Oh, no. You need a favor?"

"I do."

"Shocker. Yes, we've still got friends at the phone company. We've got friends everywhere. What do you need?"

"I need to find out the phone number that called 925-555-0702 on Saturday around seven a.m."

"Is that 925 number a cell phone?"

"If it was a cell phone, they would have seen the number."

"Not so fast, smart guy. I know people who can block their number from being seen."

As usual, Paddy knew more about this type of thing than I did.

"I stand corrected," I said. "It was a house phone anyway."

"Alright. Those are generally tougher to track, but I'll put someone on it. My guess is twenty-four to forty-eight hours."

"Thanks so much, Paddy. I'd like to see you and Dennis when this ends."

"Are you in trouble?" he asked.

"When am I not?"

"Stay safe, Quint."

"I'll do my best."

~

Wednesday's meeting at Ellie's office began at ten a.m. sharp.

It was the usual suspects: Ellie, Archer, A.J., Grace, Gene, Cliff, and me.

"Let's start with you, Quint. What have you learned?"

For the most obvious of reasons, I wouldn't be mentioning my meeting with Dickie Faber. While I thought of what to say, I pressed record on my phone, while subtly setting it on my thigh below the conference room table. If the phone somehow fell off my thigh and crashed to the floor, I'd just pretend it had fallen out of my pocket.

"Not a whole lot," I said. "I'm getting stonewalled by everyone who works for Lancaster Construction. It's not just the employees who are refusing to talk to me, but secretaries and people from corporate too. It's from on high. I can tell they've been given an ultimatum not to talk about it."

"How about the murder of Jan Goddard?"

"I know they are looking for Dickie Faber," I said.

And I know where he's staying!

"Any luck from the cops on that front?" Ellie asked.

"No. As you all know, he was gone when they raided his house Sunday. They are trying to ping his cell phone and look for his car, which was not at his home. No luck on the phone or the car yet."

I was now making half-assed assumptions mixed with things I'd heard on the news. I must have really believed Dickie Faber because I had fallen off the deep end.

"Are the police convinced it's the same killer as Gracie's?" Gene Bowman asked.

"Yeah, I think so. Which means, if they catch Jan's killer, the charges against Archer would have to be dropped."

I was just repeating what Ellie and I had talked about. I must have been nervous.

Archer gave me a slight head nod when I'd mentioned the charges being dropped. The confident man I'd met the first time was no longer with us. Who could blame him? The ups and downs of this case were maddening. And it was his life on the line, not ours.

"That's what we're hoping for," Grace said.

A.J. nodded.

"Are you guys still staying at your father's?" I asked.

"Yeah. In the guest house," he said.

"Good. I think it's important you guys are there for him. I don't have to tell you guys, but this is a crucial five days or so."

"We're not going anywhere," A.J. said.

I nodded in her direction.

"I have a question, Ellie," Grace asked.

"Shoot."

"What happens if they don't catch Dickie Faber this week? What will the judge do?"

"That's the million-dollar question, Grace. And I don't have an answer. Cliff, you got a guess?"

"In my forty-five years as a lawyer, I think it would be one of the tougher decisions a judge has ever had to make. I truly don't know what Vicky Kilgore would do. If I had to harbor a guess, she would either push it back one more week or rule it a mistrial."

"What would that mean for my father?" Grace asked.

"It means they could try him again down the road, but if they caught Ms. Goddard's killer, they never would. A mistrial would be a good result for Archer."

"Can they just rule him not guilty and never be able to try him again?" A.J. asked.

"You can't do that unless this goes to the jury. And considering Ellie and I aren't even close to finishing our defense, that's an impossibility."

"The law is complicated."

"Not always, but it sure is in this case."

Like Archer, Gene Bowman had been a commanding presence when

I'd first met him. He'd also become quieter and quieter as the trial had moved along.

Maybe he sensed that himself because he asked the next question.

"What if by some miracle, Judge Kilgore decided to proceed with the trial?"

Ellie took this one.

"I've thought a lot about it. It would be like nothing I've ever come across. I'd want to call Dickie Faber and we all know that's impossible at the moment. Jan Goddard was going to be one of my star witnesses and that's sadly also impossible. So I just don't know."

I jumped in.

"How about calling a Pleasant Hill homicide detective and he can testify that they suspect Dickie Faber of murdering Jan Goddard. And maybe you could get a Walnut Creek homicide detective who will admit they are now looking at Faber for the Gracie Keats murder as well."

"Brilliant," Cliff said.

It was the second time I'd been called brilliant in two days. Once, by Dickie Faber. And the second time, when I just suggested hanging Dickie Faber out to dry. This case was all sorts of crazy.

Archer spoke next.

"Is there anything we can do while we wait?"

"Not much," Ellie said. "But don't think of that as a bad thing. We are in an appreciably better position than we were after Kirk Stroud spoke last week."

"That lying jerk," Archer said. "I wonder who got to him?"

Was it the same guy who called Dickie Faber? I think that was pretty likely.

Assuming Kirk Stroud had perjured himself on the stand.

As I sat there waiting for someone to answer, I realized there was a conundrum.

If someone got Kirk Stroud to lie under oath, it was to make Archer look guilty.

Whoever killed Jan Goddard and told Dickie Faber to flee were making Archer look innocent.

They couldn't be the same person, could they? Were there conflicting forces competing against each other?

I had no answer.

Finally, Ellie answered Archer's question.

"I have no idea who got to Kirk Stroud. But I know our P.I. hasn't given up hope."

That snapped me out of it.

"I'll keep trying," I said, although my emphasis was now on what I'd learned from Dickie Faber.

I hoped my phone was recording all of this.

"If there's nothing else, I think we can end this meeting," Ellie said. "We'll have another one tomorrow. Monday will be here before we know it."

As people stood up to go, I leaned down and pressed the right button on my cell phone, knowing that would stop the recording. I cautiously grabbed my phone and set it in my jeans.

Mission accomplished. No one was any the wiser.

I drove home and started editing down the conversation.

Dickie Faber didn't need to listen to the whole thing. What he did need was to hear everyone's voice at least once. And that included Ellie and Grace. I know that Dickie had said it was a male voice, but I wasn't ruling out a woman. Not just yet.

Once I finished, I sent it to the burner phone I'd bought him the day before.

And then I waited for his response. Or Paddy Roark's.

As I expected, I heard from Dickie Faber first.

He couldn't positively ID anyone from the recording. He reiterated that he thinks they were using a sock, or a towel, or something else to obscure their voice when they called him.

Was it time to go confront Brad Lacoste again and get his voice on tape?

Who else?

Parker and Caleb Johnson?

Vic Parsons?

Yes, I was kidding about that, but where did my list of suspects end?

I decided to wait until I heard back from Paddy Roark.

Most of Wednesday passed and I hadn't heard back from Paddy.

If he wasn't able to get the number, I couldn't decide on my next course of action.

Even if I got the number, what was I going to do?

Have someone call the number at the next meeting and see if someone picks up their phone?

Not the worst idea, but I figured that phone was either at the bottom of a river or sitting in someone's sock drawer, never to be turned on again.

Maybe, just maybe, Paddy would come up with a name as well.

Finally, at ten minutes to ten, he called me.

He was one of the few people who still preferred talking on the phone. The reason was obvious. Texts leave a trail. No one knows what you discussed on the phone.

"Hey, Paddy."

"Got some good news and some bad news, Quint."

"Hit me with the bad news first."

"It was a burner phone. We have no idea who it's registered to."

"And the good news?"

"I got you a number."

"Hit me."

"925-555-3825."

"You're the best, Paddy. What can I do for you?"

"Get out of this in one piece."

"Don't I always?"

"You have so far, but luck runs out on everyone."

"Even Irish leprechauns like yourself?"

"Don't make me come over to the East Bay and kick your ass."

I laughed.

"Thanks so much, Paddy. I'll come to see you after this is over."

"Take care of yourself, Quint. I mean it."

CHAPTER 32

I woke up on Thursday morning and the first thing I thought of was Ellie telling me to go rogue this week.

She never could have guessed just how rogue I'd be going.

I took a twenty-minute shower. Most of the time was spent debating my next course of action as water spilled down my face.

No great idea sprang to mind.

I stepped out of the shower, toweled myself off, threw on some deodorant, dressed, and took a seat on the couch.

I decided to find a payphone - if they still existed - and call the phone number myself. In all likelihood, it was turned off, but just in case someone answered, I didn't want my phone number appearing on the screen.

I'd had burner phones on previous cases, but none at the moment. I told myself to grab another one sometime soon. They did come in handy now and then.

As I was about to leave my apartment, a better idea sprang to mind.

"Hello?"

"Paddy, this is Quint again."

"You can't get enough of me."

"Very funny. Can you do me another favor? It's a small one this time."

"How small?"

"Can you use one of your burner phones to call that number I had you find? I just want to make sure it's disconnected."

"Sure. I'll call you back in a minute."

He actually called me back in less than that.

"That was quick."

"Straight to voicemail. No welcoming message," Paddy said. "But on the bright side, it wasn't disconnected."

That was good news. The phone was still out there.

"Thanks, Paddy."

"Let me guess. I'll bet you're going to go on a wild-goose chase to find that phone?"

"You know me too well."

"I might as well sign off like I always do. Take care of yourself, Quint."

Now all I needed to do was break into every possible suspect's house and search for the mysterious phone.

Easy as pie.

Maybe I could accumulate a few breaking and entering charges in the process.

Maybe a possession of stolen property charge.

No, thanks. I wouldn't be breaking into any houses.

I tried to think of another way.

It wasn't hard getting everyone from Archer's defense team together. The problem was whoever was in possession of the phone wasn't going to bring it to a meeting.

And that was just for the people on our defense team.

What about any other potential suspect?

Did I have to think up a different plan for each one?

I racked my brain. Nothing.

Just as I was about to focus on something else, I looked outside of my apartment. It was a beautiful day and the sun was shining. It was the March that was headed towards spring, not the March still hanging on to the winter that was February.

And the weather is what led to my crazy idea.

I dialed Ellie's number.

"Hey, Quint."

"What time is today's meeting?"

"Not till two."

"Let's do it at Archer's. I was just out walking around and it's a beautiful day."

"It's tempting."

"C'mon. All we do is go from the courthouse to your law firm. We're always inside. Maybe the sun will lift our spirits a little bit."

"Alright, you sold me. I'll call Archer. I'm sure he'll have no problem with it."

"Great. I'll see you there at two."

Phase one had worked to perfection.

I arrived at Archer's house ten minutes before two.

I was tired of always being the last one at these meetings.

Being early did me no good. As usual, everyone was already there.

There was no Gene Bowman, but that didn't bother me.

Today's mission was about Archer.

And possibly A.J. and Grace.

"Shall we start early?" Ellie asked.

"Sure," Archer said.

He had two pitchers of water lying on the outdoor table. We took our seats and I poured myself a glass of water and took a huge sip. It would help with my plan.

"Let's keep the tradition going of asking Quint first. Any luck, Mr. P.I.?"

I wanted to make something up. Throw them off the scent of what I'd really been doing. So I made up a bullshit story. To my friends, who I'd fought tooth and nail with this whole case. I better have been right about Dickie Faber telling the truth.

"Kirk Stroud has an ex-wife who lives in Stockton. I'm going to call her after this meeting. If she agrees to meet with me, I'll drive out there. Maybe she can shed some light on why Mr. Stroud would lie on the stand."

"Maybe they haven't talked in years," Grace said.

"Maybe. But if he was an asshole, she'll probably be more willing to talk. And maybe she can give examples of him lying in the past. Anything to impugn his reputation."

I took another big sip of my water.

"He did serve time in jail," A.J. said.

"Yes, he did, A.J. I'm looking for something else, though. Lying, as I said. Or maybe he ran a scam on people. Things like that. Obviously, if the ex-wife had an example of him committing perjury, that would be ideal."

"Regardless, that's good work finding his ex, Quint," Ellie said. "I'd like to say something before we continue. There's still a very good chance that this case gets dismissed by the judge or the prosecution drops the case entirely. However, we should prepare ourselves as if this will continue on Monday. That's why we are having these daily meetings. If the case did proceed on Monday and we weren't prepared, I couldn't live with myself."

I took another big sip.

"Well said, Ellie," Cliff said. "It doesn't cost us anything to be prepared. Now, if we weren't prepared? That would cost us dearly."

"You two are great attorneys," Archer said. "I'm glad I chose you. Quint, I know you're not an attorney, but I'm grateful we hired you as well."

"Thanks, Archer," I said.

It was the most upbeat I'd seen him in days. Maybe the sunlight had actually helped, despite it just being the impetus for my plan.

"Very nice of you," Ellie said.

Cliff just nodded.

No one said anything and I saw my opening.

"Are you done with me for a second, Ellie?"

"Yeah. Why?"

"I've had to use the bathroom since I got here, but didn't want to interrupt the meeting."

"Well, it doesn't help that you've finished three-quarters of your water."

I laughed.

"That's true."

Archer stood up and pointed twenty feet away.

"Just use the guest house. It's closer."

That's what I was expecting.

"Thanks, Archer."

As I walked towards the guest house, I heard Ellie say, "Alright, let's talk about next Monday."

I knew I had some time.

I entered the guest house, but not with the intention of using the bathroom.

In the "family room" area, there was the bathroom, a futon, pool table, a Ms. Pac Man machine, and a bar.

There weren't any drawers where you'd hide a phone.

I quickly glanced on the top of the bar and the pool table. No cell phone.

Next, I hit the bedroom on the left. It was the small one. If I had to guess, Grace was in that room, A.J. was on the futon, and Archer was in the big bedroom.

The room was tiny and there was only one dresser, which had four drawers. I quickly dug my hand through each, careful not to make it obvious someone had rummaged through them.

It was female clothes so I was right about Grace staying there. No stray phone, however.

I quickly went to the closet, but all I saw were a couple of dresses. I scanned the ground and the railing above the clothes. Nothing.

I'd probably just passed the time it would take to urinate, but I had to hit the main bedroom. If Archer or one of the kids walked in, I'd have some explaining to do, that's for sure.

I speed-walked the twenty feet to the other room. This room was twice the size. There was an eight-drawer dresser. There was also a small desk with two tiny compartments.

I tried the dresser first. I scanned the top of each drawer when I opened it and then dragged my hand along the bottom. If they hid a phone in the middle of six sets of t-shirts, well good for them, I wasn't going to find it if that were the case.

I probably spent only five seconds on each drawer.

As I finished the eighth and final drawer, I heard a noise.

Or, I thought I did.

Was my mind screwing with me or were one of the Keats about to open the door?

It was the middle of the day, the sun was out, and still, I was nervous as hell.

I moved to the two-drawer desk. If there was nothing there, it was time to go back. I didn't have time to check the closet. Someone might be coming to check on me.

I opened the first drawer. Nothing. Just a pen and some computer paper.

I opened the second drawer. Nothing. It was empty

Or, so I thought. As I moved my finger further back, I happened to touch something. I slid it towards the front.

A fucking phone!

I knew my time was running short, but I had to know.

I quickly press the power button.

If someone walked in, I'd have no excuse. Nothing could explain this away.

Why are you turning on our phone, Quint???

I'd be caught red-handed.

The next forty-five seconds were the longest of my life. Every second felt like a minute.

I thought my heart was going to leap out of my chest.

I knew there were two things I had to do once it powered on. And I'd have to do them as quickly as humanly possible.

The phone powered on. With my heart in my throat, I called the number Paddy had given me.

For a second, maybe a second and a half, nothing happened.

And then to my horror - or was it delight - the phone lit up and started to ring.

I almost froze from dread, but I couldn't lose a second.

I turned their ringer off immediately and then went to their call log.

As I grabbed my phone to take a picture of their call log, I heard another noise.

It caused me to jump, but I didn't hear anyone enter the guest house.

I took a picture of the outgoing phone numbers dialed.

Lastly, I had to power down the phone. I pressed the power button and as I saw it turning off, I shoved the phone back into the corner of the drawer.

I quickly walked towards the door, just knowing someone was going to walk in any second. It didn't happen, and I was able to make it outside.

I wiped my forehead with my shirt. I was sweating. Hopefully, they wouldn't notice.

"You're back," Archer said. "Thought we were going to have to send a search party."

I tried to make the most convincing fake laugh of my life.

"Sorry. It turned out to be more than just pee."

I saw a few of them laugh. Hopefully, that would lighten the mood and take the focus off of me. My anxiety was still off the charts.

I was just hoping none of them could sense it.

I intentionally didn't talk much over the next ten minutes of the meeting.

Instead, my brain just ran through all of the possibilities. None of which were good.

As we stood up to leave, I had to know something. I looked at Archer, my thoughts on him having done a complete 180. My working assumption - albeit, newly formed - was that he had killed Gracie and somehow, someway knew that Jan Goddard had been killed. Maybe he had a partner.

"I like the guest house, but it must be pretty packed with the three of you," I said.

The others had walked past us and just Archer and I remained.

"You're right. It would have been too packed. I'm in the main house now."

"Oh, really?"

"Yeah, I let Grace and A.J. take over."

My heart was sinking, knowing what this meant.

"Did you take your stuff with you?"

"Sure did. Cleaned the whole thing out. What kids want their Dad's shit lying around?"

I laughed, but it was a sad clown's laugh. I was mortified by what I'd discovered.

"Are the kids relishing being home?"

"Well, it's not exactly a time for relishing."

"You're right. I'm sorry."

"But it's nice to have the kids bonding. I'm not sure they've always been that close."

"I didn't know that."

"How could you? This case is about Gracie and me. It doesn't involve the kids."

That was about to change.

CHAPTER 33

I arrived back at my place and the sheer weight of everything came crashing down on me.

What had already been a crazy case had just been ratcheted up even further.

Did I now think A.J. Keats might be the killer? Yes, it was certainly a possibility.

Could it have been Grace? I'd found the phone on A.J.'s side of the guest house, but I wasn't eliminating her.

Was there another option I wasn't thinking of?

Could someone have planted the phone there?

If so, how could they know I'd find it?

With every piece of evidence I found with this case, a new wave of questions remained unanswered.

I threw on another jazz album, *Bitches Brew* by the incomparable Miles Davis. I was wearing my jazz collection out this week, but I needed my thinking cap on.

I began going back over some of the trial's testimony in my head. A few things stuck out. One, during Natalie Slater's testimony, she said that her son didn't really get along with A.J. I didn't realize it at the time, but looking back, it was an odd thing to bring up.

I'd become pretty good at using social media to find people. I typed in "Natalie Slater, Walnut Creek" in the Facebook search area and got two matches, clicking on the woman I recognized.

I went to her "About" info, hoping to see a phone number listed. No such luck.

Next, I went to her Friends list and typed in Slater. Three names popped up. One was quite old and obviously not her son. The second was a young woman. Possibly her daughter or her niece. The third one was someone named Steven Slater. I clicked on his profile and then the about tab.

He listed his job title as "Temp at Vincent and Collier, attorneys-at-law."

It listed their phone number and I dialed it.

"Thanks for calling Vincent and Collier, how can I direct your call?"

"I need to talk to Steven Slater, please."

"Okay, give me a minute. May I ask who is calling?"

"His uncle," I said, thinking he'd be more likely to accept the call. Assuming he had an uncle.

Two minutes later, a voice came on the phone.

"Uncle Larry?" the voice said.

"Hello, Steven. I'm sorry this isn't Uncle Larry, but I hope you'll hear me out."

"Who the hell is this?"

"My name is Quint and I'm a private investigator."

"What's going on?"

"Did you know your mother testified in the Archer Keats murder case?"

"Yes, but what does that have to do with me?"

He was agitated, but who wouldn't be?

"She testified that you and A.J. Keats didn't get along. Is that true?"

"Hmmm, interesting. You said you're a P.I.?"

"Yes. I've been working on the case."

I felt no need to tell him I was with the defense.

"No, I didn't like him."

"How so?"

"He was just one of those guys who came from money. Do you know how I know his father opened twenty-one restaurants?"

"How?"

"Because every time you saw A.J., he'd bring it up. I've known him since 5th grade. Back then he'd say ten restaurants or whatever it may have been. In 8th grade, he'd say thirteen restaurants. It was the worst running joke of all time."

"Did your classmates dislike him as well?"

"Some. Others thought it was cool to hang out with a rich kid. And listen, there are plenty of rich kids in Walnut Creek, but it's boring if you say your father is in finance or was a doctor. Those were a dime a dozen. To say your father was a restaurateur was much cooler."

This made me think less of A.J., but it was hardly evidence he was a killer.

"How did he get along with his parents?"

"I'm not sure. He sure didn't mention his mother as much as his father, that's for sure."

"Did you ever see him get violent?"

A slight pause was followed by this:

"You think he killed his mother, don't you?"

"No, I don't. I'm just following every possible lead."

I sounded like a robot, spitting out the most basic response possible.

"I understand. You can't tell me if you are, anyway."

"I'll ask again. Did you ever seen him get violent?"

"He could occasionally be a bully. Pick on younger, dorkier, poorer kids. I don't know if that's what you mean."

This wasn't the impression that I'd gotten from A.J., but should I really be surprised? He was only going to show me his best face. Especially with his father on trial for murder.

Unlike Grace, who had shown me the worst of her the very first time we met.

"Is there anything else you can tell me?"

"I heard he wasn't doing much in Tahoe. Eighteen million smackeroos would have helped."

"You've been following this trial pretty closely, haven't you?"

"The mother of a family I knew was brutally murdered and my own mother was called to testify. You're damn right I'm keeping track closely."

"You're to repeat none of this conversation to anyone. Do you understand?"

I'd tried to sound official like I was a lawyer and this was binding.

"I know how to keep a secret."

"Can I get your cell phone in case I want to contact you again?"

"Sure. It's 925-555-4928."

"Thanks for your time, Steven."

"Of course."

I set my phone down and exhaled deeply.

Was the phone concrete evidence that A.J. had killed Jan Goddard? Maybe not concrete, but the police hadn't even found her body by seven a.m. on Saturday. If he didn't kill her, he knew who did. And why would he alert Dickie Faber? How would having him on the run help A.J. out?

It would help his father, I guess. Take suspicion away from him.

Could they have been in this together? I shuddered at the idea.

As usual, a million questions and only a few answers.

I decided to talk my way through it.

If - and this was still by no means a certainty - A.J. killed his mother, you'd have to figure it was for money. There had been testimony that Gracie was going to tell her family she was asking for a divorce. Maybe she told the kids and that's when A.J. realized his mother was taking her inheritance with her. Had Gracie told the kids they weren't going to get any? What would have provoked A.J. to do something so horrific?

Next, did he kill his mother while she was at home in order to frame his father? As terrible as it was to say, there was logic behind it. If his father was convicted of his mother's murder, A.J. and Grace were set to inherit Gracie's money.

If Archer wasn't convicted - or never even tried - then Archer would receive Gracie's inheritance and A.J. might have to wait decades.

Which brought me to Jan Goddard and Dickie Faber.

Why would he kill Jan Goddard and notify Dickie Faber?

That didn't make sense. It would make it far less likely that Archer would be convicted. And if he'd killed for the inheritance, his father's conviction would insure he'd get ir right away.

My head hurt.

After an hour of trying to decompress, I grabbed my phone and looked at the picture I'd taken of the four dialed phone numbers.

925-555-0702. That was Dickie's.

925-555-2057.

530-555-7241.

925-555-3786

I quickly realized a mistake I'd made. I didn't need to call the burner phone to see if it rang. If I'd just looked down and seen that the phone had called Dickie's house phone, I'd have known it was the right one.

Oh, well. In the moment, scared out of my mind, it was understandable.

I was immediately struck by the third number. It was a 530 area code and I knew that to be Lake Tahoe, which happened to be where A.J. lived.

I called that number first and was greeted with a voice mail.

"This is Mason Fry, Lake Tahoe's foremost expert on wills and living trusts. Please leave your message at the beep and we can talk about setting up a meeting."

I couldn't believe what I was hearing.

"Mr. Fry, my name is Quint Adler and I'm a private investigator down in the Bay Area. Can you give me a call when you get a chance?"

I hung up.

Maybe this wasn't the final nail in the coffin, but things were starting to add up.

Did A.J. Keats really kill his mother and Jan Goddard? That would have been unfathomable a few days ago. Shit, a few hours ago.

And yet, it was now a very real possibility.

I dialed the second number.

"Lancaster Construction," a woman's voice answered.

I hung up the phone. Another nail in the coffin.

I dialed the final number listed and as I looked down at the number, it registered. Hearing this voice was going to be painful.

"Hi, you've reached Jan. Please leave a message at the beep."

To say A.J. Keats was now firmly in my sights would have been a gross understatement.

He was the primary suspect, bordering on the lone suspect.

I probably had enough evidence to go to the police.

I looked at my watch. It was now 4:45.

I decided to give myself the rest of the day and then I'd go to the police in the morning.

Was I betraying the trust of Ellie, Archer, and the rest of the defense team?

Maybe, but my loyalty was to the truth, and the truth was that A.J. Keats was now my number one suspect.

If I went to Ellie with my suspicions, there's a very good chance it would get back to Archer and/or A.J. I couldn't take that chance.

Something hit me that should have registered earlier. Once again, I'll blame it on my nerves while in the guest house.

A.J.'s burner phone now had my number in it. If he turned it on and saw the incoming call, he'd do all he could to find out who'd called him.

And when he discovered it was me, he might come calling.

On the plus side, A.J. knew that phone could now connect him to Jan Goddard - and Dickie Faber - so my guess was that he was unlikely to turn it on.

Unless absolutely necessary.

Still, I vowed to stay vigilant the rest of the day.

I didn't want to be the third person with a knife through the heart.

∾

I was getting more done from the comfort of my couch than I had in three weeks of interviews to begin the case.

I remembered the first time I'd met with Grace and thinking she was the evil one in the family.

Boy, was I wrong.

A.J.'s alibi - not that he was ever a serious suspect - was that he was in Lake Tahoe. It's about a three-hour drive to Walnut Creek. Gracie was killed between midnight and two a.m. which meant A.J. would have had to leave between probably 8:30 or 10:30 at night to arrive in time.

He'd then get back on the road at approximately 12:15 to 2:15. Plenty of time to get back to Lake Tahoe and claim to your roommate that you'd never left your house.

His alibi was really a non-alibi. It just sounded like one because he was a good distance away.

It could be done, without question.

∾

I spent the next few hours trying to find out more details on Jan's murder.

And then even more time trying to find out anything I could on Kirk Stroud. Without any luck.

I couldn't even find his address online.

Had A.J. reached out to Stroud? Bribed him to lie about Archer wanting to kill his wife?

If A.J. had been trying to frame his father for murder, Stroud's was the perfect testimony.

∾

Ellie called and we talked about the case, but I made no mention of A.J. I didn't even want to bring the name up in fear that might lead me down a rabbit hole, and knowing Ellie, she'd notice. I hung up and told her we'd talk tomorrow.

Before I knew it, it was 8:30 p.m.

The day had sailed by at breakneck speed.

My phone rang and it startled me. I'd been deep in thought and the noise brought me back to earth.

I recognized the number as Dickie Faber's burner.

"How are you?" I asked.

"Anything new to report? I'm scared shitless. I feel that at any moment the cops are going to bang down the door and arrest me."

Even though I believed Dickie's story, I wasn't ready to tell him everything I'd learned.

"I'm making headway," I said. "Stay in that hotel one more night. I think this might all settle itself out by the end of tomorrow."

"You've learned something, haven't you?"

"I have, but I'm not ready to divulge it," I said.

"I guess I understand. Just do something before the cops come here with guns blazing."

It gave me pause.

Was I putting his life in undue jeopardy just so I could prove A.J.'s guilt beyond a reasonable doubt?

I wasn't a lawyer, after all. As I'd already told myself, I had enough evidence to take to the cops. Why did I have to wrap it up with a bow like I was an attorney for the prosecution?

"Are you there?" he asked.

"Just a second," I replied.

I thought it over and decided I was trying to play the hero.

I'd done this before and it had almost got people killed.

I wasn't a homicide detective - nor an attorney - and yet I was acting like both. I should turn this case over to the experts. They could do more with the information on A.J. than I ever could.

"Alright, I've decided. I'll go to the police first thing tomorrow morning. Just wait out the night. When I talk to them, I'll reinforce that you had nothing to do with it and tell them you will turn yourself in. I'm sure they'll be alright with that."

"Thank you, Quint. Look forward to your call tomorrow morning."

With that, I hung up.

CHAPTER 34

At 10:30, I got ready for bed.

With everything going on, I knew it wouldn't be easy to fall asleep.

I started to ponder how Ellie was going to take this. Was she going to hate me? Be grateful that we caught the real killer? I leaned towards the former.

How about Archer Keats? There was no way he was going to be happy with me. His freedom would matter less than the fact that I'd exposed his son as a killer.

This jarred my memory. I'd remembered thinking something was wrong with this case. Some overriding thing that I didn't like. I knew what it was now. Archer and Ellie had repeatedly asked to keep the kids out of it.

I'd never thought they were suspects, but why did they get treated with kid gloves? Did Archer suspect his own son? I thought back to A.J.'s testimony. I remember Ellie asking him how long it took him to drive from Lake Tahoe to Walnut Creek after finding out about his mother. It seemed an unnecessary question. Was she trying to get on record that he could do the drive in three hours? Did she have suspicions also?

From the very beginning, the cops stated that no one broke into the house to kill Gracie Keats. Despite this, I spent the majority of my time looking at Gracie's affairs and expecting a killing that was rooted in sex or infidelity.

And part of that was because Archer had said his kids were off-limits.

They were two of the three surviving people who had the house key. I shouldn't have avoided looking at them for as long as I had.

I heard a quick beep.

A text message was coming through.

"I see you found me."

Holy shit!

It was A.J.'s phone. I sat up in bed and a million thoughts flooded my brain.

What do I say?

Do I just call the police now?

Do I call Archer?

Instead, I decided to interact with him.

"Yes, I guess I did." I texted back.

"How?"

"Through Dickie Faber's house phone."

"He should have just left town forever."

"You should turn yourself in, A.J."

"That's not going to happen."

"Why did you do it?"

"I won't bore you with the details. I was a greedy SOB. Let's leave it at that."

"Why kill Jan Goddard? I can't figure that out."

"I panicked. I thought my testimony was terrible and people didn't believe Kirk Stroud. I was afraid the truth might come out so I tried to frame Dickie Faber."

"And killed an innocent woman in the process."

"No different than my mother."

I was thoroughly disgusted by the indifference he felt towards the death of his own mother. A.J. Keats deserved whatever he had coming.

"How did you pick Kirk Stroud?"

"I was at my parents' when he and his construction buddies were fixing the garage. I overheard some people saying what a maniac and tough guy Stroud was. How he'd do anything for money. When I decided to kill my mother, I thought of him."

"I don't get it. He had nothing to do with the death of your mother."

This was both surreal and all too real. I would be calling the cops the second we were done texting. I didn't want to call them just yet. I needed to know what A.J. was going to say.

"Oh, but he did. Did you think I was going to kill my mother and then wait thirty more years until my father died to get the money?"

A shiver went up my spine.

"You were trying to frame your father so you would inherit the money immediately?"

"Bingo, Quint. That's why I reached out to Kirk Stroud. I knew he'd be the nail in my father's coffin. Pretty brilliant if I do say so myself."

"You're evil."

"Let's be honest, I can't really argue against that with all I've just disclosed."

"How did you meet with Kirk Stroud? That would have been a huge risk being seen publicly with him."

"That's why I never met in person."

"I don't understand."

"I set up a fake email account and did it that way. It took me several tries to convince him. I kept telling him, all you have to do is lie on the witness stand about being approached by my father and for that, I'd pay Stroud 100k. He wouldn't budge, so I left him 5k cash as a down payment. After that, I think he knew I was serious. And it's not like he had to kill anyone. Just make a few white lies in court."

"You're good. I'll give you that."

I hated paying him a compliment, but the plan was the work of an evil genius.

"Yes, I am."

"What precipitated all of this? Did your mother tell you she was filing for divorce?"

"Well, what really precipitated it all is that I'm an asshole who has never cared about anybody but himself. But yes, her telling us she was filing for divorce set this all in motion. She also told us she was having two affairs, even telling us the names of the assholes."

"Are you the one who left the note on my door about Dickie Faber?"

"That wasn't me. At that point, I didn't want any more suspects coming to life. I was hoping my father would be convicted. Maybe it was innocent little Grace trying to get you to look at someone besides our father."

That made sense. It was on the day that I first met Grace that I received the letter. She probably did it beforehand, knowing I was at the office.

"And you drove from Tahoe to kill your mother?"

"No, I took a time machine. Don't ask dumb questions, Quint."

I would have preferred talking on the phone, but I couldn't risk breaking the rhythm of these texts. I was learning everything.

"And you were able to find Jan's address online?"

"Not exactly. I told her I was you."

I wasn't going to like this.

"I don't understand."

"Our case file had her phone number. So I called her on Friday night and told her I was your assistant and that we needed to stop by and ask a few more questions. At one point, I tried to sound just like you, and muzzling my voice I said,

'It's Quint, we'll see you soon.' I don't know if she bought the whole thing, but she opened the door when I got there. That was enough."

I was sickened beyond belief.

"You're certifiable."

"Yeah, probably."

"Why are you telling me all of this? I have to know."

"When you were in the bathroom for ten minutes this afternoon, I got suspicious. Unfortunately, my father had other plans for us today, and he drove Grace and me up to Stinson Beach. It was a favorite spot of our mother's. It was odd, having to smile at all my father's recollections and stories about her. If only my father knew what I had done. He wouldn't have been smiling."

"When did you finally see that I'd called."

"An hour ago."

"Why admit all this to me?"

"Because I'm not going to jail."

"Actually, by telling me all this you're guaranteeing you'll go to jail."

"I'll say it again. I'm not going to jail."

"You're going to try and outrun the cops?"

"I wouldn't have texted you if that were my plan. No, I don't think I'm going anywhere."

And that's when I knew he planned on killing himself.

"You're going to kill yourself, aren't you?"

There was no text back, so I sent another one.

"It doesn't have to end like this, A.J."

He was a sociopath and I probably should just let him do it, but I was a human being. I had to try and talk him out of it.

"I'll say it for a third time. I'm not going to jail. Tell everyone I'm sorry. Although let's be honest, I'm not that sorry."

It was the second time he'd used the phrase, *'Let's be honest.'* He was a lying, murdering sociopath. Honesty was the last thing he should be mentioning.

"Stop texting 'Let's be honest.' You're the furthest thing from honest."

I regretted it right away. He was alluding to suicide and I was calling him out for being dishonest.

"You're probably right there, Quint."

"You don't have to resort to this. Maybe you could go to a mental hospital and get the help you need."

"I did this of sound mind and body. I don't belong in a damn mental hospital."

"Don't kill yourself."

I had too much humanity to just let him do it. I'm sure others would have taken a different path.

"You're too late. I've already made up my mind. This will all come full circle.

I'll stab myself through the chest. Of course, it probably won't get all the way to my heart."

"I'm calling 9-1-1."

"Then I guess I better get on with this. Tell everyone I'm sorry. Even though I'm not."

"A.J., don't do this!"

There was no response and no dots telling me he was texting back.

I called 9-1-1.

"Hello. What is your emergency?"

"Someone is about to kill himself. Send people to Archer Keats' home. It's on Civic Drive."

I couldn't remember the address. I leaped out of bed and ran over and grabbed the initial police report.

"3027 Civic Drive."

"Okay, stay on the line, please. How do you know this person is trying to kill himself?"

"Because he just told me. Tell the paramedics he'll be in the guest house. When you get to the driveway, the guest house will be on the left."

"Okay, we are dispatching someone now."

There was nothing more I could do, so I hung up the phone. I ran and grabbed a pair of jeans and quickly slipped on a pair of flip-flops.

Within seconds, I was out my door and took the elevator to the parking garage. I started my car, exited the garage, and turned left on North Main. I took another left on Civic and started accelerating, hoping to get to Archer Keats's house before it was too late.

Maybe it's better if he dies.

As I approached the house, I saw a police car and an ambulance just pulling in. I knew I wasn't going to be able to get up to the driveway, so I parked my car on the side of the road and started running up.

One of the police officers suspiciously looked in my direction.

"What are you doing, sir?"

"I'm a friend of the family. I'm the one who called 9-1-1."

That seemed to allay his fears.

But as we reached the driveway together, he wasn't going to let me approach the house.

"Stand back," he said. "I don't care who you are."

The paramedics ran towards the guest house.

I could do nothing but wait.

And hope.

Hope that a sociopathic murderer was still alive.

In an absurd case, this might have been my most unnatural instinct of all.

Five minutes passed and nothing happened.

Finally, I saw Archer and Grace walking towards me, tears streaming from their faces.

They looked in my direction.

Archer looked confused.

"How did you know to be here?" he asked.

"Is he dead?"

"Yes," Grace said through her tears.

"I asked why you were here," Archer repeated.

"I was talking to A.J. before he did it. I'm the one who called 9-1-1."

"Why the hell were you talking to him?"

"You don't want to know," I said.

"My son just killed himself. And you're telling me you were the last one to talk to him. You 're damn right I want to know."

"Alright," I said.

"And you better fucking tell me everything."

And so I did.

CHAPTER 35

A few days passed.
    Pretty much everything had played out the way A.J. had told me during our texts. They found his DNA at Jan Goddard's house. Not on the body itself, and not on the knife, but on a couch. He'd been careful, but not careful enough.

The police arrested Kirk Stroud and he confessed that he'd perjured himself. He and A.J. had done all of their communication online. He'd received $5,000 cash from an envelope at a special pick-up location. After that, he'd agreed to lie in court.

Dickie Faber was picked up the morning following A.J.'s suicide. He spent five hours answering questions but was released as a free man later that day. He texted me, thanking me for all I'd done. I didn't respond. He'd helped crack open the case, but I still held a grudge for how he'd treated Jan Goddard. I'd reach out to him at some point, but it wasn't a priority.

Needing a break from all of the madness, I spent a night out with Tre Larson and some old friends. I tried to steer the conversation away from the A.J. Keats case, which it had now become.

No such luck.

It's all anyone wanted to talk about.

Tre told me that it wasn't just our friends. The bars and restaurants in Walnut Creek couldn't get enough of it. Neither could the news, but after the first night of being inundated with story after story of A.J. Keats, I vowed to stop watching.

~

Archer Keats had become a shell of himself. It was horrific enough that his wife had been killed, but to find out his son had committed the murder, followed by his suicide, seemed to send Archer spiraling. He rarely said a word in those first few days after A.J.'s death.

We all appeared in court on the following Monday. There were still fifty news vans, even though everyone knew it was going to be anti-climactic. Judge Kilgore was going to toss the case against Archer Keats.

Which is exactly what she did.

Archer Keats was a free man, but he couldn't even muster up a smile.

I guess you couldn't blame him.

~

We had planned to all meet for lunch after court. One last get-together.

Archer said he just wanted to go home and sleep. I worried about what was to come of the man. Gene Bowman said he had to get back to work.

It was just going to be Ellie, Cliff, Grace, and me. We'd lost a few along the way.

We walked up to a little cafe called Millie's, only a block west from the courthouse. People affiliated with the trial had told me to try it, but this was my first trip there.

Considering the circumstances, I doubted I'd be too hungry.

Cliff and Grace walked into the restaurant ahead of Ellie and I.

I shuffled her a few feet away from the door.

"Now that this trial is over, I have to know why you had sex with me. Was it because you found me attractive or because you thought it would keep me beholden to you on this case?"

"Yes."

And then she leaned up and quickly kissed me on the cheek.

"Let's go eat," she said.

We walked into the restaurant. The other two were already seated at a four-person table. I sat down. Grace was on my left, Ellie on my right, and Cliff was across from me.

The walls were filled with framed pictures of famous legal cases. Surely ones that had taken place at this courthouse. Sadly, this trial would probably be up there someday.

The waitress handed us each a menu.

"Is your father going to be alright?" I asked Grace.

"Who knows? Can you blame him?"

"No. Are you going to stay and look after him?"

"Yeah, I think I'll be staying in Walnut Creek for a while."

"Are you going to be okay?"

"I'll get through this."

"I have to say, you're handling this better than I ever could have," Cliff said.

"What choice do I have?" Grace said and we all nodded. "If I think about my mother or A.J. for too long, I'll just break down. So I choose to put on a brave face."

I could tell she was eager to change the subject.

"So, Ellie, the judge referred to my brother being charged posthumously. What exactly does that mean."

"They'll convict him of your mother's death as well as Jan Goddard's. The cases will then be closed. Joe Blow from the mental ward could come to confess and it wouldn't matter. Your brother will now stand guilty of those charges."

"Thanks," she said.

Grace seemed to relax after that. Maybe it felt like despite all the death, and all the terrible things her family had been through, she could try and move on now. As much as you could move on with only a father left from a family of four.

A few minutes later, Cliff turned to Grace.

"Tell us a good story about A.J. Something from when you were kids."

It was hard to think of a sociopath as a carefree child, but I knew what Cliff was doing. Trying to have Grace remember him back when they were young.

"We tried to make our own little language. And we mistakenly thought we were the only two people who could understand it. He'd talk like a girl and I'd talk like a guy."

"Give us an example."

"Oh, I haven't done it in forever."

"Just one," Cliff said.

Grace picked up a napkin and spoke through it.

"Hey Grace, it's me A.J."

"You sound just like him," Cliff said and he and Ellie laughed.

I did not. The hairs on my arm started to stand up.

I was thinking of the phone call to Dickie Faber.

It couldn't be? Could it?

"I'm sorry," Grace said. "This is probably inappropriate."

"It's my fault," Cliff said. "I asked you to do it. I just want you to try and remember some good times. Lord knows you've had enough bad ones recently."

Ellie chimed in.

"I think you're going to be alright, Grace. In time, obviously. You're not the woman I first met."

"I intentionally come off as a bitch at first. And then, when I start acting more diplomatically, people start to think I'm a good person."

I could feel her eyes making their way toward me.

I was in a daze.

Please, please tell me I was overthinking this.

"But you are a good person," Cliff said.

Grace didn't respond and my terror intensified.

How had everything changed in a matter of minutes?

"What are you going to order, Grace?" Ellie asked.

"The Turkey Club sounded good," she said and then put her arm on my shoulder. "But let's be honest, it might be a little early for that."

I heard 'Let's be honest' and my whole world shattered. This was no coincidence.

I slowly moved my eyes to meet Grace's. She had the vilest smile I'd ever seen.

I knew at that moment - with the utmost confidence - that it had been Grace all along.

She'd killed her mother. Walnut Creek was only thirty minutes from Napa. Her alibi was that she closed a bar tab that night. My bet was she killed her mother and then returned to close out her tab right around two a.m. or so.

"Look, I was ordering drinks at nine p.m. and then closed my tab at two a.m. I couldn't have been in Walnut Creek."

It was genius.

I was also positive Grace had killed Jan Goddard. I'm sure she'd left A.J.'s DNA at the scene. I remember Dickie Faber telling me that the person who called him - Grace, in her disguised voice - had told him she'd used flypaper to collect his DNA. It was a half-truth. Grace had collected DNA from flypaper, but it was to frame her brother. Shit, maybe she'd left some of Dickie's as well.

Finally, Grace had stabbed her brother to death, likely as he slept. She had to make sure it looked like suicide so there wouldn't be twenty-seven stabs this time. One deep stab in the direction of the heart was enough. And then I'm sure she wrapped A.J.'s dead - or soon to be dying - hands around the handle of the knife.

The burner phone had always been hers. She'd called a Lake Tahoe attorney who specialized in wills. Clearly, to make it look like A.J. was asking questions about his mother's will. The other phone calls also fit perfectly to frame A.J. as the killer. He hadn't been the killer, though. It had been Grace all along. She was the one who said it might be her father when I first met her. She's the one who testified so poorly, hoping it would increase the chances of her father being convicted. It was Gracie who'd left blood in the courtyard and on the door of the guest house in order to frame her father.

She'd been the one emailing Kirk Stroud. She was the one who'd called Dickie Faber, using the man's voice she'd just demonstrated. Grace knew at some point that the phone would be found in A.J.'s room. Dickie Faber would tell the cops that it had been a male voice that had called him. It would have been game, set, and match against A.J. Keats, but that wasn't enough for Grace. She had to kill him. The longer this went, the more likely A.J. might have figured out that his sister was behind all of this.

I'd been investigating the wrong sibling. A.J. hadn't done anything wrong. It had been his sister all along. She'd played us all.

And for her final ingenious move, Grace texted me, pretending to be A.J. It would not only set the stage for his suicide but would lay everything out that "A.J." had done. It would be a slam dunk for the cops. An open and shut case. The guy had threatened suicide minutes before. Of course he'd done it. What was there to investigate? Not much. Which is surely what Grace wanted.

My guess was that those texts were almost entirely truthful, if you just subbed A.J. out for Grace, the one actually sending them. She probably had panicked after her own testimony and thought people were going to suspect her. So she killed Jan Goddard to frame Dickie Faber. The inheritance would have to wait, but better that then being under suspicion of murder.

This is why she called Dickie Faber and forced him go on the run, taking away any heat she thought was coming her way. Dickie may have been able to convince the authorities that he hadn't killed Jan Goddard, but not if he was on the run. And Grace knew this perfectly well.

And then, just as Grace had planned, the police quickly ruled A.J.'s death a suicide.

Only, A.J. hadn't committed suicide. He'd been killed by his sister. The true sociopath.

That cunning witch I'd met the first day had been the real Grace all along. She'd basically admitted as much a few minutes ago. She felt showing her true colors to begin with, and then morphing into a nice, polite young woman would fool us all. And she was right.

The tragedy of it all was that nothing was going to happen to Grace.

What did I have? That she'd said 'Let's be honest.' That she could talk like a guy?

Her brother was about to be posthumously convicted of Gracie and

Jan's murders. No homicide detective would reopen this case. This case was over and I knew it.

And so did Grace. That's why, after Ellie said this case was closed, Grace started behaving so brash.

She'd committed the perfect murder. Or, in this case, the perfect murders.

She wanted someone to know. And that someone was me.

I heard a voice in the background say, "He must be deep in thought."

"Quint, are you alright?" Cliff asked.

I snapped back to our conversation at hand. All eyes were on me.

"You didn't answer, Quint," Grace said, that evil, manipulative smile still tattooed to her face. "Do you think I could get a Turkey Club this early?"

I chose my words wisely.

"I'm sure you could get away with it."

"You know me so well," Grace said.

And then she winked at me.

ALSO BY BRIAN O'SULLIVAN

First off, a huge thank you for reading *A Knife Through The Heart.* I really hope you enjoyed it and the end managed to shock you.

I'd be honored if you left a review. Thanks so much! Reviews mean a great deal to me.

Quint will be making a comeback later this year, but I haven't set up a pre-order date yet. If you've missed a Quint book along the way, here's a link to all of them: Quint Adler Series

If you want to read a standalone novel and a PERSONAL FAVORITE of mine, here's a link to The Bartender. It's probably my craziest!

And if you like political thrillers, then my first two novels are for you! *The Puppeteer* and *The Patsy.*

Lastly, I'd like to thank you - yeah, YOU - for giving me a chance. It means more than you'll ever know and I hope you'll tell a friend or six about my novels.

Thanks so much for your support!

Sincerely,

Brian O'Sullivan

Printed in Great Britain
by Amazon

44941836R00138